Books by Meg Cabot

The Princess Diaries series

The Mediator series

The Airhead trilogy

All American Girl
All American Girl: Ready or Not

Avalon High
Avalon High manga: The Merlin Prophecy
Teen Idol
How to Be Popular
Jinx
Tommy Sullivan Is a Freak
Nicola and the Viscount
Victoria and the Rogue

For younger readers

The Allie Finkle series

For older readers

The Guy Next Door
Boy Meets Girl
Every Boy's Got One
Queen of Babble series
The Heather Wells series

Also available in audio

This book may be returned to any Wiltshire
Library. To renew this book, phone or visit our
website: www.wiltshire.gov.uk/libraries

Wiltshire Council
Where everybody matters

LM6.108.5 (CH 2017)

to trade lives with a celebrity after all

air head
Runaway

meg
cabot

MACMILLAN

First published 2010 by Macmillan Children's Books

This edition published 2011 by Macmillan Children's Books
a division of Macmillan Publishers Limited
20 New Wharf Road, London N1 9RR
Basingstoke and Oxford
Associated companies throughout the world
www.panmacmillan.com

ISBN 978-0-330-45384-4

1 3 5 7 9 8 6 4 2

A CIP catalogue record for this book is available from
the British Library.

Typeset by Nigel Hazle
Printed and bound in the UK by CPI Mackays, Chatham ME5 8TD

For Benjamin

One

So according to the tabloids, I'm on a secret love getaway (not so secret any more now though, is it? Thank you, *Us Weekly*) with Brandon Stark, the only son and sole heir of billionaire Robert Stark, currently the fourth richest person in the world, after Carlos Slim, Bill Gates and Warren Buffett.

There are paparazzi staking out the oceanside mansion where Brandon and I are holed up. They're hiding in the dunes all along the beach. They're stretched out in ditches up and down the road, their telephoto lenses pointed through tufts of sea grass in the hopes of capturing me topless on a chaise longue by the pool (like that's going to happen).

I even saw one perched in a tree, trying to get a shot of me and Brandon Stark together that time we came out of the house to go grab a takeaway at the local crab shack.

It's big news, I guess, the Face of Stark and the heir to the Stark fortune hooking up with each other over the holidays. My room-mate, Lulu, texted me that she heard a picture of us together can fetch upwards of ten grand . . . as long as I'm facing the camera and smiling.

So far, Lulu says, there hasn't been a single shot of me facing the camera and smiling. Not in any magazine or on any website anywhere.

I know people are wondering how that's even possible. I'm the girl who has it all, right? The little white poodle, yawning delicately at my feet; the thick, luxurious blonde hair; the perfect body; the gorgeous boyfriend with the limitless credit card, who seems to care so much about me that he'll buy out the local women's boutique in my size just because I said I can't come down to dinner because I have nothing to wear.

That same gorgeous boyfriend was currently pacing up and down the hallway outside my room, so eager was he for me to join him that he could hardly wait to escort me down to the sumptuously set modern steel-and-glass table.

'How are we doing in there?' he asked, tapping on the door for the umpteenth time this hour at least.

'Not so good,' I croaked. I glanced at my reflection in the mirror hanging over the dressing table in front of me. 'I think I have a fever.'

'Really?' Brandon sounded sweetly concerned. The best boyfriend a girl could ask for. 'Maybe I should call a doctor.'

'Oh,' I said through the door, 'I don't think that's necessary. I think I just need fluids. And bed rest. It would probably be better if I stayed in my room tonight.'

I knew anyone who might have been watching – for instance, through a high-powered telephoto lens – could only have been thinking, What is wrong with this girl? After all, I was faking sick to get out of dinner with the amazing-looking son of one of the richest guys in America. I was staying in his palatial, Frank Lloyd Wright-inspired mansion. It came complete with a huge heated outdoor pool (with vanishing edges, so that the water appeared to be dropping off into the horizon). Along one wall there was an aquarium big enough to hold Brandon's pet stingray and shark (it so figures that Brandon Stark would have a pet shark, doesn't it?), a home theatre built to seat twenty, and a four-car garage that housed Brandon's European sports-car collection, with a brand-new buttercup-yellow Lamborghini Murciélago, a Christmas gift from his dad, of which Brandon was immensely proud.

Any other girl would have swapped places with me in a second.

But no other girl had my same problems.

Well . . . maybe one other girl.

'Don't think this means I like you,' Nikki informed me, bursting into my room from the connecting door to hers wearing a brightly coloured maxidress, a leather motorcycle jacket, fringed wedges and an enormous jewelled 'statement' necklace that looked like a drunk frat boy threw up on her chest.

'No worries,' I said. Nikki had made it more than clear that she doesn't like me – that she doesn't want to spend one waking minute with me unless she absolutely has to.

'It's just that your mirror is bigger than mine,' she said, clip-clopping across my room to check out her reflection in it, 'and I want to see how I look in this.'

'You look nice,' I said.

I was lying.

Nikki beamed at the compliment I'd given her though. This was a relief. It was the first time she'd smiled at me – or at least in my direction – since the private plane we took to get to this subtropical resort town touched down a few days earlier.

And who could blame her really? It wasn't just that it was boring for her, being cooped up in this house, palatial as it was. She couldn't go into town, or one of the paparazzi might get a snap of her.

And even though they wouldn't have any idea who she was if her photo showed up in a magazine, someone who had known her from her body's previous life might recognize her and wonder what the heck a girl who was supposed to be dead was doing walking around alive and kicking in ugly statement necklaces.

Because, like me, Nikki is a member of the Walking Dead.

But unlike me, Nikki's body was supposed to be dead and *buried*.

'You think?' Nikki stared at herself in the full-length mirror on the far wall of my room, across from a bank of floor-to-ceiling windows that face the curling waves of the Atlantic – black and ominous-looking at that time of night – just a few dozen yards away.

Then she distractedly tucked a strand of her medium-length auburn hair behind her ear and made a face.

'Ugh,' she said. 'What is the point? Why do I even try?'

'What are you talking about?' I asked. 'You look amazing.'

OK, I was exaggerating. But only a little. Actually, if she'd just worn make-up that suited her new skin tone, and quit straightening her hair until it didn't have a hint of body left in it, and put on some clothes that weren't my cast-offs from the boutique Brandon had raided on my behalf – which she didn't seem to realize were way too tight and long on her – she'd have been totally cute.

But no way was I going to tell her anything that wasn't one hundred per cent positive. I wanted Nikki on my side even more than Brandon did.

'But do you think Brandon will like me in this?' Nikki asked anxiously.

Now we were getting to the root of the problem: the whole reason why I was faking sick . . . so she could get some one-on-one time with Brandon, without me being there to hog the limelight from her.

'Of course he will,' I lied.

He'd better. I knew how desperately she craved Brandon's attention.

Not that I could blame her. Really, who wouldn't be in love with Brandon Stark? He had everything most girls could want in a guy: stunning good looks, an enviable sports-car collection, a Greenwich Village brownstone *and* a beach house in the tropics, not to mention access to a private jet to go from one to the other.

Brandon really would make some girl a great boyfriend.

Except for the part about him being a low-down, two-faced snake of course.

I stared at the back of Nikki's skull as she turned towards the mirror again. I couldn't help lifting my hand to finger the spot on my own scalp where, more than three months earlier, surgeons at the Stark Institute for Neurology and Neurosurgery had cut open my head, slipped out Nikki's brain, and inserted my own.

It sounded like something out of a cheesy made-for-TV movie, one that would be awesome to curl up in front of and watch on a rainy Sunday afternoon with a big bowl of popcorn.

Except for the fact that it was actually happening in my real life.

And little had I known that at the exact same time my brain was being inserted in Nikki's body, one of those neurosurgeons was secretly taking Nikki's brain and slipping it into the head of this girl standing in front of me.

Nikki – her brain, anyway – was supposed to have died.

And the secret she carried was supposed to have died along with her.

Unfortunately for Mr Stark – but fortunately for Nikki – Nikki was still very much alive. Both her brain, and her body. Just in two separate locations.

The secret she knows, however? That's still a secret.

And Brandon hadn't done a very good job of sweet-talking it out of her . . . mainly because he'd been too distracted lately, trying to sweet-talk me.

And, God knew, Nikki hated me way too much because of that to utter a barely civilized word to me, no matter how often I've tried to get her to open up to me.

I wondered how much of that is because her scar still aches sometimes, the way mine does.

'I'm sure you're right,' Nikki said, her nose in the air as she left my room. 'Brandon loves the colour blue.'

He does? This was news to me.

But I was finding out that there was a lot about Nikki Howard's ex-boyfriend that was news to me. His favourite colour was the least of it really.

What about the fact that he has a secret beachside lair where he likes to stash girls he's either kidnapped against their will, the way he has me, or intends to seduce, then blackmail to get what he wants, the way he does Nikki . . .

. . . which, in this case, is information to use against his father so Brandon can take over his company himself. Super!

Yeah. If it turned out Brandon Stark also likes to dress up like Strawberry Shortcake while playing croquet with his miniature pony collection, I totally wouldn't be surprised any more.

'Em?' Brandon thumped on my door again.

'What?' I said, more sharply than I meant to. I had a headache that I *really wasn't faking*.

'I think I found a cure for what you have,' Brandon said through the door.

I looked up in surprise at this.

Because there is no cure for what I have, since what I have is *one hundred per cent fake*.

'Really?' I said. 'What is it?'

'It's called You better get out here,' Brandon said in a

different tone of voice, 'or you'll be sorry.'

Oh. Right. I forgot.

Because the tabloids have got it wrong.

I'm not on a secret love getaway.

I may not exactly be behind bars.

I'm not sporting shackles or handcuffs.

There aren't even men in black suits standing on either side of me, speaking into little mini-microphones in their sleeves.

But I'm Brandon Stark's prisoner just the same.

Two

I opened the door and stood there in the long black velvet evening gown Brandon had had sent over for that evening's festivities – a gourmet dinner being prepared by the cordon-bleu-trained chef Brandon had stolen away from a nearby five-star hotel to come work for him for the week.

One thing about Brandon Stark: he doesn't mess around when he's trying to impress a lady.

The question was, why couldn't he figure out the right girl to impress? It was Nikki he was supposed to be trying to win over, not me.

Not that he'd even have to try that hard with her. If he'd expended *half* as much energy on her as he kept expending on me, he'd have had her eating out of his hand.

Why couldn't he understand that?

Probably for the same reason he thinks it's cool to hang out in Ed Hardy shirts with reality-show stars on his dad's yacht: he's kind of stupid.

And yet at the same time he's completely evil.

It turns out the two combined are deadly. Well, for me.

Brandon didn't say anything for a minute. He just stared at me.

Which was good. It meant plan B – which I'd come up with in case plan A, faking sick, didn't work out –

was working. I may seem like a defenceless blonde on the outside, but I actually do have a few weapons in my arsenal.

One of them was the Armani I was wearing. I realized the moment I saw it on the rack of clothes that had been sent over from the expensive designer boutique that this particular gown was totally going to be my ally.

I may not have known a thing about fashion a few months ago when I'd been the worst-dressed girl in the entire eleventh grade at Tribeca Alternative High School.

But I've always been a fast learner.

'Brandon,' I said to him. The long hallway – which was glass on one side so you could see the ocean and dunes (when it wasn't so dark out) – was empty except for us two (and the paparazzi, of course. But I'm fairly certain the private security guards Brandon had hired, and who were patrolling outside the house, had flushed any photographers out). I closed the guest-room door behind me so there was no chance Nikki would overhear what I was about to say to him.

I figured it was probably useless. I'd tried reasoning with him before.

But never in Armani.

'This is ridiculous,' I went on. 'You're supposed to be trying to seduce Nikki, not me. She's the one with the secret your dad tried to have her murdered for. The one you want to steal so you can kick your dad out and take over.'

Brandon just stared down at me. He's no smarter, in

some ways, than Jason Klein, the king of the Walking Dead (aka the jocks) back at my high school.

Just richer and with fewer morals.

'Which is great, but I have to get back to the city,' I said to him. I was trying to speak slowly and clearly, so he would be sure to understand me. 'I have the Stark Angel fashion show in a few days. You know I can't miss that. This romantic getaway over the holidays with Brandon Stark? The press is eating it up.'

Though the truth was, I couldn't imagine my mother was too happy about it. Not that I'd spoken to her. I'd been letting her calls go to voicemail. I knew if I spoke to her, the hurt I'd heard in her voice – *Really, Em. Spending the week with a boy? What's the matter with you?* – would be like a stab wound to the chest.

But what was worse was that no one else besides her – and of course Lulu and my agent, Rebecca, who'd called me approximately a zillion times – had left me a voice-mail.

No one else, meaning the single person whose feelings I was most anxious about having wounded by taking off with Brandon Stark.

Right: Christopher Maloney, the love of my life, hadn't called.

I don't know why I thought he would have, after what I'd done to him – which was lie and tell him I didn't love him any more . . . that instead, I loved Brandon. It wasn't like I *deserved* a call. Or an email, or a text message, or anything at all from him.

I guess I just thought he'd get in *some* kind of contact . . . even if it was only to send me a letter of bitter recrimination or something. Sure, I wouldn't have enjoyed being on the receiving end of a *Dear Em, thanks for ruining my life* email. I mean, Christopher didn't know Brandon had forced me to say what I had.

But even a Dear Em letter would have been better than this cold stone silence . . .

But no. Nothing.

Better not to think about that now.

Or ever.

'But eventually,' I forced myself to go on to Brandon, 'the people I'm close to are going to start getting suspicious. They know, Brandon, that you and I aren't . . . well, what you're trying to make them think we are.'

I was lying, of course. The people in my life had no idea that I wasn't in love with Brandon, and that this whole thing was a fake. They didn't know. Hadn't I been the one going around basically hooking up with every cute guy I'd come into contact with ever since I'd gotten my brain slipped into this hot new bod? How was anyone supposed to have known which of those guys I actually cared about and which of those guys I didn't? Right: I had made the mess I was in right now.

And I was the one who needed to get myself out of it.

Which I was actually trying to do at the moment. Although it may not have looked like it.

'I've got to get back to the city,' I said to Brandon again, stalling for time. 'Just let me—'

12

Brandon reached up to lay a finger over my lips. And left it there.

'Shh,' he said.

Uh-oh. His reboot was apparently completed. His pupils stopped looking like twin spinning beach balls of death. He'd taken a step forward.

Now he was standing just inches away from me, looking down at me with an expression I couldn't quite read.

But, like a lot of things about him lately, it scared me a little.

'Everything's going to be all right,' he said in what I suppose he thought was a soothing voice.

Except I was about as soothed as a Dalmatian puppy at Cruella de Vil's house.

'I know what I'm doing,' he went on.

'Uh,' I said, from behind his finger, 'actually, I don't think you do. Because Nikki's not going to tell you anything if you don't start paying less attention to me and more attention to—'

Then he removed his finger and started to lean his head down to place his lips where, a second before, his finger had been.

Ugh, no. Seriously? Again?

I had goosebumps, and not because I was in a sleeveless dress.

Look, I couldn't blame Brandon. I'd been giving him mixed messages for months. And straight up using him, basically. That's the kind of girl I'd turned into since I'd become Nikki. It wasn't nice to admit, but it was the truth.

But things were different now. I finally had my head – pun intended – on straight.

Nevertheless, I knew what I had to do. What I'd been having to do all week.

It's what models have to do all the time: pretend like we're actually comfortable in what we're wearing, or enjoying what we're eating, or aren't completely freezing standing there in the ocean, waves crashing over us.

It's not the hardest thing in the world. I've actually gotten pretty good at it. And in this particular case, that was a really good thing.

Because prisoners are treated better when they get along with their jailers.

And there's more of a chance their jailer might slip up and let down his guard if he thinks his prisoner might actually like him a little.

And that would allow the prisoner to escape.

The problem is, I can't escape until I get what I need. Which happens to be the same thing Brandon needs: the piece of information that got me into this mess in the first place.

Which means no matter how bitchy Nikki is to me, I have to put up with her until she spills her guts.

So no matter how much Brandon grosses me out, I have to put up with him.

Nobody said it was easy being a prisoner.

So I did what I had to do: I let Brandon kiss me.

Fortunately, just as I saw Brandon's lips looming closer and closer to mine, I heard a nearby door thrown open.

14

It wasn't plan C.

But it was enough.

I hastily pulled my head back, relieved I had an excuse to, since even Brandon would have to admit he couldn't afford to let Nikki see him making out with me.

Footsteps – sturdy ones, not the tippity-tap of fringed wedges – sounded on the polished marble floor, and I turned to see Nikki's older brother, Steven, coming towards us.

'Hey,' he said, nodding to us both at once.

'Hello,' Brandon said, his response almost comical in its lack of enthusiasm. His attitude towards Steven this past week had been cool at best. While he had to pretend to be at least somewhat enthusiastic about seeing Nikki every time she came stomping into the room, he didn't have to pretend to be enthusiastic about seeing her brother.

'So,' Steven said as he walked slowly by us. 'What's up?'

'Dinner's being served downstairs in the dining room,' Brandon said coolly. His tone clearly suggested, *So why don't you get down there and leave us alone?*

'Yeah?' Steven didn't look like he was in any kind of hurry. And why not? Steven, like his sister, couldn't leave the house, for fear he too might be photographed and tracked down by Robert Stark, who wasn't supposed to know where Steven or his mother were . . . or he might have them eliminated as well, the way he'd tried to do to Nikki.

'And what culinary delight are you going to stun us with tonight, Brandon?' Steven asked.

The funny part was, Brandon was too dumb to tell that Steven was totally being sarcastic. I had to hide my smile. Steven didn't care what was for dinner. He hated Brandon as much as I did. He'd never said so . . .

. . . but I could totally tell.

'She-crab soup,' Brandon said, 'and some kind of crab salad – peekytoe, I think – along with foie gras or something.'

As Brandon was speaking, Steven started heading for the floating staircase to the ground floor. Because he usually left the room while Brandon was talking. That's how much Steven hated him.

In my mind, I was screaming, *Don't go, Steven! Don't leave me alone with him!*

But of course I couldn't say anything like that. I had to be polite. On the surface.

'And then,' Brandon went on in a bored tone, 'filet mignon. There's a chocolate soufflé for dessert.'

'Sounds great,' Steven said over his shoulder. He was wearing some of the clothes Brandon had bought for him, a pair of black jeans and a dark grey cashmere sweater, the sleeves pushed up to the elbows. All of us – with the exception of Nikki and her mom, who'd had time to throw a few things into some bags before we left – had arrived at Brandon's with nothing but the clothes on our backs (and our dogs . . . those of us who owned dogs), trying to escape from Robert Stark.

Brandon had been more than generous about making sure Steven and his mom had the things they might need,

16

since they couldn't use their credit cards for fear Stark Enterprises might be able to trace them.

But I could sense that Steven seemed annoyed at being beholden to the son of the man who'd caused his family so much heartache. He never actually *said* anything that was outright rude to Brandon.

But he did *do* things that someone who was a little more self-aware than Brandon might have found rude. Such as walk out of the room while Brandon was still speaking.

'Filet mignon again. Great,' Steven tossed over his shoulder as he headed down the stairs. 'Oh, hey, Brandon,' he added casually. 'You know your Lamborghini is on fire, right?'

Brandon's hand went to the wire-suspended steel banister and froze.

'What?'

'Your new Lamborghini,' Steven said. 'I noticed it just now when I looked out across the driveway. It's in flames.'

Yes. *Finally*. Plan C in action.

Brandon glanced out of the bank of windows that looked over the front of the house, seeming a little scornful, like, *Yeah, right. My car is on fire.*

A second later his demeanour changed entirely. He let out a curse word that singed my ears.

'My car,' he cried. 'It's on fire!'

'That's what I said.' Steven shook his head, looking up at me from the bottom of the stairs, as if to say, *What a loser.* 'Isn't that what I just said?'

17

Brandon let out another curse and, grabbing his hair with both hands, tore past me, nearly shoving me down the stairs in his haste to get by, and then barrelling by Steven.

'Call 911!' he screamed.

Three

Nikki chose that exact moment to come out of her room.

'What's wrong with Brandon?' she asked as she click-clacked down the hall towards me.

'His car is on fire,' Steven said with a shrug.

'What?' Nikki's voice rose to a high-pitched shriek. 'Not the new Lamborghini!'

I had to flatten myself against the wall again in order not to get knocked down as she hurried off after Brandon, her heels making a huge racket on the shiny marble floor.

'Brandon,' she cried, racing after him. 'Wait! I'm coming!'

I wanted to remind her not to go outside or the paparazzi might get a shot of her, but it was too late. She was already gone.

Cosabella, my miniature poodle, who'd followed me from my room, rushed down the stairs after Nikki, her claws skittering on the slick floor. She gave a few excited barks and then, when Nikki slammed the front door in her face, gave herself a good shake and came trotting back, looking proud of herself for a job well done.

'So.' Steven folded his arms and stared up at me as I made my way down the long staircase. It was a little treacherous to navigate in high heels and a skin-tight

Armani evening gown, I found. 'You set the guy's car on fire?'

This caused me to freeze in my tracks.

'Me?' I arranged my face into a suitably shocked expression. 'What makes you think it was *me*, and not one of the paps trying to lure him outside so they could get a photo op?'

'Because I found your fuse,' he said, holding up what used to be a wooden mixed-bead necklace Brandon had given me . . .

. . . at least until I'd rolled it in a mixture that included hot water, sugar and another substance, and let it dry overnight.

'You're a liar,' I said when I reached the bottom of the stairs. I plucked the singed necklace from his hand. 'You said you saw the car burning from the windows.'

'Actually,' Steven said, 'I did. And I went out to investigate. That was a little while ago. I found it so interesting, I thought I'd let it keep going, to see what would happen. Where did *you* of all people learn to make a slow-burning fuse?'

'YouTube,' I said. I dropped the charred necklace into the neck of a Greek amphora that was sitting at the bottom of the stairs. 'And I resent the implication that a girl wouldn't necessarily know her way around explosives. I go to an alternative high school, you know.'

'Of course.' Steven nodded. 'Stupid of me. But let me ask you a question,' he said as he followed me into the dining room, where I'd gone to sit down at the massive, already set table. 'Why would you want to blow up Brandon Stark's new car?'

Because he's holding us prisoners here. And Christopher doesn't love me any more.

'It's not going to blow up,' I said. 'I just made a decorative design on the hood with lighter fluid. And there are plenty of fire extinguishers out there. I checked. If Brandon has any sense, he'll get the fire out before it does any permanent damage to anything but the paint job.'

And I hadn't timed the fire right. It was supposed to have gone up *before* he got a chance to kiss me.

'You didn't need to destroy his car,' Steven said, joining me at the table. 'The guy is a tool, but that's going a little far, don't you think?'

'No,' I said shortly. Cosabella curled up at my feet beneath the table.

'Wow.' Steven stared at me. 'You really hate him.'

I pictured Christopher's face growing smaller and smaller in the distance as the limo Brandon had forced me into snaked its way down the road.

You have, my voicemail's robotic voice said in my head, over and over, *no new messages.*

Yeah. I guess I did hate Brandon.

'I told you,' I said. 'I was only trying to mess up the paint job a little.'

Steven shook his head. 'I'm not falling for it, Em.'

Of course he wasn't. Nikki's brother is a trained military officer. He isn't stupid.

But I widened my eyes and went for the innocent act

anyway. Because of what Brandon had said would happen if I didn't.

'I don't know what you mean,' I said.

'Convincing,' Steven said. 'But spill now while we have five minutes alone together for once. You're not in love with Brandon Stark. What's going on, Em? Why are you pretending to be in love with Brandon on the one hand, then setting his car on fire behind his back?'

Whatever she knows about Stark Quark, if it's worth killing Nikki Howard for – and then giving her a brain transplant to keep her image alive – it's worth knowing. And I want in, Brandon had whispered to me that cold grey morning back in New York just a week ago.

Why should I help you? I'd demanded.

Because, he'd said, *if you don't, I'll tell my dad where the real Nikki Howard is. And,* he'd added, about Christopher, *no more of that other guy, the one in the leather jacket, who seems so into you. Just me. You're mine now. Understand?*

I'd looked up at him then like he was crazy.

But now I know better. Brandon Stark isn't crazy. Dumb, maybe. Desperate to leave his mark on this planet, the way his father has, but with no real idea of how to go about doing that.

But not crazy.

And if you tell them that I'm making you do it, I'll tell my father about the girl.

Would he? Would Brandon tell?

He certainly didn't care about Nikki – or about Steven or Mrs Howard. Sure, he was willing to house – and clothe –

them, since they had nowhere else to go thanks to his dad's company essentially stalking them.

But he was only doing this because of what he thought he was going to get out of it: me (only not the real me. The me he thought I was, this made-up girl whose name he didn't even really know, who looked like Nikki Howard).

Oh, and whatever it was Nikki knew that he thought was going to make him so much money.

'Em.' Steven was staring at me, his face – so much like the one I saw reflected in the mirror every morning when I put on my make-up, only masculine – tight with anxiety. 'Whatever he's threatened you with, I swear to you, I can make it better. You just have to tell me what's going on.'

I wanted to believe him. I really did. I'd never had a big brother before, but I was starting to really love Nikki's. He was so comforting, with his wide shoulders and steady gaze. I almost believed that he *could* make it all better.

But of course he couldn't. No one could.

And if you tell them that I'm making you do it, I'll tell my father about the girl.

Except Brandon wasn't going to tell his father a thing about Nikki. He couldn't. He needed her too much. She held the key to everything.

But Christopher. He'd tell his father about Christopher.

'Oh, there you are,' Nikki's mother called as she came down the floating staircase, holding carefully on to the handrail as both her poodles, Cosabella's siblings, skittered down the steps in front of her. 'Is everything all right? What was all that ruckus I heard before?'

Talk about saved by the bell . . . a real southern belle, as a matter of fact: Nikki and Steven's mom had the drawl and the gently fading beauty of one. You could see where both Nikki and Steven got their good looks. Mrs Howard was still what my dad would call a knockout.

But before anyone could say anything else, the chef's assistant came out of the kitchen holding a silver tray.

'She-crab soup,' he said, trying to ignore the obnoxiously dancing poodles at his feet, all hoping they might be able to trip him and that he might spill some of what he was carrying. He seemed more disconcerted by the fact that there were only three of us than by the dogs.

'Oh,' he said. 'Is Mr Stark not ready for dinner yet?'

'There was a little emergency,' I said. 'He'll be back in a few minutes. I guess you could tell the chef to go ahead and serve.'

The assistant nodded, holding the tray for Steven and his mother to help themselves to the first course, then he retreated back into the kitchen, his rubber clogs soundless on the black marble floor. Cosabella and Mrs Howard's dogs, Harry and Winston, followed after him, still eagerly hoping he might drop something.

'What kind of emergency?' Mrs Howard asked.

'Em set his car on fire,' Steven said.

Mrs Howard, about to lift her shot glass of soup to her mouth, gasped instead. 'Em! Why would you do such a thing?'

I shrugged. I couldn't tell her I'd done it because Brandon was a great big lying fake who'd caused me and my boyfriend to break up forever. She, like everyone else, thought I was in love with Brandon, and that he was protecting her and her daughter from his evil father.

And, in a way, he was.

I didn't want to worry her more than I had already. She'd left everything behind – her business, her home, her friends, her life – for her daughter.

Who actually didn't seem all that grateful for it, if you asked me.

'Shouldn't we call the fire department?' Mrs Howard asked, still looking shocked.

Just as she was saying this, one of the glass side doors opened and Brandon came in, Nikki tripping at his heels.

'I'm telling you, it was those jerks from *OK!*,' Brandon said. 'And I'm not standing for it. Not a second longer. I'm calling my lawyers. I'm suing for the cost of replacing my car.'

'You're so right, Brandon.' Nikki wobbled along after him in her too-high – and several sizes too big for her – platform wedges. 'It had to be them. Who else would do such a thing?'

'Is everything all right?' Mrs Howard asked. 'No one was hurt, were they? Is the fire out? Nikki, no one got a photo of you out there, did they?'

'Oh, it's out,' Brandon said as Nikki shook her head. Brandon had his iPhone glued to his face. 'And Nikki's fine. But the paint job on my car is ruined. Ruined! Hello, Ken?'

He started shouting into his cellphone. 'Ken, it's Brandon. They trashed my car. What? The Murciélago, that's which one. Why? How the hell should I know why? To get a reaction out of me that they can plaster all over their damn magazine covers, that's why. Why else?'

'I don't know how any of us is supposed to be able to eat,' Nikki said with a sigh as she sat down, unfolding her white linen napkin with a snap, 'after what just happened. The paparazzi have just gotten so out of control. How could they do such an awful thing to poor Brandon?'

'What makes you think it was the paparazzi?' Steven asked, not looking in my direction, as the chef's assistant came into the dining room carrying a tray. He was trying very hard not to trip over the dogs again.

'I don't know who else it would be,' Nikki said. 'Brandon's never hurt anyone. He's completely sweet and adorable.'

I choked a little on the sip of sparkling water I'd just swallowed. If Brandon was sweet and adorable, I was Satan's bride.

'Maybe,' I said when I'd recovered, 'it was his dad.'

'What?' Nikki looked confused. 'Why would his dad send him a nice car for Christmas, then set it on fire?'

'Because,' I said, 'maybe Mr Stark knows *you're* here.'

Nikki turned visibly pale.

'You think he knows?' she asked.

Yeah. I was evil. I was a car-burning, lie-telling super-model. Whatever. I didn't care any more. They'd already given me a brain transplant, made me dump my boyfriend, and were going to make me parade around in a million-dollar bra on national television in a couple of days. What more could they do to me? Kill me?

Well, guess what? I was already dead.

'He could suspect,' I said. 'And if he does, we don't have much time. We need to know what it is he tried to murder you for. That way we can get the proof we need to prosecute Brandon's dad and have him put away where he can't try to hurt you any more.'

Nikki's chin slid out stubbornly.

'Like I already told my *mother*,' she said, putting an unpleasant emphasis on the word *mother*, 'when she tried to bring this up the other day: Brandon's dad did not try to have me murdered. I don't know where you all keep coming up with this story—'

'Because we all sat in the same room with Doctor Fong,' Mrs Howard explained patiently. 'And heard him reveal that you didn't have an embolism, Nikki—'

'But they forced him to do the surgery anyway,' Steven interrupted. 'They were going to *throw your brain away*. He saved your life by transplanting it into the body you have now. Why don't you get that? Just tell us what you were going to blackmail Robert Stark about, and we can all go back to our old lives.'

'Oh.' Suddenly Nikki's eyes were bright with unshed tears. 'Can we? Can we all go back to our old lives, Steven? I'm sorry, but you seem to have forgotten that that isn't possible for some of us. Because *there's another girl living in my old body*.'

She shot me a look that sent chills up my spine. No one – not even Whitney Robertson, back at Tribeca Alternative, who I'm pretty sure had disliked me more than any human being in the entire universe, and only because when I was on her volleyball team during PE, I'd sometimes miss the ball – had ever given me a look of such pure, unadulterated hatred.

'So I can't go back to my old life,' Nikki said to her brother. 'That girl right there is living in my apartment, using my money, taking my gigs, even *my dog* likes her better than me.' She pointed through the glass tabletop at Cosabella, who was sitting at the side of my chair, panting up at me eagerly, hoping I might slip her a piece of whatever food was about to be served (which, I have to admit, I'd been known on occasion to do).

'So excuse me,' Nikki went on, 'if I'm not exactly in a rush to get out of here. I happen to like things exactly as they are, considering the alternatives. Because if you think I'm going back home to live in redneck Gasper, USA, with you and Mom, Steven, well, you can just think again. I'm never going back there. *Never.*'

'Nikki,' I said. I felt terrible about what had happened to her. I really did. Even though none of it had been my fault – hey, I definitely hadn't chosen to be the new brain behind the Face of Stark – I felt like I owed her something.

But I had to get out of Brandon Stark's control before I went crazy.

Or set something else of his on fire. Like his trousers, for instance.

28

'Maybe we could work something out.' I lowered my voice just in case Brandon, even tied up as he seemed to be in his phone call, happened to overhear me.

She narrowed her eyes at me.

'What do you mean, work something out?'

'Well,' I half-whispered, 'like, I could give you the money back. The money in your bank account. I'd also offer you a cut of anything I make in the future. You know, from future jobs.'

Nikki leaned back in her chair. The chef's assistant had set decoratively arranged plates of peekytoe salad in front of each of us, including in front of Brandon's empty seat. Brandon was still pacing at the bottom of the stairs, on the phone to his lawyer. Every once in a while a burst of his conversation would reach us. It sounded like, 'What do you mean, I need proof?' and 'No, I don't see why I should have to do that!' He was clearly lost in his own little world.

'That sounds fair, Nikki,' Mrs Howard said, moving some of her peekytoe salad around on her plate. 'You really ought to consider it.'

'I don't have to consider anything,' Nikki said. 'She's not offering me anything I wouldn't have if none of this had happened in the first place. She's offering me less, actually, than I would have had.'

'But you ruined your career,' Steven pointed out, his voice raised a little in frustration, 'by trying to blackmail your boss. Which he should have fired you for. But instead, he tried to have you killed. Either way, Emerson's the one who would be doing all the work.'

Nikki stared at him like he was stupid.

'You think modelling is work?' she demanded. 'Getting paid to stand around in five-thousand-dollar dresses while people airbrush make-up on to you and compliment you while taking your picture? That isn't work. That's freaking fun, dude.'

I had no idea what she was talking about. Modelling was totally work. Sure, it wasn't standing over a fryer at McDonald's in a polyester uniform, getting grease all over you, for the minimum wage, while people yelled at you that they wanted a Diet Coke with their Big Mac, fries, McNuggets and apple turnover. And Supersize it.

But I had never worked so hard in my life on most of the shoots I got sent out on. That whole thing where Tyra was going on about smiling with your eyes? Yeah, not so easy, it turns out, when you're in nothing but a bustier and a thong and standing in freezing cold water up to your butt and you're shivering and all you want to do is go home and cry.

'Look, Nikki,' I said, feeling like we were getting off topic, 'with that kind of money you wouldn't have to live in Gasper. You could live in a duplex with a doorman and an in-house gym in SoHo.'

'And do what?' Nikki demanded.

'Go to college,' Mrs Howard said promptly.

Nikki snorted again. 'Oh right, Mom,' she said, rolling her eyes.

'What's wrong with that idea?' her mother asked. 'There're all sorts of things you could get degrees in, things you already know all about and could bring a specialized knowledge to because of your background . . . photography, fashion design or merchandising, business, publicity, media, entertainment law—'

Nikki cut her mother short.

'There's only one thing I want,' she hissed.

'And what's that?' I asked.

Not the dog, I prayed. I wasn't sure I could part with Cosabella. In the months that I'd gotten to know her, the two of us had really bonded. True, it was kind of annoying having a four-legged little shadow follow me everywhere I went.

But I had kind of gotten used to it.

Yet what else could Nikki want? I'd already offered her all the money I had, and a split of my future earnings? Should I offer her *all* my future earnings? It was going to be tough to figure out how I was going to pay the mortgage on the loft . . .

Wait. Did Nikki want the *loft*? Was I going to have to move? What about Lulu? Lulu paid me rent to live in the loft.

Well, I guess we were just going to have to find some other place to live.

'What I *want*,' Nikki said, in the nastiest voice I think I've ever heard – and that includes when Whitney Robertson used to ask me if I'd ever even heard of conditioner – 'is my old body back.'

Four

Stunned, I looked down at the body Nikki was talking about. *Her* body. The body I'd woken up in a few months earlier, in so much confusion. The body I had had to get accustomed to seeing myself in, to walking around in, to *living* in. The body that had caused me so much pain and heartache and astonishment as I'd tried to get used to it.

The body I had hated, railed against, refused to believe was now my own, and had cursed.

The body I'd been convinced was ruining my life.

And then later, the body in which I'd experienced so much laughter, having whipped-cream fights with Lulu in the kitchen. And wonder, as I'd felt what it could do on a treadmill, actually experiencing runner's high for the first time in my life (I'd certainly never exerted myself in my old body, especially in PE . . . except to try to duck the volleyballs Whitney Robertson spiked at my head).

And finally joy, as I'd lain beneath Christopher and felt his mouth moving over my lips, his heart drumming against mine.

And I realized, with a shock like the cold seawater I'd felt once pouring over me when I'd flung myself backwards off a cliff into it, I wasn't giving this body up.

No way.

I may have hated it at times – I may have longed for my old life back.

But this was my new life. It was the only life I had.

I wasn't about it to give it up.

'Over my dead body,' Mrs Howard burst out, basically summing up my feelings exactly.

'Well,' Nikki said, looking over at her mother, 'good thing it's not your body we're talking about, isn't it? So why don't you just butt out?'

'Nikki,' Mrs Howard said. Nikki had pushed back her chair and risen from the table angrily, 'Doctor Fong and I spent weeks nursing you after you nearly *died* the last time they did the surgery. Your new heart couldn't take the strain of being under anaesthesia for so long. It was a miracle you even survived. And without brain damage.'

'I'm not so sure she *didn't* suffer brain damage,' Steven remarked with the sarcasm only a sibling could display.

'Shut up,' Nikki snapped at him. Her chin was sticking out again, a sign, I had figured out, that she'd made up her mind. To her mother she said, 'I'm willing to risk it. I want my old life back. *All* of it. That includes my old body. Give it to me, or no deal.'

Wow.

I had seen Nikki in a lot of moods since we'd moved into adjacent bedrooms . . .

. . . but I'd never seen her this adamant about anything.

'You're being ridiculous. I don't see how that surgery would even be possible,' Mrs Howard went on, throwing a beseeching look at Brandon, 'considering the fact that the only doctors who can perform it work for Brandon's father at the Stark Institute for Neurology and Neurosurgery. And how is he possibly going to get them to do it without his father finding out?'

'Doctor Fong can do it,' Nikki said. 'He did it once for me. He can do it again.'

Well. That much was true.

I looked down at the elegant hands I'd grown so accustomed to seeing at the ends of my slender wrists. The hands that had shaken so badly the first time I'd tried to feed myself. The hands with which I'd been forced to learn to write a new name – Nikki's, not my own – on all the slips of paper autograph seekers had thrust at me every time I'd set foot in public. The hands that had slipped under Christopher's leather jacket – had it really only been a few nights ago? – and felt his skin burning beneath mine.

But I guess they'd never really been my hands after all.

They were her hands. Nikki's hands.

And now she wanted them back.

I clenched Nikki's hands into fists.

They may have been her hands.

But it was *my* brain that had made them do all those things.

'Doctor Fong doesn't have his own facilities to perform a complicated procedure like that,' Mrs Howard was saying. 'You know he doesn't. Why do you think your recovery took so much longer than Em's, besides the fact that you nearly died during it, because the body you have now isn't as strong as your old one? Because he didn't have access to—'

'Well,' Nikki said, 'we can just set up an operating room here. If Brandon wants this information badly enough, he'll pay whatever it costs to give me what I want. Right, Brandon?'

'Oh, Nikki,' her mother said. 'Don't be so—'

'Right, Brandon?' Nikki said, interrupting her mother.

Brandon, who'd shoved his iPhone into his pocket and stridden over to sit in his chair at the head of the dining table, looked up from his plate and said the words that sent a chill through my heart . . . Nikki's heart:

'Uh . . . I guess.'

Wait – he was actually *considering* this? Did he even realize what we were talking about?

'See?' Nikki turned shining eyes on us. 'It's all set then.' Her eyes, I saw, weren't shining because they were tear-filled. They were bright with triumph. *Goody*, her eyes seemed to be saying. 'Now that that's settled—'

'Nikki,' Steven said, raising his head and swivelling it to send a steely eyed look at his sister. 'No.'

The word was simple. And final. Just *No*.

I realized then how much I loved Steven. He may have been Nikki's brother.

But he was my hero.

'What do you mean, no?' Nikki demanded, whipping her head towards her brother. No one ever said no to Nikki. I should know. 'If they took it out, they can put it back in. You asked what I wanted in exchange for telling what I know, and that's what I want. I want my body back.'

'Well, you can't have it back,' Steven said. Steven's tone was brusque. 'It could kill her. And you. You can't ask her to risk her life. She's already done it once. You can't ask her to do it again.'

'*Yes*,' Nikki said, her eyes narrowed, '*I can*.'

And in that *Yes, I can* I finally saw the girl from the tiny town who was so determined to make it big that she was willing to break her mother's heart by having herself declared an emancipated minor before the age of sixteen.

And had signed her first million-dollar contract a week later.

'*No*,' her brother said, with just as much determination. And I saw in him the self-made man, the soldier who my loft-mate Lulu was so head over heels in love with, and who she asked me so breathlessly about every time she called. 'You're asking too much.'

Now the shininess I saw in Nikki's eyes really was tears. She glared at all of us.

'Nobody thinks about *me*,' she said. The flintiness wasn't gone. It was just being directed somewhere else. At forcing herself to appear sympathetic by crying, I suspected. 'How *I* feel. I mean, how do you think it feels for *me*, to know I'm going to have to go around for the rest of my life in *this* body, looking like this hideous hag?

She flung herself into the nearest chair, lowering her head on to the table, and burst into dramatic sobs.

Brandon and Steven exchanged incredulous glances,

while Mrs Howard hurried over to comfort her weeping daughter.

'Nikki,' Mrs Howard was saying, 'how can you say that? You're a normal, healthy-looking girl. No, you don't look like you used to. But you're not hideous. You're still beautiful to me, just different from how you used to be—'

'*Normal?*' Nikki echoed, in a tone that suggested her mother had used a dirty word. '*Healthy-looking?* Are you kidding me, Mother? I don't want to be *normal*. I don't want to be *healthy-looking*, or *beautiful to you*. I want to be freaking gorgeous, like I used to be! I don't want to be stuck in this stubby-looking body, with this plain-Jane face and this useless, ugly hair! I want to be hot! I want to be sexy! *I want to be Nikki Howard!*'

I don't know if it was my imagination or not, but the phrase *I want to be Nikki Howard* seemed to bounce off the cold hard windows around us and echo around the room. *I want to be Nikki Howard! I want to be Nikki Howard! I want to be Nikki Howard!*

'Well, you can't,' Mrs Howard said exasperatedly. 'And you're not going to get anywhere if you don't stop putting yourself down. Just look in that window there and see what I see: a bright young girl, with so much to offer . . .'

But Nikki wouldn't look up. She was too busy crying into her statement necklace.

And because Nikki wouldn't look up, I did. What I saw was my own reflection . . . the reflection Nikki used to have.

Perfect. Not a feature, not even a hair, out of place. Exactly what you would expect to see on the cover of a magazine or modelling an expensive dress or piece of jewellry in an ad. Telling you what to buy or where to go or what was hot now.

And because she looked so perfect – or what we'd been told for so long was how a perfect person was supposed to look – you would believe her. You'd want to buy whatever she was selling you, or go where she said to go. You'd want to make sure you had whatever it was she assured you was hot now.

That was if you weren't one of those people, like I'd always been, who hated her on sight. What did I need Nikki Howard for, telling me what to wear, what to buy, where to go? I'd never been able to stand the sight of her perfect, vapid face and body, towering over me on the sides of buildings or winking out at me from the pages of magazines.

And now that face and body were mine. I couldn't get away from them. No matter where I went, or how far I tried to run. Her face was my face. What she touched, I touched. What she experienced, I experienced.

But the thing was, I couldn't imagine *not* being her. Not any more. She and I were one . . .

. . . and, I had to admit, I *liked* being her. I did. It wasn't always easy, being Nikki.

But it was me. I was Nikki now.

Beneath me, I felt Cosabella – realizing I wasn't going to drop any food tonight – give up on her vigilant stand at my side and lay down to rest her head on my foot with a sigh. It was where she lay at every meal. It felt warm and natural to have her head there, soft as velvet . . .

My heart jerked.

If what Nikki wanted to happen actually happened, I'd never feel Cosabella's head on my foot again.

Oh, I supposed I could get a new dog . . . if I lived through the surgery. She wouldn't be exactly like Cosabella, but it would be all right.

Wouldn't it?

Even if I ran – even if I took off tonight, with Cosabella – they'd find me. Where could I go that Brandon couldn't find me? I had the most recognizable face in the world. Maybe there was some tribal village in the wilds of the Amazon where they'd never seen Nikki Howard before.

But how long was I going to last without cable? I'm not even talking about the premium channels, but Bravo and BBC America? I started freaking out after even a few hours without the Internet.

I had to face it: I was screwed.

'*No*,' Steven said again. 'Nikki. It's not going to happen. It's too dangerous. And it's not medically necessary. No surgeon in his right mind would do it. Not even Doctor Fong.'

'Why,' Nikki sobbed, lifting her head and revealing that mascara had begun to run down her face, 'does everyone hate me?'

'Nikki,' her mother said. 'No one hates you. It isn't that. It's because you two aren't—'

'*It's not up to you,*' Nikki yelled, just as the chef's assistant came out with a tray to collect the empty plates from the second course. '*It's up to Brandon!*'

The assistant turned around and headed right back into the kitchen, Harry and Winston looking after him disappointedly. Apparently he'd realized now wasn't the best time to interrupt the conversation.

'Uh,' Brandon said, shifting in his seat as he realized all eyes were on him. 'If Nikki wants her body back, then that's what Nikki's gonna get. She's what matters here.'

A coldness – like the cold of the glass tabletop beneath my fingers – began to seep into my heart. It felt as if it was spreading from my heart to each of my limbs. Soon the only warmth in my body was the warmth radiating from Cosabella's head, resting on my foot.

'And Doctor Fong will do it,' Brandon went on. 'Or I'll haul his ass in front of the AMA for violating ten thousand different medical ethics in doing this whole switcheroo thing in the first place. Right, Nik?'

Now? He decides to start being Nikki's best friend *now*, right when I need him the most?

Oh, God. I was sure I was going to throw up.

Nikki stopped crying at once. Instead, she squealed with excitement. She jumped up from her seat and ran over to where Brandon sat, throwing herself into his lap so that she could fling both her arms around his neck.

'Oh, thank you, thank you,' she cried. 'I love you so much, Bran!'

'I don't believe this,' Steven muttered. He stood up and walked out without another word, heading up the stairs and back to his room.

Don't go, Steven, I wanted to say. *Don't go.*

But I couldn't speak. Because my lips, like the rest of my body, were frozen.

Nikki, noticing he was leaving, asked confusedly, 'Steven? Don't you want to stay for filet mignon? I mean . . . we have something to celebrate.'

'No,' Steven said over his shoulder. 'We don't.'

A few seconds later, we all heard a door slam.

Nikki, still in Brandon's lap, threw an accusing look at her mother. 'What's his problem?'

'He's upset, Nikki,' Mrs Howard said, looking distressed. 'I'm upset too. I don't think you or Brandon have thought this thing all the way through. Or considered poor Em. It's completely absurd – not to mention unethical – to perform a risky and life-threatening operation on two perfectly healthy young women because of *vanity*—'

'It's not vanity, Mother,' Nikki said coldly. 'It's my *life*. And I want it back. Steven can pout about it all he wants, but he's never been in this situation. He doesn't *know*. Does he, Brandon?'

'Uh . . .' Brandon said. He'd been texting someone on

41

his cellphone behind Nikki's back as she'd been talking. 'What was that, babe?'

She turned her head. 'Brandon. Are you *texting*?'

'Sorry,' he said, grinning his perfect, boyish grin. 'It's my lawyer. About the car. He thinks I may be able to pursue it in civil court.'

'Oh.' Nikki gave him a very brittle smile. 'Maybe you should be calling Doctor Fong and starting to arrange having medical supplies shipped here instead.'

'Uh,' Brandon said. 'Sure. Can we eat first?'

Nikki laid a loving hand along his cheek. 'Sure, babe,' she said, and kissed him very tenderly on the mouth.

I sat there. All I could think about was the weight and warmth of Cosabella's head on my foot. I didn't dare let myself think about anything else. If I did, I knew I would just start sobbing, the way Nikki had a few minutes earlier.

If anything could break through my frozen tear ducts, that is.

I don't know what I'd been expecting really. I was a prisoner, after all. I always had been, ever since the surgery. I guess I just hadn't realized it until now. I had no rights, no say in what happened to me. If Brandon wanted to set up some whacked-out operating room in his garage and have a surgeon come remove my brain and stick it in some other girl's body, I guess I had to let him.

Didn't I?

Well, didn't I?

If I hadn't felt so isolated, so rigid – as if ice had

formed in my veins – I might have been able to think straight.

But as I sat there, staring at my reflection in the plate-glass windows looking out over that cold black sea, I could think of nothing except how completely frozen and alone I was . . .

I was on my own, and there was no one at all who was going to be able to help me out of this one.

Five

I was in my bed at Brandon's beach house, and I was dreaming.

In my dream, Christopher had come to rescue me. He wasn't, it turned out, mad about the whole thing where I'd told him I loved Brandon and not him.

Quite the opposite, in fact. Our reunion was joyful . . . and passionate. It was turning the ice that had been flowing in my veins back to blood . . . warm, rich blood that was making me hot . . . shove-the-covers-down, hair-sticking-to-the-back-of-my-neck hot.

In my dream, Christopher was kissing me . . . gently at first, playful kisses on the lips, light as the down feathers in the comforter that I'd already pushed past my bare thighs.

Then, as I kissed him back, proving that it was true – I had never loved Brandon. How could I? – the kisses became longer . . . deeper . . . more passionate. My lips parted beneath his as his hands found their way into my hair – spread like a fan across my pillow – his mouth cool against mine because of the chill outside, the zipper from his leather jacket almost unbearably cold as it pressed against my warm skin as he leaned over my bed, whispering my name . . .

I was so relieved to learn he hadn't even believed me

that bitterly cold morning outside Dr Fong's house when I'd said I didn't love him. He'd known Brandon had been making me say it.

He just hadn't known why.

The reason he hadn't believed it was because he'd loved me – the real me – all along. Not me, Nikki, the girl who'd torn his heart out of his chest and thrown it to the ground and then squashed it underneath her Louboutins.

Me, Em. The girl in the photo he'd kept over his desk all those months.

The girl he'd thought was dead for months.

Except if that was true . . . if Christopher hadn't believed me . . . why hadn't he called?

Because, a voice inside my dream reminded me, *Christopher doesn't love you any more.*

Wait a minute. I wasn't actually liking this dream after all.

I opened my eyes with a gasp to find a hand pressed to my mouth. This was no dream. This was really happening.

I knew who it was, of course. Who else could it have been? Who else had been trying my doorknob (unsuccessfully, since I'd been careful about locking it every night) all week? The hand over my mouth was masculine. I could tell that just by its size and heaviness, even if, in the darkness of my room, I couldn't see who owned it.

So of course I did the only thing I could: I clamped down on it with my teeth as hard as I could.

What else was I going to do? Brandon had snuck into

my room in the middle of the night to do what guys like Brandon do to girls when they're asleep. How dare he try to take advantage of me when I was dreaming about someone else? Someone I actually *liked* . . .

I bit down and didn't let go until I heard bones crunch.

'Ow. Jesus, Em!' the voice cried in a hoarse whisper. The hand ripped away from my face and, for a second, I heard the sound of leather rubbing on leather . . . a sleeve lifting away from the body of a jacket as someone waved his hand back and forth.

Wait. My sleep-muddled mind tried to make sense of this. Why would Brandon be wearing a leather jacket *inside*?

'What did you go and *bite* me for?' Christopher wanted to know.

My mind reeled. Christopher? In my room? Here, at Brandon's house? What was Christopher doing here? How had he gotten in? Had I not been dreaming after all? Had he really been kissing me?

I sat up so fast I jostled Cosabella, who'd been curled against my neck.

'Christopher?' I whispered. 'Is that really you? Oh my God, did I hurt you? Are you bleeding?'

'Of course it's really me,' he whispered. He sounded so annoyed I wanted to grab his face and go back to kissing it, just like in my dream . . . if that *had* really been a dream, and not real. Only Christopher could sound that irritated with me. Wonderful, amazing, easily annoyed Christopher. 'Who else would it be? And don't tell me

Stark has been sneaking in here. Was that why the door was locked? I had to use my library card to jimmy the lock. Seriously, if he's been trying to get in here, I'll kill him –'

I forgot that I was supposed to be giving Christopher the cold shoulder, on pain of Brandon destroying everything and everyone I loved.

I forgot that I was supposed to be pretending that Brandon and I were an item now.

I was so overwhelmed at finding Christopher sitting on the side of my bed, just like in my dream, that I threw my arms around him, pulling him close and swearing to myself that I was never going to let him go. I didn't even care that the metal rivets and zipper of his leather jacket were icy cold against the parts of my bare skin that weren't covered by the matching pink tank top and sleep boxers I was wearing. Just like in my dream.

'Oh my God, Christopher,' I whispered, breathing the crisp outdoorsy scent that was still clinging to his short hair. 'I'm so glad to see you.'

'I'm glad to see you too,' he said, putting his arms around me to hug me back. Hard. 'And don't worry about my hand. I'm sure it's just a flesh wound.'

I laughed. I think I was semi-hysterical.

But I didn't care. It felt so good to be in his embrace.

Christopher. Christopher was *here*.

'But what are you *doing* here?' I whispered.

His hold on me loosened just enough so that he could look down into my face. Sometime while I'd been sleeping, a partial moon must have come out . . . I could see its faint glow through a crack in the curtains on the far side of the room. It didn't let in enough light for me to see him by, because his back was to it and he was thrown into silhouette by its glow. But he, I knew, could see me.

'Did you really think I'd believe you, of all people, were in love with Brandon Stark?' he asked in a softly chiding voice. 'It may have taken me a while to figure out who you really are now, Em. But give me some credit. And now that I do know it's you, I'm certainly not going to let you go that easily.'

My heart gave a little somersault inside my chest. I don't think I could have let go of him, either, even if he'd wanted me to. Which, thank God, he didn't.

'But you never called,' I said, a throb in my voice. I couldn't help it. I knew I sounded like one of those pathetic girls I hated – *Why didn't you caaaaawl me?* – but I couldn't help it.

'He's not checking your messages to make sure you're not talking to the outside world?' Christopher asked, sounding genuinely surprised. 'I didn't want to get you in trouble.'

'Uh, no,' I said. 'I don't think that's occurred to him.' What Brandon was planning to do to me was way, way worse than monitoring who I was texting on my cellphone.

'Well, I'm here now,' Christopher said. He leaned down and kissed me, and I realized, as our lips touched, that I *hadn't* been dreaming . . . that really *had* been him

48

kissing me. Kissing me awake. No wonder I'd been so hot . . .

And that his kisses were doing to me again what they'd done to me before, making me feel warm and protected in a way I hadn't felt since . . . well, since the last time I'd been in his arms, all too briefly, back in my room at the loft during Lulu's holiday party.

And just like then, before I was entirely aware of what was happening, Christopher's hands were gently cradling my face as his lips moved over mine . . .

. . . and then I was sinking . . . sinking slowly back against the soft pillows behind me, with Christopher on top of me. Somehow he'd shed that annoying leather jacket, and he was half on, half off the bed.

But definitely half on me, a sensation I couldn't say I didn't find enjoyable. I knew there were things we needed to say. Things I needed to know, things I needed to tell him.

But how could I when his lips were doing such interesting things to mine, and his hands – oh, his hands – had moved away from my face to tug at my . . .

'Christopher,' I said breathlessly, pulling my lips from his. It was the hardest thing I think I'd ever had to do. In the darkened room, there was nothing I wanted to do more than just let him keep doing what he was doing.

But I couldn't. Someone had to stay sane. And I had a pretty good idea that it wasn't going to be him.

'We have to focus,' I said.

'Focus,' he repeated. I could see that his blue eyes, so

close to mine, were half-lidded and looked dazed. 'Definitely.'

He lowered his head to kiss me again.

But as much as I longed to let him, I knew I couldn't.

'No.' I ducked out from beneath him and moved to the far side of the bed, where Cosabella was sitting licking herself. I pulled her on to my lap to use her as a kind of doggy boy-defence shield. 'I'm serious. I'm happy to see you. But we have to talk. What are you *doing* here?'

Christopher seemed to pull himself together. He lost the dazed look – well, some of it – and said, sitting up straighter, 'I think it should be obvious what I'm doing here, Em. I'm here to rescue you.'

My heart gave another one of its crazy somersaults. Seriously, everything this boy said – and did – was causing my internal organs to do acrobatics.

'Rescue me?' Never in my life had anyone said anything as sweet to me. He had come all the way from New York to *rescue* me? Just when I had given up all hope that anyone I knew was even thinking about me. Except Lulu and my mother. And my agent, Rebecca, of course. 'Oh, *Christopher* . . .'

It was all I could do to keep from crawling back across the bed and into his arms.

But that, I knew, would be a huge mistake. Because I wouldn't have the strength to crawl out of his arms again . . . not until things had gone way further than either of us was ready to handle . . . at least right now.

Pushing some of my sleep-tossed hair out of my eyes, I resolved to follow my own advice and focus.

'How did you even get in here?' I asked. 'Brandon keeps this place locked up tighter than Fort Knox.'

He pulled a small, sleek box from the pocket of his coat.

'Universal code grabber,' he said. 'Just the latest of my cousin Felix's many do-it-yourself hacking devices he's been working on to keep himself entertained. This one can run something like a million potential code combinations a second before it finds the right one. Used it to open Brandon's garage door.'

I stared at the little metal box in his hand. OK. *This* was definitely something I wouldn't dream. I wasn't so sure Christopher's cousin Felix belonged under house arrest in his mother's basement. I think maybe he belonged on the payroll of some tech corporation in Silicon Valley.

'I suppose that's how you bypassed the security system too,' I said.

'Oh, no,' Christopher said, casually slipping the box back into his pocket. 'I just typed in Brandon's password for that once I got inside. I figured he'd be stupid enough to use his name – and I was right.'

I couldn't help smiling at that one.

'So we're just supposed to walk on out of here,' I said, 'the way you came in?'

'Pretty much,' he said. 'You ready?'

I had to laugh at that. The idea of me just walking out

of Brandon's house with Christopher and away from my problems as if – well, as if it was that easy.

Where could we even go? It wasn't like with my face, we wouldn't be instantly recognized anywhere we went.

And what about Steven and his mom? I know I'm not related to them – except by blood – but I owed them something for the way they'd fought for me, even if it hadn't worked. Steven had gotten so mad at Brandon for agreeing to Nikki's insane plan, he'd finally had to leave the dining room entirely, for fear – he'd told me later when I'd met him in the hallway as I'd been coming up to bed – that he'd smash Brandon's face in. Later, he'd come into my room, telling me that we all had to get out of there before both Nikki and I ended up dead.

But go where? Steven could always rejoin his naval unit and slip back under the sea in the submarine he'd left to look for his missing mother. But what about Mrs Howard, who couldn't even use her credit cards or pay a bill for fear of Stark Enterprises tracking her down?

Or Nikki, who chose to remain so blindly ignorant of the role she'd played in causing all this heartache?

I wanted to tell Christopher all these things.

But first I had to tell him the most important thing of all – besides the fact that I was madly in love with him, which I was pretty sure from the previous few minutes' make-out session he already knew.

'Christopher,' I said breathlessly, 'Nikki told us. She told us what she tried to blackmail Brandon's dad over.

What she overheard that got her killed . . . and me into this mess in the first place.'

He reached out and smoothed some of my hair away from my face. I closed my eyes for a second or two, relishing the warmth from his fingers as they swept my skin. A wave of desire slammed into me with all the force of a dodgeball hurled by Whitney Robertson.

Bad. I had it bad for this guy.

'Go on,' he said.

'It just . . .' I said, opening my eyes again when his hand fell away from my face. 'It doesn't make any sense, is the thing. Nikki says she overheard Mr Stark and a bunch of his cronies chuckling in his office over the fact that the new Stark Quarks are going to arrive with some kind of undetectable spyware – bundled with the new version of *Journeyquest* – that's going to upload all the information the user taps into it. Any information they ever enter into any websites, Priceline, Facebook, emails, that kind of thing. And all of it is going to be stored on the mainframe at Stark Corporate. All of it.'

I looked at Christopher and shrugged.

'That's it?' he asked, his eyebrows raised.

'That's it,' I said, nodding. 'Nikki swears. She didn't hear them say anything else. She says they were all congratulating one another and toasting over it. I mean, I guess an undetectable tracking software is pretty advanced, but one in three PCs in America has spyware on it already and their owners don't even know. What's the use of having all that information – and we're talking about data from hundreds of thousands of homes, maybe millions, because the Stark Quark is going to be the lowest-priced laptop in history – if Stark's just going to store it on the mainframe? It's not like they said they were going to use it for anything. And you know the people who are going to be buying the Quarks – they're pretty low-end – aren't rich. It's not like Stark's going to be getting the credit-card numbers of, like, millionaires or anything. That's why I don't understand how this could be worth killing Nikki Howard over. What's the big deal?'

The moon had shifted. Now a shaft of its light fell full on Christopher's face, and I could finally see him properly for the first time since I'd woken to find him in my room . . . and in my bed.

And for a second, I thought I spotted a glimpse of the dark supervillain that I had been convinced he'd turned into after reports of my 'death', and his decision to try to avenge it . . . that supervillain I thought was gone for good when he realized I wasn't dead after all.

But no. The darkness – and hate – were still there. Maybe they would never go away.

And I was going to have live with the knowledge that I was the one who was responsible for that.

'Why does anyone commit murder?' he asked in a low voice.

'I –' I blinked. 'How should I know?'

'Three reasons,' Christopher said. He held up one finger. 'Love.' Another finger. 'Revenge.' And finally, a third finger. 'Profit. They tried to kill Nikki Howard when she threatened to expose the truth about them.'

'So?' I shook my head. 'I still don't—'

'Robert Stark definitely has a plan for how he's going to profit from the information he's stealing from the people who buy his new PCs,' Christopher said. 'What we need to do is figure out what that is. And how we're going to make him pay. We've got a lot work ahead of us. We better get on it. Get dressed and let's go.'

I started disentangling my legs from the sheets. 'Steven and his mom are going to be fine,' I said. 'I can probably get them up and out, no problem. But I'm not sure how we're going to convince Nikki to come along with us willingly. She likes it here just fine. And she's expecting a brain swap in the morning.'

'Wait,' Christopher said, putting a large hand on my shoulder. 'What are you talking about?'

'Nikki,' I said, looking at him in the moonlight. Something about his expression told me that the evil supervillain was not only back, but here to stay. 'She's not going to want to go. But she has to, of course. It's not safe for her here.'

'Em,' Christopher said. His voice was cold. 'I don't care about Nikki Howard. I'm here to rescue you. Not her.'

'But . . .' I blinked at him. 'We can't just leave her behind.'

'Oh yes,' he said, 'we can.'

Six

I was trying to wrap my mind around a world where the guy I loved would refuse to help a damsel in distress.

Although it *was* kind of hard to think of Nikki as any kind of damsel.

'If she wants to stay with Brandon,' Christopher said, his tone uncompromising, 'let her. Now put some jeans on so we can get out of here.'

'She's a severely damaged person,' I argued. 'She doesn't know what she wants. She's been through a lot.'

'So have you,' Christopher said. 'And you aren't going around trying to blackmail people. Though I can't say I've been too impressed by how you've handled the situation so far.'

I glared at him, stung. 'What's *that* supposed to mean?' I demanded.

'You really thought I was going to believe you'd run off with *Brandon Stark*, of all people, because he's just so damned irresistible?' His tone was slightly scornful. 'I'm not a complete idiot, you know.'

My heart gave a warning *ker-thump* inside my chest. Uh-oh.

He sounded mad. Not just annoyed. But really, really mad.

And also, maybe, beneath the anger, a little hurt.

'Christopher,' I said when I was able to find my voice, 'I can explain all that. Brandon told me if I didn't pretend like he and I were –' I swallowed. Uh-oh. Snot. And some tears too. Not a good sign – 'you know. That he'd tell his dad where he could find Nikki.'

'And you believed him?' Christopher demanded. 'What was the likelihood of that happening, when Nikki holds the key to Brandon getting back at his father for taking away his Super Soaker when he was a kid, or whatever the hell it was Robert Stark did that Brandon's so mad at him for?'

Wow. Christopher was right about that one. Why hadn't I ever thought of that? For a smart girl, I can be really dumb sometimes.

I may be able to figure out how to make a slow-burning fuse off YouTube.

But boys? That's where I seem to have a big, fat blind spot.

'He was really convincing, Christopher,' I said. The tears were starting to overflow. I hoped he couldn't see them in the dark. I tried to hold them back. I felt so stupid. He was angry, and I responded by crying? How big a baby was I, anyway? No wonder he liked McKayla Donofrio better than me. I bet she never cried. She was too busy watching CNBC's stock-market report and double-checking her retirement portfolio. 'Brandon's dad tried to have Nikki killed. I think you're right, and he maybe even tried to have me killed . . . or at least that TV dropping on my head at that exact moment wasn't quite the accident everyone made it out to be. So how was I supposed to know he wouldn't try to have someone else killed, maybe even someone I love, like Mom or Dad or Frida, or even . . . you?'

I thought that might cause him to warm up. I mean, I'd just admitted I loved him. You would think the guy would throw me a bone.

But no. He still wasn't having any of it.

'And you couldn't call or text me to tell me any of this?' Christopher demanded. 'Seriously, Em? This past week, not a single message? What, Brandon's been watching you every second of the day?'

'No,' I said, wiping tears from my face with the back of a wrist. I was mad now too. Mad at myself for crying, but mad at Christopher too. What did he want me to do? 'But what was I supposed to say, Christopher? How do I know they aren't tapping your phone? You don't know what it's been like. It's like they're everywhere, watching. And besides, I promised Brandon—'

'Oh, you promised him,' Christopher said. And this time, he wasn't being a *little* harsh. 'Jesus, Em, for a smart girl, you can be really dense sometimes. Almost,' he added, with a self-deprecating smirk, 'as dense as I was, for taking so long to figure out who you really were.'

'Well, *you* never called or texted me,' I said, a throb in my voice. I couldn't help it.

'You kicked me to the kerb!' Christopher cried, spreading his hands out wide. I noticed for the first time that he was wearing black leather fingerless gloves, the kind cool bad guys – who always turn out to not really be bad – wear in movies. I supposed that's what Christopher was now, though.

Except that he was actually kind of bad. Or he was acting that way, at least.

'What am I,' he went on, 'your fricking dog? You can treat me like crap and I'm just going to come crawling back to you every time? Oh no, wait – you treat your dog better than you treat me.' He pointed at Cosabella, curled up beside me. 'You let her in on everything.'

I blinked at him. This had gone from really, really great to really, really bad in a matter of minutes. In my dream, Christopher had totally forgiven me. And then he'd made out with me.

But it didn't look like that was going to happen in real life.

'Face it, Em, you don't really love me,' he said harshly. 'You say you do, but you don't. You know how I know that? Because you don't trust me. Through this whole thing, you've never trusted me enough to let me in completely.' He got up from the side of the bed. 'Well, you're never going to be able to have a real relationship until you stop thinking Emerson Watts is the smartest person in the whole world, and start trusting other people and let them try to help you. It's called being an adult, Em. You might want to give it a try.'

'Wait,' I said, my voice cracking. 'You're just going to *leave*?'

'Well,' he said, 'are you going to come with me if we don't take Nikki?'

'No,' I said, lifting a wrist to wipe furiously at my eyes.

'Then yeah,' he said, 'I guess I am. Because you said yourself she's not going to leave willingly.'

I couldn't believe this was happening. It was my big Princess Leia moment – I was being rescued, only not, thankfully, by my own brother – and I was blowing it. My rescuer was just walking out, and leaving me behind like dryer lint.

But what was I supposed to do? I couldn't leave Nikki behind.

However much she might not deserve or even want my loyalty.

'Fine,' I said. 'I guess this is goodbye then.'

'I guess it is,' he said.

And he turned and walked out of the room, closing the door behind him.

I sat there in my bed, expecting the knob to turn and for him to come back any minute. He'd be all awkward and sweet – or maybe still angry and defensive – and say it was my fault. Only, of course, what he'd really be saying was, *I'm sorry, Em. I still love you. Come with me. Please come with me.* Whichever. It didn't matter.

But he'd come back. Of course he'd come back.

He couldn't have just walked out. He couldn't be gone. He just couldn't.

But he was. The minutes on my bedside clock ticked by, and he didn't come back. The house was noiseless. Nothing. No sign of Christopher, coming or going.

It took a while for reality to sink in, but eventually it finally did. He'd ditched me. He'd completely ditched me!

I couldn't believe it. This was the worst thing that had ever happened to me.

Well, OK, not really. Getting a brain transplant in the first place. That was the worst thing that had ever happened to me.

But this was totally the second worst thing.

Besides the fact that tomorrow Brandon Stark was going to make me get a second brain transplant.

Yeah. I was a total idiot not to have gone with Christopher.

On the other hand . . . he'd clearly morphed back into the dark supervillain I'd seen hints of ever since I'd had my accident. I guess you can't really shake that kind of thing entirely. Maybe I'd been smart not to go with him. Of course I had! I couldn't have gone off with him and left the Howards behind. Because Steven and his mom wouldn't have gone without Nikki either. How selfish would that have been?

No, I'd made the right choice. Christopher was the one with the issues, not me. How could he even have suggested otherwise? If anyone had any growing up to do it was him, not me.

When I woke up – and I don't even know how I'd managed to fall asleep, with all the fuming I'd been doing – it was because Brandon Stark was rattling my doorknob, demanding to know when I was going to get up and come down to breakfast.

And a few seconds later, Nikki came barging into my room from the connecting door to hers, telling me to be sure not to eat too much, because she didn't want to get 'her body' back too bloated.

And my cell, over on my nightstand, was buzzing. When I fumbled for it and squinted at the caller ID, I saw it was a text message from Rebecca, demanding to know when I was going to be back in New York.

Robert Stark was throwing a New Year's party at his massive four-storey town house preceding the live Stark Angel lingerie show the day after tomorrow, and it was important that I be there to meet the shareholders. If I wasn't there, I was going to be in violation of my contract. Not only was I going to be replaced by Gisele Bündchen (who'd managed to lose all the pregnancy weight in record time and changed her mind about agreeing to be in the show), but I was going to lose a lot of money.

Needless to say, Rebecca was unhappy with me.

I lay there and wondered how unhappy Rebecca would be if she knew how much her highest-paid client was about to *really* lose. As in, her life, if Nikki had her way.

Honestly, I don't know what I had been thinking. I've never considered myself the girliest of girls or anything. I was born and raised in New York City, so I'd always thought I'd seen it all, including a broken-bottle fight once outside our local Mexican restaurant (Señor Swanky's) between two men arguing over possession of a parking space.

So was it completely unnatural of me to think, when I'd woken in the middle of the night to find my boyfriend saying he was there to rescue me, that all my problems were over and that everything was going to be all right?

Apparently so. Apparently that Aretha Franklin song my mom liked so much was right, and sisters really did need to keep doing it for themselves.

Probably it was my fault for believing that those corny happily-ever-afters at the ends of the romance novels my sister Frida was always reading, where the hero was always saving the heroine – usually from dangerous situations she'd put herself into – could actually happen in real life.

Because it turned out all those books were wrong. It turned out, in real life, the hero had problems with the heroine's 'trust issues'.

Excuse me, but *I* have trust issues? I'm not saying I'm perfect. I'm not saying there isn't a possibility – a slight possibility – that what Christopher had said was partly true.

Maybe I do have difficulty letting other people in, or allowing them to get to know me, or help me, or whatever.

But Christopher thought *I* was the only one with a problem? Oh, that was rich. That was just hilarious, coming from a guy who kept a *code scanner* in his pocket.

And OK, Christopher had gone to a lot of trouble to rescue me.

But was I rescued? Um, the answer to that question would be no.

But I told myself I didn't care any more. Not now that Dark Spider-man had taken the place of my formerly sweet boyfriend.

Even if he had only been my boyfriend for about two minutes in total.

Why hadn't I just told Christopher last night that Nikki had demanded her old body back in return for her spilling her secret to Brandon?

Not that this would necessarily have made the slightest difference to him. Probably it wouldn't have, considering how much he hated me. Which was maybe why I didn't tell him. A girl had to have some pride. I mean, I didn't want him taking me back out of *pity* or something. Nothing would be more disgusting than *that*.

So now he was gone and I was still here and I'd never know for sure if it would have made a difference or not.

And right now Brandon was probably having a secret laboratory set up where my brain was going to be sucked out and put into yet another stranger's body.

And who even knew if this time I'd even recover from the surgery? I might be lobotomized or, worse, never wake up at all. I might end up in a vegetative state for the rest of my life. Or have that icky hair that Nikki had totally fried with the straighteners.

I'll just be honest: I wasn't that jazzed about being the new Nikki. No offence, but she wasn't showing too much potential, at least the way the old Nikki was dragging her around in my cast-offs.

Plus, I had gotten used to being *the* Nikki Howard. Maybe it was shallow and, sure, I'd complained about it a few times.

But I don't care what Megan Fox or Jessica Biel say: there were definite advantages to being the hottest girl on the planet. Number one was that I got paid for it. A lot.

And number two was that people were just nicer to you when you looked pretty, as opposed to looking like the hot mess that I used to be, and that the old Nikki was now. They just were. It was a fact. Whitney Robertson was example A. Why would I want to go back to having volleyballs spiked at my head (on purpose), and my own sister refusing to be seen with me?

You could go on and on about how people were supposed to like you for what you had on the inside.

But if that was really true, why in the name of all that was holy would anyone ever have liked Nikki in the first place? I was becoming more and more convinced she was a cross between Heidi Montag and Hitler.

And I had no great faith that Christopher would ever come back. We hadn't exactly parted on the greatest of terms, so it seemed unlikely I was ever going to see him again, except maybe in Public Speaking, if I ever got back to Tribeca Alternative. I couldn't believe he'd accused me of treating him like a dog when I most definitely had made almost every decision that I had out of concern for *his* safety.

And OK, maybe, like he'd said, that *was* infantilizing him, just a little. After all, he was a grown man who could make his own decisions, and didn't need my protection.

But in my opinion my trying to protect him only proved how deeply I loved him.

Wow. Maybe Christopher was right. Maybe I really *was* turning into one of those stupid heroines from Frida's books.

The thing was, I'd just felt so *happy* when I'd woken up and found him in my room. Everything had seemed so great. I wasn't all alone any more . . .

. . . except, it turned out, I was.

And all thanks to my own stupidity.

TSTL. Too Stupid to Live. That's what Frida said they called the heroines of her books who made choices that put their own lives at risk.

And those heroines weren't just in books either. They were in horror movies too. Like when the heroine of the movie hears a noise in the basement, and thinks to herself that she had just better go check it out. Even though all the electricity in the house has blown out. And her flashlight is broken. And there is an escaped convict loose in the neighbourhood.

Really, she deserves what is coming to her.

But did I? I mean, did I deserve to have my brain pulled out of my body *again*, and have to learn to adjust to being a whole new person all over?

I texted Christopher an *I'm sorry. Can we talk? Where r u?* message that I fully didn't expect him to reply to (he didn't), then took a shower and got dressed in a pair of designer jeans and a ruffly top the boutique had sent over, pulling on the boots I'd brought with me from New York.

As I blow-dried my hair, I tried to think about something other than myself. Like how Brandon's father could possibly be hoping to profit from storing all those people's data on the Stark Enterprise mainframe. Obviously he wasn't going to use their credit-card numbers himself. He was a billionaire. What did he need with a JCPenney card?

And most of the people buying Stark Quarks were college and high-school kids. I mean, the Quarks only cost two or three hundred bucks, tops, and they came in colours like lavender and lime green.

So why was he collecting all that data?

I was still trying to figure it out when Brandon rattled my doorknob again.

'Hey,' he called. 'Are you coming to breakfast, or what?'

I strode over to the door and threw it open. Brandon was standing there, his dark hair sticking to the back of his head because he'd just showered. He was wearing, of all things, another Ed Hardy shirt, jeans and a thick gold chain around his neck. A waft of Axe assailed my nostrils.

Really, Brandon? I swallowed hard against the barf that rose up in my throat.

'I'm coming,' I said, not smiling. 'Is the doctor here?'

Brandon stared down at me blankly. 'What doctor?'

I'd always suspected Brandon had been allowed to eat way too much sugar as a child.

But this was a bit much, even for him.

'Doctor *Fong*,' I said, enunciating clearly so he couldn't misunderstand. 'To perform the *brain transplant*.'

'Oh,' he said. 'Uh . . . not yet.' He glanced down the

hallway to make sure Nikki wasn't around, then put one arm up against the wall behind me, leaning in close enough that I could smell the toothpaste on his breath. 'Listen . . . you don't think . . . I mean, you didn't think I was actually going to go through with that crazy plan of hers to let you swap brains or whatever. Did you? I mean –' He reached out and lifted the pendant I was wearing, some kind of crescent moon or something – 'she's crazy. And you . . . you're the one I want.'

I just stared at him. I would no sooner believe anything that came out of Brandon's mouth than I would believe something I saw on the cover of *Star* magazine about Jennifer Aniston's current state of pregnancy.

'Uh,' I said, 'you seemed pretty into the idea last night when you were talking about it with Nikki.'

'How else was I going to find out what she was blackmailing my dad about?' he asked with a laugh. 'I had to lead her on, you know.'

I plucked the necklace out of his hand. Seriously, his cologne was so strong it was making my eyes water.

'How do I know you're not leading *me* on?' I asked. 'You two did used to go out. So you didn't always think she was so crazy.'

Brandon stared at me with his mouth hanging open a little, giving me ample opportunity to observe his veneers.

'That was just,' he said, his Adam's apple bobbing, 'for sex.'

'Charming,' I said, wanting to throw up more than ever.

'So what happens now? To Nikki, and Steven, and their mom? Are you going to go on keeping them forever, like your pet shark?'

'Well,' he said, looking uncomfortable. 'No.'

'Then where are they supposed to go? They can't go back to their normal lives. Your father will find them. Do you want their deaths on your conscience?' I stabbed an index finger into the middle of his chest. 'Do you? Well? Do you?'

'No,' he said. He'd been backed up against the wall behind him. 'Of course not. But that's not going to happen. Because your computer-geek friend is gonna help me figure out how to use the information Nikki got about my dad and turn this all around to get back at him—'

'My computer-geek friend?' I knew exactly who he was talking about. 'And just why exactly do you think he's going to be willing to help you, after what you made me do to him the other day?'

I didn't mention the part about Christopher's problem with my 'trust issues'.

'That's not my deal,' Brandon said with a shrug. 'You're the one who's supposed to figure out how to make that work. Or Nikki might end up exactly where you're so worried she will . . .'

I don't know why I was so surprised. Everything in Brandon's life was disposable. Last night after he'd gotten off the phone with his lawyer he'd already begun making calls to purchase a new car to replace the one I'd burned up.

Why shouldn't he consider people disposable too?

Just as he was making this casual threat, Nikki appeared in the hallway from her room, wearing a lantern dress that was exactly the wrong colour green for her new complexion, and patterned tights that made her legs look chunky. Her hair, as usual, was a disaster, and it looked like she hadn't even tried with her face. Maybe because there was no make-up artist around to do it for her.

'Good morning,' she said. 'Ready for breakfast?'

I gave her a tight smile. 'Can't wait,' I said, dropping my finger from Brandon's chest and brushing past him to head down the stairs. Behind me, I heard Nikki purr, 'Hello, tiger.' She was apparently speaking to Brandon. I hadn't any doubt from the slurping noises I heard next that she'd wrapped her arms around him for a big good-morning kiss.

Was it everyone's intention to make me throw up before I'd even had my breakfast?

What I saw when I got to the dining doom, however, made me completely forget what I'd just heard.

And that was my little sister, Frida, pouring orange juice into glasses at our place settings.

Seven

Oh, she was wearing a disguise. Or what I suppose she considered a disguise: red plastic-framed glasses, black and white checked trousers, a white chef's coat, and her hair was stuffed up into a tall white chef's toque, like the kind they wear sometimes on the Food Network.

But other than that, she was very definitely Frida, a freshman in high school, who was supposed to be at cheer camp over winter break.

There were any number of things I could have said or done at that particular moment. Blurted out, *What are you doing here?* Fainted. Stomped up to her and demanded she get back home this instant. Didn't she know how much danger she was in . . . how much danger she was putting the rest of us in?

I didn't say or do any of those things. Instead, I just sank down into my seat – I'm pretty sure I couldn't have remained standing even if I'd wanted to – and sat there, staring up at her. I couldn't figure out what was going on for a minute or so. It isn't often you see someone from one part of your life in a completely separate part of your life and have to meld the two together, then try to make sense of what you're seeing.

Then slowly – more slowly than I would have liked to admit – I put two and two together.

It was all starting to make sense though. The fact that Christopher had shown up last night, then left without me?

The fact that Frida was standing there in ill-fitting catering clothes, ladling out food to us – she was serving us scrambled eggs from a platter – trying not to make eye contact with me through the lenses of the red plastic-framed glasses?

I could see that she'd caught on to the fact that I'd recognized her. There were bright spots of colour blossoming on both her full cheeks, even though she was resolutely not looking my way.

My heart had begun to thump, hard, inside my chest. Not only was I afraid for Frida – afraid that Brandon (thick, dopey, dangerous Brandon) was going to show up any minute and recognize her – but I'd realized if Frida was out here, Christopher was in the kitchen. He had to be.

What was he thinking, letting my baby sister come here, of all places?

Worse, just the idea that he might be nearby was making my pulse speed up. How could I be so weak?

But I quickly put this thought out of my head. More important than that – more immediate than that – was the danger that Frida was in. My palms had gone slick with sweat. Didn't she have any idea how risky what she was doing was? If Brandon caught her . . .

. . . well, I didn't know what he'd do.

But I knew it wasn't exactly going to go down very well.

And what about Mom and Dad? Did they know where Frida was at this very moment? I very much doubted it. Because if they did, they wouldn't have allowed it.

She was so, so dead when I was through with her.

'Is there anything other than eggs?' Mrs Howard, already seated, asked politely, looking down at the yellow lumps congealing on her plate, her forehead slightly wrinkled as if she was worried about actually tasting them.

Mrs Howard, of course, had never met Frida. She had no idea my baby sister was the one serving her her breakfast.

'Pancakes,' Frida said, in the fakest Southern accent I'd ever heard. She sounded like a bad Paula Deen. Did she really think just because she'd tucked her hair into a chef's toque and had glasses on that anyone was going to believe she was over fourteen? 'I'll be right out with them, ma'am.'

'Oh,' Mrs Howard said, moving bits of egg around with her fork, 'that will be lovely.' She didn't sound convinced.

Seated across the vast glass table from Mrs Howard was Steven, who'd risen early to work out in Brandon's private gym, as he did every morning. I stretched out my legs as far as I could and tapped his foot, lightly, I thought . . .

. . . forgetting I was wearing pointy-tipped stilettos.

'*Ow*,' Steven said, reaching for his injured leg. He gave me an aggrieved look, like, *What did you do that for? Aren't things bad enough? We're imprisoned in this guy's beach-house mansion. Do you have to stab me in the leg with your shoes too?*

I jerked my head in Frida's direction. Steven glanced at her, then gave me an annoyed *So what?* look, still rubbing his leg.

When I jerked my head back at Frida, Steven looked at her again. Recognition dawned.

When Steven glanced back at me one more time, his expression was one of alarmed disbelief.

I know, the look I gave him said. *What are we going to do?*

'What the hell is this?' Brandon wanted to know.

Brandon had disentangled himself from Nikki, and the two of them came over to sit down at the table.

'Is this juice fresh-squeezed?' Nikki wanted to know, before she gulped some without waiting for an answer.

'This doesn't look like waffles,' Brandon said, glaring down at his plate.

'That's because it's eggs, sir,' Frida said, giving him a slight bow.

My heart was now thumping so hard I could barely breathe. Would Brandon recognize her? He had seen her only a week ago at the party Lulu and I had given at our loft – he'd danced with her, for Pete's sake! How could he not recognize her?

And if he recognized her, would he have one of his security people rough her up? Over my dead body would any of them lay a hand on my sister . . .

Of course, given the fact that I already was dead, this was sort of an empty threat.

'Eggs?' Brandon looked perturbed. 'Since when were eggs ever on the menu? I hate eggs.'

My shoulders sagged in relief. He hadn't recognized her. Of course not. Brandon paid no more attention to the help than he did to . . . well, Nikki, if he could help it.

'There's been a slight change, sir,' Frida said. 'Chef trusts you'll still find the food to your satisfaction.'

Jeez! Where had Frida learned to say all this stuff? She actually sounded like a real caterer. I couldn't believe it. My baby sister was all grown up!

Brandon looked down at the yellow goo on his plate. 'No Belgian waffles?' he asked, now sounding slightly forlorn.

'This is disgraceful,' Nikki said. 'You really can't find good help any more.' She threw her napkin down beside her plate and started to get up. 'I'm going to go give that chef a piece of my mind.'

'No.' I hastily threw my own napkin down, feigning indignation. 'I'll do it. There's no reason why the rest of you can't stay here and enjoy yourselves.'

I got up and made my way across the slick black marble floor towards Frida, with Cosabella, who had followed me downstairs, trotting behind me, her claws making familiar clicking noises on the marble. The whole time my heart was clattering along with my heels and Cosabella's claws. I was a little ashamed about what my heart seemed to be saying: *Chris-to-pher*, my heart beat, in rhythm to my footsteps. *Chris-to-pher.*

It was ridiculous, I knew. Now was no time for it to be thinking about boys. Especially boys who'd abandoned me because of my alleged 'issues'. My sister was the one I had to concentrate on. My sister who had stupidly, foolishly, amazingly put herself at risk because of me.

In a way, I was incredibly proud of her (not that I had any intention of letting it show while I was beating the crap out of her). How had she gotten here, all the way from New York City? She was only a freshman . . . a kid, after all. It seemed like only the other day she'd been begging me to go with her to go see Gabriel Luna in concert at a Stark Megastore.

Or begging me not to go with her, actually, since she hadn't wanted me to be seen with her and embarrass her in public because I looked and dressed so badly. That had been before I'd become Nikki Howard, of course. God, how time flies.

'Come with me, young lady,' I said, grabbing Frida's arm. 'Let's just have a word with this chef of yours.'

'Um,' Frida said. She could barely keep up with me on her much shorter legs as I hustled her towards the kitchen. 'Whatever you say, ma'am.'

He wouldn't be there. I knew he wouldn't be there. I'd seen the look on his face last night when he'd told me he was done with me.

Not to mention the look he'd been wearing that morning by the limo outside Dr Fong's house when I'd told him that things might have been different if he'd just liked me the way I was before the surgery.

But he hadn't, and so now it was too late.

No wonder he was so unwilling to forgive me . . .

. . . and was so convinced I had issues.

And OK, what I'd said to him by the limo had been a lie, though I'd told myself at the time that I believed it. I'd had to, in order to make myself say it.

The expression I'd seen on his face when I'd said it hadn't been the expression of anyone who seemed like he might later give me another chance.

Except . . . well, Frida was here. I never in a million years thought I'd see her. Miracles, it seemed, *did* happen.

So maybe . . . just maybe . . .

When I hit the swinging door to the kitchen with all the force I could, trying to give the impression, for Brandon's sake, of a billionaire's angry girlfriend, Lulu, in a white coat and toque that matched Frida's, let out a shriek.

My heart gave a deflated *zzzzzzt* like a balloon some birthday clown had stepped on with his stupid giant clown shoes.

Christopher wasn't anywhere to be seen.

Instead, Lulu, letting out a sigh of relief, smiled like I was Ryan Seacrest, telling her she was the new American Idol.

'Oh, thank God,' she said, flattening a hand to her chest. 'It's just you two. Oh, and Cosy! You *scared* me. Did you have to sneak up on me like that?'

My mind staggered as I tried to make sense of what I was seeing in front of me: my room-mate, Lulu Collins – not to mention my sister – were in the kitchen of Brandon Stark's tropical beach house.

Of course. Of course they were. Where else would they be?

'What,' I demanded, when I'd finally caught my breath from the lunacy of it all, 'are you doing here? How did you get in? And where's the chef who was supposed to be here?'

'I don't know,' Lulu said, answering my last question first with a shrug. She'd gone to turn off the stove where she'd been frying something in a pan. It actually smelt delicious, like pancake batter. When had Lulu learned to cook anything but her signature dish, coq au vin? 'I slipped him a cheque to take the day off. And we just borrowed his stuff and walked in. Well, drove in, actually. No one checked our IDs or anything. Em, are you OK? We've been so worried about you. You've been acting so weird! Cute top. Don't hug me back, I don't want to get pancake bits on you.'

Lulu went to hug me. I stood there with her skinny little arms circling my neck, glaring over the side of her toque at Frida, who stood there smiling at me sheepishly.

'Do Mom and Dad know where you are?' I demanded, even though I knew the answer.

'Mom and Dad think I'm at cheerleading camp,' Frida said. 'And before you can get even more mad, Em, let me remind you that they put off their trip to Grandma's to stay in the city to be with you. But then you just took off to be with your new boyfriend, Brandon Stark. They're not exactly happy with you.'

I blinked at her. 'But—' I started to protest.

'Yeah,' Frida said, nodding, 'I know. But I couldn't exactly tell them you weren't here of your own choice, could I? Or they'd start flipping out. So I had to be all, *Oh no, she's in love with Brandon now*. And go along with what all the tabloids were saying, just like everybody else. Even though I knew you didn't give a rat's butt about Brandon Stark. I could see it in your face, even if Mom and Dad couldn't. But just so you know, you're basically killing them, a day at a time. Happy?'

I blinked at her. So my boyfriend thinks I have trust issues, and I'm killing my parents? This wasn't exactly something I wanted to hear. Especially before breakfast.

'So when Lulu called me at camp – because Mom flipped out and said I was going to cheerleading camp, because I think she doesn't want me to turn into a boy-crazy freak like you, Em – to say she wanted to stage an intervention on you,' Frida said, 'I jumped at the chance. Because which do you think is more important: saving a beloved sister, or learning to do a ball out to high splits?'

Since I had no idea how to answer this question – a ball out to high splits had to be some kind of cheerleading move – I blew some of my hair from my lipgloss and glared at them as Lulu let go of me and stepped aside to move the heavy iron frying pan she'd been using off the heat of the stove. There was, I saw, a pancake in it.

Lulu really had been planning on serving pancakes.

Then, pulling herself up to her full height – which was more than eight inches less than mine – Lulu said, 'Really, Em, you shouldn't be mad. We're here to rescue you.'

I just stood there staring at them. I couldn't believe

they'd done what they'd done – come all this way, just to bring me home.

'Come on, Em,' Lulu said, making a little beckoning motion. 'Get Steven and his mom and Nikki and let's go. Are you ready? That's a fantastic top, by the way. Did I say that already?'

'You guys,' I said. I felt tears pricking the corners of my eyes. I couldn't help it. I couldn't believe how sweet they were being, especially after I'd been so sure no one cared. Well, except my mom. And Rebecca.

But my mom only cared because she had to . . . she was my mom. And Rebecca . . . well, she needed me for the money I made her.

At the same time, there was a hurt in my heart that I couldn't deny, and it had to do with the fact that, while they might have been there, a certain other person was so conspicuously absent.

Frida and Lulu, noticing the sudden tears in my eyes, exchanged glances.

'Uh,' Lulu said, 'OK. Christopher was right.'

My heartbeat sped up a little.

'You talked to Christopher?' I asked. 'What did he say? Did he . . . tell you?' If he had told them about my alleged trust issues, I was going to kill him.

'Yes,' Frida said, 'he did. And don't worry. I've got this. We covered it in my psych class, Em.' She turned towards me, put her hands on my bare shoulders, and started speaking in an exaggeratedly slow voice. 'What you're ex-periencing right now is called Stockholm syndrome. It's when you begin sympathizing with your captor because he's shown you kindness. I know Brandon might be hot, and he gave you that nice shirt. But he's still a bad guy. Just because he hasn't killed you doesn't mean he's your friend.'

Shocked, I flung her hands off me. 'Would you shut up? I'm not in love with Brandon. Ew, is that what Christopher said?' Talk about Too Stupid to Live . . .

'Oh, phew,' Lulu said, her fragile shoulders slumping with relief. 'Good. Look, we don't have a lot of time. I chartered a jet to take us all back to New York and it's waiting on the tarmac. They charge by the hour, so, you know, chop-chop. Go tell the Howards to come back here. By the way –' She dropped her voice – 'has Steven asked about me? Did he like the eggs? I made them special just for him. He loves scrambled eggs. By the way, he knows I like him, doesn't he? I'm being too obvious.' She poked Frida in the arm. 'I told you scrambled eggs were too obvious. I should have gone for sunny side up.'

'Ouch,' Frida said, rubbing her arm. '*Lulu.*'

'I peeked out a minute ago and saw him,' Lulu went on. 'He looks really hot in that sweater. It's cashmere and we're at the beach, for heaven's sake. Maybe he should take it off. It would be all right with you if he went around shirtless, wouldn't it, Frida? See, Frida wouldn't mind. And what's with Nikki's hair? Is she not even trying? And that green is all wrong for her.'

I took a deep breath.

'You guys,' I said. 'Seriously. We can't leave just yet. Did

Christopher not tell you? We have to—'

'Are you all right?' Frida asked. She had taken off the red plastic-framed glasses and now she blinked at me, her eyes looking very dewy. I realized this was because there were tears in them. 'Because you look horrible. I mean, underneath the make-up and everything. Do you realize you haven't smiled once since we got here?'

'You haven't smiled once since you left *New York*,' Lulu said accusingly. 'I know, I've got you on Google Alert. I've seen every shot that's been taken of you, and you look totally miserable. That's how we knew –' She shot me a meaningful look – 'that you needed to be rescued.'

'Look.' I took Frida and Lulu both by the arm and started steering them towards the back door, through which food deliveries were made. 'Thanks a lot for trying to rescue me. I appreciate it. I really do. But we have to –'

Before anyone could say another word, the swinging door to the kitchen slammed open. Lulu let out a shriek . . .

. . . for which I couldn't blame her, since Brandon Stark was suddenly standing there in front of us.

Eight

'What the hell,' Brandon demanded, glaring from Frida to Lulu to me and then back again, 'is this?'

'Oh,' Lulu said. Her dark eyes had gone the size of the pancakes she was making. 'Hi, Brandon. Did you like the eggs? I made them myself.'

Brandon ignored the question. For which I couldn't exactly say I blamed him.

'What are you doing here?' He ripped his gaze from them and instead raked it over me.

I knew I had to act, and fast. It wasn't like I had a lot of time to think over how I was going to handle this, or what I was going to say or do. No one had told me there was going to be a second rescue attempt that morning. This wasn't like the car-bomb thing, which I'd lain awake at night mulling over and planning. I mean, I really hated Brandon Stark, so I'd decided to do the meanest thing to him that I could think of, and that was set his favourite thing on fire.

But in this case I didn't have a chance to come up with something as genius as a chemical-soaked beaded-necklace slow-burning fuse. I just did the first thing that came to me.

I threw myself at him, draping an arm across his chest and snuggling my boobs up against his shoulder.

This was another advantage of being Nikki Howard. She was very distracting to men.

'My friends came for a surprise visit, Brandon,' I purred. 'And they made breakfast. Isn't that a nice surprise?'

Brandon didn't look like he thought it was a nice surprise at all. In fact, he continued to look homicidal, completely ignoring my purry voice. And my boobs. Which was quite unusual for him.

'No,' he said, fuming. 'Where's the chef? I paid a lot of money for that chef.'

'He'll be back tomorrow,' Lulu chirped. 'I promise. Look, Brandon. I was going to make you guys pancakes!'

Brandon seemed understandably unimpressed.

'Lulu,' he said. 'Were you the one who set my car on fire?'

Lulu looked confused – which made sense, since she'd had nothing to do with the destruction of Brandon's Murciélago and had no idea what he was talking about.

'What?' she asked, setting the frying pan back down on the stove with a clang. 'No . . . ?'

'I knew it,' he said, reaching into his pocket for his iPhone. 'I knew it wasn't the paparazzi who destroyed my car. That's it. I'm calling the police and having you all arrested.'

I let go of him and took a step backwards.

'Brandon,' I said, 'what are you doing?'

Except it was pretty clear what he was doing as the tones of 911 filled the air.

'Don't worry, babe,' he said to me. 'I have it under

84

control.' He pointed at Lulu and Frida as he said, 'This is trespassing, you know, and that, my friends, was destruction of property. That Murciélago was worth over a quarter of a million dollars. Lulu, your dad can afford to pay that back, even if his last movie was a bit of a dud. Yes, hello,' he said when someone on the other end of the cellphone picked up. 'I'd like to report a—'

But before the last words were out of his mouth, a muscular, charcoal-grey-clad arm appeared around his neck – seemingly from nowhere.

And Brandon's voice was cut off. He dropped the phone, reaching to claw at the arm.

But it was too late. A second later, Brandon closed his eyes. By then the arm had released him, and Brandon had sunk quietly to the floor, unconscious. Cosabella hurried over to him to sniff his ear, then give it an encouraging lick.

We all stood there, blinking down at him, completely unsure what had transpired – it had all happened so fast – until someone cleared his throat.

That's when we noticed Steven. He had apparently been standing behind Brandon the whole time he'd been talking to us. It had been his arm that had choked Brandon into unconsciousness.

'Steven,' Lulu said, her face transforming into an expression I can only describe as unmitigated adoration. 'Oh, hi!'

'Uh,' Steven said, looking a little uncomfortable, 'hi, Lulu.'

'Oh my God,' Frida cried, snatching up a spoon and bending down to hold it in front of Brandon's nose, apparently to check and see if he was still breathing. 'He's dead!'

'No,' Steven said a little diffidently. 'He's not dead. He'll wake up soon, no worse for wear. He won't even know what happened.'

'Did you learn that choke hold in *military* training?' Lulu asked as she stepped over Brandon's prone body to come up to Steven and rub her body against his like a cat. I'm not even lying when I say her eyelashes fluttered.

'Uh,' Steven said, eyeing her even more uncertainly than before, 'yes.'

'That was incredible,' Frida said. She seemed just as admiring as Lulu. Maybe even more so. I flashed her an annoyed look. She was supposed to have a crush on Gabriel Luna, not Nikki Howard's older brother.

'So,' Steven said, ignoring his new fan club, 'would someone care to tell me what's going on here?'

As he asked this, there was the sound of an explosion . . . so powerful, it actually rocked the kitchen a little, causing all the pots and pans hanging from a rack over the centre island to clatter together and make a tinkling sound. I grabbed hold of the counter to steady myself on my heels.

'What was *that*?' I asked, alarmed.

'Oh.' Lulu tugged on her chef's toque so it sat at a more rakish angle, and said, 'That was just Christopher. He was supposed to blow something up to distract Brandon's

86

security guards – and Brandon – so we could all slip safely out the back.' She looked over at Steven adoringly. 'But Steven already distracted Brandon, as you can see.'

'Wait,' I said, my heart stopping. 'Christopher's *here*? With you?'

'Of course he's here,' Frida said. 'He said you two talked last night,' just as Lulu was explaining at the same time, batting her big Bambi eyes at Steven, 'We're here to rescue you. And your mom and Em.' Then she added, with just a hint of distaste, 'And your sister too.'

'Steven!' The kitchen door flew open. It was Mrs Howard, looking pale, followed by Harry and Winston. 'What's going on? What was that?' She looked down at the unconscious Brandon. He seemed to be sleeping as gently as a baby. 'Oh dear . . .'

'He's all right, Mom,' Steven quickly assured his panic-stricken mother. He went to put an arm around her. 'Why don't you and Nikki go and get some things together? I think we're going to have to be leaving here in a minute or two.'

Mrs Howard shook her head, unable to tear her gaze from Brandon.

'We always seem to be fleeing places at the most unexpected times,' she murmured.

But her reaction was mild in comparison to her daughter's, who came in a few seconds after her mother had left, and whined, 'What's going on? What was that—'

That's when her gaze fell to the floor, and she let out a bloodcurdling scream.

'Brandon!' Nikki fell to her knees at her ex-boyfriend's side. 'Oh my God, Brandon! Are you hurt?'

Brandon actually appeared to be regaining consciousness as she asked this, partly because Nikki had yanked him into a sitting position. He rolled his head back and forth, murmuring something about how he didn't want any more peekytoe salad. When his eyelids fluttered open, he looked at Nikki and asked in a dazed voice, just like in the movies, 'What happened?'

'Steven did a secret military move on you,' Lulu volunteered to Brandon. 'Don't worry, though. You're going to be fine.'

'*What?*' Nikki cried, whipping her head towards her brother. '*You* did it? Why would you do that to Brandon, of all people? He's been so nice to us!'

Uh, maybe he'd been nice to her. To me? Not so much.

'Because he was going to call the police and have your friends arrested, Nikki,' Steven explained. 'And they're only trying to help.'

'Help?' Nikki's straightened hair flew around as she looked from Steven to her mother to Lulu and me and then back again. 'Help how?'

'Help us get out of here, Nikki,' I said. I didn't want to be the one to give Nikki the bad news. But someone had to do it. 'Now that you told Brandon what you heard about the Stark Quarks, he has no use for you any more. He's going to cut you and your family lose.'

Brandon didn't dispute this. To be fair, he didn't look as if he was in the greatest shape to.

'No.' She shook her head back and forth so rapidly that a lot of that shiny hair got a bit staticky and started sticking straight up into the air. She didn't seem to notice though. 'No he's not. He's getting me my operation. Aren't you, Brandon? Tell them.' Brandon was still a little groggy from whatever Steven had done to him, so Nikki, I guess to be helpful, gave his face a few smacks. 'Did you hear me, Brandon? Tell them!'

'Uh, Nik?' Steven said. 'Slapping him isn't really going to help.'

It was at this moment that the back door to the kitchen tore open and Christopher came bursting in, a smudge of something that looked like oil on his cheek, his jeans dirty and his leather jacket flapping open. He stopped on the threshold, apparently surprised to see us all gathered there, and particularly Brandon on the floor . . .

. . . and me, standing above him.

It only took him a second or two, however, to gather himself together.

And it only took a heartbeat for my breath to be knocked completely from me by the sight of him.

Which was infuriating. Because I was really, really mad at him. And I definitely wasn't in love with him any more.

Why would I be in love with such an infuriating, stubborn person?

Or at least, that's what I told myself.

'Oh, good,' he said. 'You're all here. Let's go then, we don't have much time. I'm pretty sure one of the security guards called 911. They're all over on the beach now, putting out the fire. Still, we need to go now.'

Oh, the fire. Right. Of course.

'What do we do about him?' Steven asked, nodding at Brandon.

Christopher looked down at the heir to Robert Stark's vast fortune. 'What happened to him?' he asked curiously.

'Steven used a secret military choke hold on him,' Lulu volunteered again, just as chipperly as before.

'Excellent,' Christopher said with a congratulatory nod at Steven. 'Tie him up.'

Tie him up? I stared down at Brandon, who looked about as freaked out as I felt. I couldn't believe Christopher – *my* Christopher – had just casually suggested someone tie up Brandon Stark. Who had Christopher turned into? A week ago he'd been a relatively geeky – if hot – straight-A junior at Tribeca Alternative High School in Manhattan.

Now all of a sudden he's John Connor from *Terminator Salvation*?

'Tie him up?' Nikki looked up with tears brimming in eyes that were already mascara smudged. 'You can't be serious. You are *not* going to tie him up.'

'Here's some cooking twine,' Lulu said after opening a few kitchen drawers.

'Perfect,' Christopher said, and reached for the spool of twine Lulu handed to him. 'Steven, want to help me out here?'

'It would be my pleasure.' Steven bent over to begin

wrapping Brandon's legs in lengths of cooking twine, while Christopher went to work on his wrists.

'Are you crazy?' Brandon demanded. He seemed to be coming round, but not enough to fight what was happening to him. Except vocally. 'Do you know who I am? When my father hears about this—'

'When he hears about what?' Christopher wanted to know. 'How you had a girl he tried to murder here in your house for nearly a week and never told him about it, because you were trying to get her to tell you what it was he tried to have her killed for in the first place?'

Christopher did have a point. On the other hand . . .

Frida edged over to me and whispered, 'What's going to happen when Brandon gets out of that string or whatever? I mean, isn't he going to be mad?'

'I would think so,' I said.

'Then won't he just come after all of us?' she asked worriedly.

'Probably,' I said.

This had been exactly what I'd been thinking. I was a little surprised Frida had figured it out. Frida had lately begun showing startling growth and maturity for someone who, just a few short months earlier, had been willing to stand for hours in line just to get the autograph of some guy I had never even heard of.

Suddenly I became aware that Nikki's sobs had reached a pitch where they sounded like keening. I'd never heard actual keening before, but I'd read about it in books. It sounded like wailing, only higher pitched. Nikki was hugging herself and rocking back and forth on her knees like a little kid who'd had her favourite toy taken away.

'No, no, no, *no*,' she was saying, the nos growing progressively louder. 'I am *not* leaving here! Not without Brandon!'

Lulu, I noticed, was viewing Nikki's theatrics a little less sympathetically than anyone else in the room. Since I'd never seen Lulu behave anything but kindly towards anyone, I couldn't help feeling a little surprised when she said with more than a hint of prickliness to Nikki, 'You seem awfully devoted to Brandon now, Nikki. But you weren't so devoted to him back when you were sneaking around behind his back – and mine – with my boyfriend Justin, were you?'

This cut Nikki's keening off like a siren that someone had suddenly silenced – just as, in the distance, we heard the wail of a real-live siren.

The police were on their way.

Brandon looked over at Nikki in surprise – almost as if he really was seeing her for the first time.

'You?' His dark eyebrows furrowed. 'And *Justin*?'

Nikki's mouth fell open, and she looked from Brandon to Lulu and then back again, seeming to be gulping a little for air as if she was one of the fish from Brandon's aquarium . . . one that had accidentally leaped out of the safety of its soothing blue waters.

'You – you found out about that?' she asked, sounding a little stunned.

'He tried to perform mouth-to-mouth on Em,' Lulu

said, pointing at me. 'Only she wasn't experiencing any trouble breathing, if you know what I mean.'

I winced. I'd always wondered if Lulu had been looking out the window that day Justin had snuck up on me outside the loft.

Now I knew. Poor Lulu.

And poor Nikki. She blinked as if someone had slapped her. Her mouth was still moving noiselessly, as if she was trying to say something.

Only no words were coming out of her mouth.

'As much as I'd love to stand around and continue this very special episode of *America's Next Top Model*,' Christopher said, 'we need to get moving before—'

The doorbell rang.

'I think that's our cue,' Steven said.

Mrs Howard reappeared in the kitchen doorway, holding the same bag I'd seen her leave Dr Fong's house with nearly a week earlier.

'I'm assuming,' she said, 'I shouldn't get that.'

'No,' Christopher said, 'you should not.'

Nikki leaped to her feet and threw herself at her mother.

'Mom,' she cried, 'they're making us go with them! And leave Brandon behind!'

I looked at Christopher. I knew he hated me now, and everything. And maybe he had reason to.

But he still had to listen to me. Because this was my escape too.

'We have to take him with us,' I said.

Christopher looked back at me like he'd never seen me before in his life. In fact, it was a lot like those early days back in Mr Greer's Public Speaking class, when Christopher hadn't known it was me, Em, looking out at him behind Nikki Howard's famous sapphire-blue eyes.

'Absolutely not,' he said emphatically. 'That is not part of the plan.'

I walked up to him and stood so that my face was just inches from his.

'We have to change the plan,' I said. 'Because if we don't, the minute the plane lands, we're going to be surrounded by a bunch of Feds. Brandon's going to call them. I guarantee it.'

'He's not going to tell anyone,' Christopher said. 'He can't. What's he going to say? That he kidnapped you, and you escaped?'

'He'll make something up about all of us,' I said. 'He'll say horrible things about what we did to him, and next thing we know, Steven will be on *America's Most Wanted*.'

'I don't think that show is even on any more,' Christopher said, looking down at me with his eyebrows furrowed. His lips, I couldn't help noticing, were very close to mine.

I hated myself for noticing this.

'Oh, that show is still on,' I said. 'And you know who's going to be starring on it soon? You, if you keep on the way you've been acting. What did you blow up, anyway, when you were out there "distracting Brandon's security guards"? How do you know none of them got hurt?'

He bristled.

'Because none of them did,' he said. 'I was there. It was only a pipe bomb, and I threw it towards the beach, away from everyone.'

'Including the paparazzi?' I demanded. 'They've been hiding in the dunes.'

'I checked it out beforehand,' Christopher snapped. 'No one was there. God, Em, what do you want from me?'

Obviously I couldn't tell him what I wanted from him. Because it wouldn't have been exactly appropriate to say in the mixed company in which we were standing, part of it having to do with his tongue in my mouth.

'I want you to be responsible for your actions,' I said instead. I didn't know what was wrong with me. Why was I yelling at him when he was only trying to help me, which was quite generous of him, considering the fact that he didn't even like me any more? 'Not run around acting like your *Journeyquest* avatar, who by the way always attacked before thinking too, which is exactly how you always got pwned—'

'You never pwned me,' Christopher snapped. 'I pwned you—'

'Um,' Mrs Howard said. The thumping on the door was growing louder. Now someone was ringing the doorbell too. 'I hate to interrupt. But I really think we ought to be leaving now – and I think taking Brandon along with us is probably the wisest course,' Mrs Howard continued. 'Otherwise I think he might do something . . . impulsive.'

'If you lay one hand on me,' Brandon roared, thrashing

on the floor, 'I'll call my lawyers! I'm going to sue all of you! You too, Lulu! Just because your mother and my mother both once lived in the same ashram, don't think I won't do it!'

Lulu looked down at Brandon with narrowed eyes. It was clear he'd made a big mistake bringing up her mother, about whom Lulu'd never been able to speak without emotion.

'He's coming along,' she said, producing a dishcloth from her apron pocket. 'Gag him, Steven.'

It only took a few seconds for Steven to thrust the dish towel into Brandon's wide-open, protesting mouth. The next thing I knew, he and Christopher were half dragging, half shuffling Brandon out the back door and around the side of the house towards a parked minivan. The sound of the waves hitting the beach a few dozen yards away was loud . . .

. . . but not as loud as the sound of even more approaching sirens.

The air outside was crisp and smelt of mingled woodsmoke and salty ocean spray. Cosabella, excited to be on what she assumed was her morning walk, hurried along in front of me on the path, sniffing everything she came across and doing her business, along with Mrs Howard's dogs.

Nikki kept stumbling as she walked in her platform heels and looked back at the house.

'My operation,' she said faintly. 'If we leave, I'm not going to get to have my operation.'

'Yeah,' her brother said in a voice that was as unsympathetic as Lulu's had been over Justin. 'Well, that's for the best. Mom said it would kill you, remember?'

'But,' Nikki said mournfully, 'I just want to be pretty.'

I won't lie: when I heard that, *I* stumbled.

I could barely look at her. *I just want to be pretty*. Oh my God.

Nikki didn't stumble again as we all got into the car (well, Brandon had to be scrunched down behind the back seats of the rear of the minivan, an indignity he did not seem to enjoy one bit, if the grunting that could be heard from back there was any indication) and started at top speed towards the airport, passing fire engines on our way. Lulu, who still had on her chef's hat, waved cheerfully at the handsome firemen, and some of them actually waved back at her, blithely unaware we'd been the ones who'd started the fire they were racing towards.

But Nikki's face, when I glanced at it, was just about the saddest thing I had ever seen.

I just want to be pretty.

I may not have been a prisoner any more . . .

. . . but Nikki suddenly looked as if she felt she was.

Nine

We told the pilots and flight attendants that the reason Brandon was tied up was because we were taking him to rehab against his will.

They knew enough about Brandon Stark from having read about him in the tabloids – and from even having flown with him once or twice – to believe it. They walked around during the flight shaking their heads to themselves as if thinking, *Oh! Those poor, spoilt billionaires' kids! I'm so glad my own kid doesn't have any of* those *kinds of problems.*

But that still left the problem of what Brandon was going to do to us when the plane landed.

'Have each and every one of you arrested,' he snarled at us once, when he worked the gag out of his mouth.

Lulu, rolling her eyes, popped the dishcloth right back in.

Mrs Howard thought we should hold a press conference, like the impromptu one I'd held when I'd been trying to find her.

'Nice idea,' Steven said, leaning his elbows on the slick table top in front of him. 'But what exactly are we going to say at this press conference?'

'Well, the truth,' Mrs Howard said. 'That Robert Stark attempted to murder my daughter.'

'And where's the proof?' Christopher wanted to know.

'You're looking at her,' Mrs Howard said, pointing at me.

Christopher had most definitely not been looking at me. He had been studiously looking everywhere *but* at me. Now that we were broken up – because of my alleged trust issues – he had taken the furthest seat from me on the large plane, at the dining table for six.

Not that I'd cared. Or pretended to, or even noticed. I'd taken a seat in front of the flat-screen TV and started flicking through the DVDs to check if they had anything new I hadn't seen yet.

'But she's clearly alive and well,' Steven pointed out, nodding at me. 'I think it's going to be a bit difficult for the average American viewer to understand that Em isn't Nikki Howard. I think by proof Christopher means something a little more substantive than just Em's word that she's not Nikki on the inside. Because she actually is, on the outside.'

'She's got a scar,' Frida said. 'Em could show them her scar from the surgery. Where they did the surgery.'

'I suppose we need more,' Steven said thoughtfully. 'We need an actual *witness*. Maybe someone who was there when they performed the surgeries.'

'Well, you can forget Dr Fong,' I said, moving back from the front of the cabin. I'd just hung up the jet's phone.

'They killed him?' Lulu cried in horror.

Steven gave her a wary look. I really couldn't tell whether he liked her or not. Sometimes I thought he did, and sometimes I wasn't sure. While I considered her an utter delight, Lulu seemed to scare Nikki's brother sometimes with her intensity.

I guess I could sort of see why. Since getting back on to the plane, she'd changed from her chef's uniform into a leopard-print bodysuit and a purple tutu and sequinned jacket, along with a cherry-red beret that sat on her bleached-blonde pageboy at a rakish angle and brought out the cafe au lait tone of her skin.

Still, I thought she looked cute.

Steven, on the other hand, seemed to regard her as a sort of species he'd never observed before, in the wild or captivity or anywhere really.

I suppose there hadn't been many girls in Gasper like Lulu.

'Uh, no,' I said. 'I think he's on the run, like we are. The operator says his house phone is no longer in service, and when I called the Stark Institute for Neurology and Neurosurgery and asked for him, they said he had given notice.'

From the very back of the plane I heard a mournful sob. Looking round, I saw that it had come from Nikki, curled up in a seat by a window.

I guess I shouldn't have been surprised. Dr Fong had been her last hope for getting her old body back.

I just want to be pretty, she'd said, in the most mournful voice I'd ever heard.

Who didn't?

Well, OK . . . I didn't. Pretty was the last thing I used to care about. Back in the days before that plasma screen had hit me on the head, I never used to make any effort whatsoever to look good.

That's why Frida had never wanted to be seen with me. I'd just throw on whatever of my clothes was lying closest on the floor. A haircut was whatever was cheapest at Supercuts. Make-up was . . . nothing. I guess maybe I'd tried once or twice to make an effort, but only half-heartedly, and it had always ended in disaster. It was, like, I'd just decided, *Well, I can't look like Nikki Howard, so I guess I'll just give up completely*.

Which could be partly why the guy I'd liked had never noticed I was actually female . . .

The trouble was, from what I now had been able to observe, Nikki Howard herself had never been too pretty either . . . on the *inside*, anyway. Maybe if she could just work on being that now, it might start showing on the outside too . . .

On the other hand . . . if I had to look at somebody else walking around in my body, I guess I wouldn't be feeling too pretty on the inside either.

'What about the thing about the computers,' Frida asked. She held up her Stark Quark, which she'd received as a gift from Robert Stark. 'Can't we tell the press or the police about that? The thing Nikki overheard?'

'But we don't have any proof regarding that either,' Steven said, reaching for the laptop. 'At least, not yet.' He looked questioningly over at Christopher.

But all Christopher did was hold up both hands, still in their fingerless gloves, in a helpless gesture.

'Don't look at me,' he said. 'I'm out.'

I narrowed my eyes at him.

'What do you mean,' I asked, 'you're out?'

Lulu looked at me and, pressing her cherry-red lips together – she was using a pretty heavy hand with the gloss these days, due, I knew, to a certain someone whose initials were S.H. – said, 'Christopher said he'd come with us to help get you away from Brandon, because he felt that was the right thing to do and he owed you that much. But after that he didn't want anything more to do with any of this.'

'So,' I said, still regarding him through narrowed eyes. I couldn't believe he was serious. 'We're just supposed to figure this whole thing with the Stark Quarks out on our own?'

'Hey,' he said. 'You're the one who's so concerned about putting the rest of us in danger. It's probably for the best then that I just walk away. For my own safety. Right?'

I glared at him. 'Whatever happened to *Take it down*?' I asked. 'Wasn't that your plan? To take Stark down? You're just going to forget about all that?'

'Em Watts isn't dead any more,' Christopher said, giving me a brittle smile. 'Is she?'

'So it's all good?' I couldn't believe what I was hearing. 'What about that speech you gave in class? The three hundred billion dollars in profit Stark made last year that just went to line Robert Stark's pocket. The cheap, Chinese-made knock-offs they sell that our American-made products can't compete with. The locally owned businesses the Stark Megastores drive out of town. How, if we're going to keep from going the way of ancient Rome, with a collapsing economy and a society dependent on imported goods, we have to become producers again, and stop consuming so much . . .'

Christopher shrugged.

'Not my problem,' he said. 'You don't need my help. You don't even trust me enough to *ask* for my help. Remember?'

I looked at him, not sure if he really meant it or not. A part of me was pretty sure he did. His gaze on mine was steady and unblinking, and there was an upward curl at the corners of his mouth . . . he was smiling like he was actually *enjoying* this.

But I couldn't help feeling as if, behind those blue eyes, there was a different Christopher – the old Christopher – begging me to call him on his asinine behaviour. To say, *I'm asking for your help now. Will you help us? Will you help* me?

Only I didn't.

Because I was too angry with him. Why was he acting like such a four-year-old? I'd already explained to him why I'd made the decisions I had. They'd been perfectly decent, rational decisions.

So why was he acting this way?

'We don't even know that they're necessarily doing anything wrong with the information, other than storing it,' Steven said hesitantly. 'Do we? If we just knew what they were collecting it for . . .'

I watched as Christopher turned his head to look stubbornly out one of the jet's many windows.

'*I don't care any more,*' he said, to the window.

But I knew he wasn't saying it to the window.

He was saying it to me.

And it wouldn't be exaggerating to say I felt like he had thrust his hand past my ribs, ripped my heart from the walls of my chest, pulled it out, and tossed it thirty thousand feet to the ground (I think we were somewhere over Pennsylvania at the time), just like I had that morning outside Dr Fong's.

Really? All this because I hadn't wanted to leave without Nikki last night, and he'd had to switch to plan B, calling in Lulu and Frida for support?

Or was it really because of my *issues*?

Well, if you asked me, Christopher was the one with issues.

I glanced at Lulu to see what she was making of all this, and wasn't too surprised to see her roll her eyes. *Boys,* she mouthed. Then she made a gesture like I should go over and sit down next to him.

I'm sorry, but had Lulu been nipping at the emergency oxygen? Because no, this was not going to happen.

Instead, I turned my attention back to the conversation at the table, ignoring Christopher, who was ignoring everyone else . . .

. . . even though I'd known what was coming. I'd known it before it had even come out of Frida's mouth.

'Maybe,' she'd said, 'maybe if Christopher doesn't want to help, his cousin could figure it out.'

Of course. Christopher's computer-genius cousin,

Felix, who was already under house arrest for having bilked a televangelist out of tens of thousands of dollars for programming a local payphone to autodial his show's 1-800 number several hundred thousand times in a row (who knew the owners of 1-800 numbers actually had to pay every time you called them?).

Why not drag Felix into all this, even though he was Frida's age? Felix had nothing more to lose, after all.

'No,' Christopher said, turning his head back sharply to face us. I knew he'd been paying attention. 'If I'm out, he's out too.'

I couldn't help wondering how Felix was going to feel about this decision. Felix seemed like the kind of kid who, once involved in a project, wasn't going to let go of it quite that easily.

And Felix had already found a way into Stark's computer mainframe because of me.

I couldn't even deal with Christopher any more. Instead, I decided just to ignore him. There were too many more important things to think about.

One of them was Brandon, and how we were going to get him to leave us alone. I decided I'd handle this one.

I sat down across from him in one of the Gulfstream's soft, cream-coloured leather seats.

'Brandon,' I said, leaning forward to lay a hand on one of his . . . which were getting a little puffy from having been tied up for so long. 'If your dad's company goes down, there's going to be a great big opening for a new CEO. It would be a shame if you couldn't step into his shoes because you'd been arrested too, for all the stuff you did to me. You know, like blackmailing me and threatening me and taking me across state lines against my will even though I'm a minor and all. That's going to look *really* bad on Fox News. I mean, I don't *want* to press charges against you for doing all that stuff. Because the way I see it, you're still a Stark, which isn't exactly a good thing . . . though at least you don't seem to be into killing people. But I totally will go to the Feds about you if you mess with my friends after we all get back to New York.'

Brandon, looking at me with wide eyes above the huge green-and-white-striped dishcloth sticking out of his mouth, said a lot of stuff.

But I couldn't tell what any of it was, on account of the gag.

'The thing you need to know, Brandon,' I said, leaning back in the seat and crossing my legs, 'is that I'm the one who set your Murciélago on fire.'

Brandon's eyes got a lot wider and he said a lot more things in a louder voice. I still couldn't tell what any of them were though. Well, any of them that weren't swear words.

'Yeah,' I said, 'I know. You totally deserved it. You can't treat women – or anyone – the way you treated me. Do you understand? And no, I'm not going to pay for a new car for you. Instead, I'm going do a lot worse to you if you mess with me again. I'm going to call Oprah's people and schedule an in-depth interview on her show about how you used me, and what a total and complete loser you are. You will become the most detested man in America. And then you will have zero chance of the Stark Enterprises shareholders letting you take over when your dad goes down.'

Brandon quieted when I said all this. He stared at me with wounded eyes, looking almost like Cosabella when I scolded her for chewing on a pair of Jimmy Choos, which for some reason she seems to find irresistible.

'So, what's it going to be?' I asked him. 'Are you going to play ball? Or are you going to continue going through life acting like a total butt-head? Because at some point, Brandon, you are going to have to decide.' I lifted both hands like they were the scales Lady Justice held. 'Butt-head? Grown-up? It's up to you.'

He studied my hands. Then, nodding towards the hand signifying grown-up, he said something. Only of course I couldn't tell what, because of the gag.

'Did you say grown-up, Brandon?' I asked.

He nodded vigorously. I leaned over to remove the gag.

'Oh, thank God,' he said. 'And I forgive you for the Murciélago. Really, I do. I admit, what I did to you was really, really crappy. Like you said, I *can* be a loser sometimes. I really can. Now, could you please, please untie me and get the stewardess to get me a drink and a turkey sandwich? I'm dying here.'

'Flight attendant,' I said.

'What?' He looked at me like I was crazy.

'She's a flight attendant, Brandon,' I said. 'Not a stewardess. On your journey towards not being a butt-head any more, you might as well start using the correct language.

Stewardess is sexist. And I will untie you and get you a ginger ale. We told them you're on your way to rehab so it would be better for you not have anything alcoholic.'

'Whatever,' Brandon said. 'Thanks. And I'm sorry.'

Getting up from my seat, I stopped and looked at him in surprise. Those were the last two words I'd ever expected to hear from Brandon Stark . . . *I'm* and *sorry*.

Was it actually possible for guys like him to grow and change?

I glanced over at Christopher, who was bent over his cellphone, pounding away at the keys with his thumbs.

Hey, if guys could change for the worse, why couldn't they change for the better?

But maybe that was just wishful thinking.

Ten

It felt good to be home.

Oh, there was a ton of mail I was going to have to go through – not just bills that needed to be paid, but gift bags and packages from appreciative clients and sponsors and even, I supposed, some of Nikki's old friends, wanting to wish her happy holidays. Someone had sent her an entire case of Grey Goose vodka, someone else a three-thousand dollar Chanel bag, someone else four different iPods, still in their boxes.

Happy holidays, indeed, for someone – at the Memorial Sloan-Kettering Thrift Shop where I was going to donate all this stuff so they could sell it to raise money to give to people who needed cancer treatment (although I wasn't sure they'd take the vodka).

And of course I wasn't going to be able to avoid my voicemail – or Mom and Dad – forever.

But it was amazing to be in my own place, surrounded by my own things, in my own beloved New York City.

Except of course it wasn't *really* my own place.

And they weren't *really* my things.

And who knew for how much longer I was going to be able to enjoy any of them? I was still going to have to worry about giving them back to their rightful owner. Or maybe not, since I also had the whole my-boss-might-be-trying-to-kill-me thing to worry about, as well.

Because things hadn't ended particularly well with Christopher. Or Nikki.

I'd tried my best with both of them. I really had.

Now, stretched out on my bed, I remembered how, Brandon taken care of, I'd gone to try to make amends with Nikki. I don't know why I'd felt like I owed her something. She'd been nothing but nasty to me.

But I couldn't stand to see her sitting there crying in the back of the limo we'd taken into the city from the airport (well, all of us except for Frida, who'd taken the charter jet back to Florida, to finish out the rest of her week at cheerleading camp).

I just want to be pretty.

Hadn't all those times I'd sat in our living room, wishing that Christopher would notice me as something more than just someone to play *Journeyquest* with, I sort of longed to be pretty too? Frida had always been the one who'd said the actual words though.

'I wish I could be pretty,' she'd say, and sigh, looking at a photo spread of Nikki Howard in some kind of ridiculous $20,000 gold metallic dress in *Elle* magazine.

Mom, feminist professor of women's studies at NYU, would always huff the same thing in reply.

'Don't be ridiculous, honey,' she'd say. 'Looks don't matter. What matters is the kind of person you are, how much character you have.'

110

And Frida would snort: 'Yeah. All the boys in school really care about my *character*, Mom.'

'Looks fade,' Mom would go on. 'But intelligence lasts forever.'

'But you do think I'm pretty,' Frida would say. 'Don't you, Mom?'

'Honey,' Mom would say, cupping Frida's face in her hands, 'I think you and your sister are both growing into strong, independent young women. And that's how I hope you'll always stay.'

I'd always wondered if Frida had noticed how Mom never really answered the question.

But when I'd laid a hand over Nikki's and squeezed it, and said softly, 'Nikki. You're going to be staying at Gabriel Luna's place for a little while until we can get this thing worked out.' This wasn't something Gabriel had been particularly delighted to hear. He'd been shocked when I'd called him from the plane and announced that the Howard family was coming to stay with him in his place.

But we couldn't exactly stash Nikki and Steven and their mom in a hotel – Stark was sure to be tracking all our credit cards.

But hiding them directly under Robert Stark's nose, in the new high-rise, super-secure apartment (into which he'd had to move to escape his hordes of screaming fans) of Gabriel Luna, a recording artist on Stark's very own label? Genius, even if Gabriel had his doubts . . . not just about Stark not finding out, but about playing host to Nikki, who practically spat at him in response to his cheerful, 'So nice to meet you,' before locking herself in his spare bedroom.

'OK,' Gabriel had said. 'This is going to go well, I see.'

'I'm going to do everything I can to try to get you back all the things you've lost,' I'd assured Nikki in the limo. Or attempt to, anyway.

'Really?' She'd whirled to look up at me with tears streaming from her eyes. 'Like my face? You're going to give me back my face?'

'Well,' I'd said, startled. My hand had risen unconsciously to my cheek. Or Nikki's cheek, I guess it was. 'I'm not sure I can give you that, Nikki. But your money and your apartment – those things are yours.'

She turned right back to the limo's window.

'Then we have nothing to talk about,' she said coldly. 'Because all I want is to be pretty again.'

And kind of like my mom, I hadn't known the right thing to say. Because pretty was the one thing I couldn't give her. Because maybe pretty was something she had to give to herself.

Lying on my bed in Nikki's loft, staring up at Nikki's ceiling, with her dog snuggled against my neck, all I could think of was what she'd said to me in the car.

Then we have nothing to talk about. Because all I want is to be pretty again.

I had never seen anyone look as sad as she had.

I could understand her loss. I'd lost the same thing. Well, not quite the same thing . . . but sort of the same, if you counted the fact that I'd lost things I probably loved

112

as much as Nikki loved her looks: my family, my home, my friendship with Christopher. . . .

I don't know how long I'd been lying there before Lulu popped her head into the doorway and said, 'I'm starving. I'm thinking of ordering in. Do you want a banana split?'

I rolled over to look at her.

'Lulu,' I said, 'banana splits are not a meal.'

'Yes, they are,' Lulu said, coming over to hop up on to my bed beside me. 'They have fruit and nuts and dairy. So they represent most of the major food groups. If you include chocolate sauce. And I'm always full after I eat one.'

'Go ahead and order me one too then,' I said, giving up and rolling back over on to my back with a sigh.

Lulu clambered over me to reach for the landline, sitting in its cradle on the nightstand by my bed. She hit the autodial for the deli on the corner and ordered us two banana splits for delivery. Then she hung up and looked at me.

'Are you thinking about Christopher?' she asked accusingly.

'No, I'm thinking about Nikki,' I corrected her. Although of course I *had* been thinking about Christopher, even if only peripherally.

Lulu made a face. She evidently didn't consider her former room-mate worth thinking about, much less discussing.

'He still loves you, you know,' she said about Christopher.

'Oh, really?' I asked with a bitter laugh. 'That's not what he says.'

'He's just upset,' Lulu said, 'that you lied to him. Not just once, but a bunch of times. It's wrong to lie to the person you love. Unless it's to tell him that his hair looks good, even when it looks awful.'

'What if it's to protect his life?' I asked, rising up on my elbows to look at her.

'Especially then,' Lulu said, shaking her head gravely. 'Guys *hate* that. They're supersensitive, especially now, with feminism and stuff. It's completely confused them. They don't know where they stand. Are they supposed to do stuff for you like open doors and pay for dinner when you go out, or let you do it all? They don't know. Then he tried to rescue you, and you wouldn't even go with him. So you're going to have to let him do things for you once in a while. Even if you know he's just going to screw it up. Especially when you, you know, have so much going for you, and he . . . doesn't.'

I glared at her, feeling a little hurt. How dare she say my boyfriend (well, ex-boyfriend, I suppose, technically) didn't have anything going for him.

'Christopher has a lot going for him,' I said. 'He's a total computer wizard and he's really funny and sweet – when he isn't being all supervillainy about avenging my death, and stuff. Or mad at me about running off with the son of his mortal enemy.'

'I'm sure he is,' Lulu said diplomatically. 'But right now, he's hurt. And so you're just going to have to work on breaking through the protective wall he's built up around himself for fear of getting hurt again.'

'Well,' I said, collapsing back against the pillows. 'It wasn't just to protect him. It was to protect my family. And Nikki too. I explained that to him. And he still hates me.'

'I told you –' Lulu had found some black nail polish in Nikki's nightstand drawer, and now she was applying it to her toenails, having kicked off her purple platform mules – 'He doesn't hate you. But you're going to have to find a way to make him understand how much you really do need him, so he can see how important he is to you.'

'He *is* important to me,' I cried. 'I love him!'

'But he can't really *do* anything for you,' Lulu said, concentrating on her toes. 'You're the one with all the money and power. He's just a high-school boy. He can barely afford to buy you dinner at Balthazar. At least, not dinner *and* an appetizer *and* the crème brûlée there. He probably couldn't even afford to buy a bottle of this nail polish.' Lulu closed the cap on the bottle and shook it. 'It's Chanel. More than twenty bucks. Like I said back at Brandon's—'

'But he had the opportunity to do something for me today,' I cried. 'To help with the Stark Quark thing. And he wouldn't!'

'He's still mad now,' Lulu said. 'Let him cool down. Boys need cooling-off periods, just like my nails are going to need to dry off before I can put my shoes back on and go over to Gabriel's to give Nikki a makeover. She needs one just like you and Christopher need some relationship counselling from Doctor Drew.'

I gave her a dirty look. 'Christopher and I don't need relationship counselling. He just hates me, is all.'

'He does not. Going to rescue you was totally his idea,' Lulu pointed out. 'He was the one who called me and was completely gung-ho about sweeping in and getting you out of there. It was way Luke Spacewalker.'

This made me want to cry, it was so sweet.

'Skywalker,' I corrected her. 'It's Luke Skywalker.'

'So what are we going to do?' Lulu asked, looking at me with her huge brown eyes. For once, she'd foregone one of her many pairs of tinted contacts, which often gave her eyes an eerily catlike glow against her dark skin. 'I mean, about this mess? We can't hide the Howards at Gabriel Luna's forever. Brandon's totally scared of you now since you told him you're the one who set his car on fire, so he won't tell. But his dad—'

'– is the fourth-richest man in the country,' I said. 'And also the most powerful. I know.'

I stared back at Lulu. Why was she asking *me* what we were going to do? I had no idea. I had never wanted for any of this to happen.

And I had no idea how to fix any of it either.

We were sitting there looking at each other blankly when something rang, loudly enough to make us both jump practically out of our skins.

'Ahhh!' Lulu screamed. 'What *is* that?'

We jumped off the bed and began running around the

loft, trying to find the source of the ringing, while Cosabella dashed up and down, barking.

'Is it the banana splits?' I asked. 'Are they here already?'

'That's not the buzzer,' Lulu said, meaning the intercom the doorman used to let us know when someone was waiting for us in the lobby.

'Then what is it?' I wailed as the ringing continued, loud as ever, at regular intervals.

'Oh, my God!' Lulu cried, stopping by a side table. 'It's the house phone!'

'The house phone?' I didn't even know that we *had* a house phone, we were both so dependent on our cells. 'Are you kidding me?'

Lulu reached down and picked up the phone. 'Hello?' she said, a curious expression on her face. Someone said something, and Lulu looked over at me.

'Oh,' she said. 'Yes. Oh, hi! Of course she's here. Hold on one moment.'

Then Lulu covered the receiver with her hand and said to me, in an excited way, 'It's for you. It's your mother.'

I immediately threw both my hands into the air.

'*My mother?*' I whispered back to her. '*I don't want to talk to my mother! Tell her I'm not here!*'

Lulu looked confused. 'But I just told her that you *were* here. Why don't you want to talk to your mother?'

'Because she's mad at me!' I whisper-yelled. 'I just spent the holidays at a boy's house without his parents being there! You might have read about it in every tabloid

117

in America? I'm in big trouble with her.'

'Ooooh,' Lulu said, nodding, as understanding dawned. 'I get it. Do you want me to explain that you were being blackmailed and that if you didn't do it, Brandon was going to tell his dad where he could find Nikki, and then Mr Stark would kill her? I'm sure Karen will understand that.' Lulu took her hand away from the receiver and said, 'Hello, Karen? It's me, Lulu. Listen, if it's about Em going to South Carolina with Brandon Stark, I can—'

I don't think I've ever moved as fast before in my life. I literally dived for the phone in Lulu's hand, landing with it on the couch and then pressing it to my ear. Lulu looked down at me in shock as I said to my mother, 'Hi, Mom!' in the fakiest voice you could imagine.

'Emerson,' my mom said.

Uh-oh. This was bad. My mom only called me by my full name when she was really, really mad.

Plus, she wasn't even supposed to be using my real name on the phone, let alone Nikki Howard's house phone.

Something in her tone, however, suggested that this might not be the best time to remind her of this.

'So,' I said, lying full length on the couch as Cosabella, excited by all the activity, leaped on the cushions around me. 'How's it going? How's Dad?'

'Your father is fine,' Mom said in the tightest voice you could imagine. She sounded like she'd just gotten Botox in her lips or something, she was speaking in such a cold, controlled, tiny little voice. It was clear that she'd been bottling up her anger with me all week, just saving it for the moment when she could see me, so she could explode all over me like one of Christopher's pipe bombs. 'Thank you for asking. I've been leaving messages for you on your cellular telephone. Have you not received any of them?'

Cellular telephone. She had actually said the words *cellular telephone*. I was so, so dead.

'Uh, no,' I said. 'You know what happened, actually? It was the funniest thing. I dropped my cellphone in the ocean, and I haven't gotten around to replacing it . . .'

Beside me, Lulu stamped the floor and gave me a dirty look. *'No more lying,'* she mouthed. *'To anyone!'*

I rolled my eyes at her.

'Well,' Mom said. Her voice was still insanely small and cold, 'it's lucky I happened to catch you at home.'

'Yes,' I said, trying to get Lulu to go away by making shooing motions with my hand. Unfortunately it wasn't working, because she was still jumping around, going, *'Stop lying! Don't lie!'* which wasn't at all annoying (yes. It was). 'So how's Grandma?'

'Your grandmother is fine,' Mom said, still sounding as frosty as a lemon-ice. 'Emerson, your father and I would like to meet with you. Would fifteen minutes be enough time for you to get to the Starbucks on Astor Place?'

'What?' Feeling panicky, I flung a glance at the windows of the loft. It was, as usual for late December in Manhattan, sleeting outside. 'Um . . .'

'Your father and I are already sitting here waiting for you,' Mom went on, 'since I understand from TMZ dot com – the only way I seem to be able to keep track of

119

my own daughter's activities any more – that you're back in Manhattan. The adult thing to do would be, of course, to show up to meet us. However, if you just want to leave us here waiting for you like complete idiots, that's fine. But—'

'Oh my God, Mom,' I said, sitting up. 'I'll be there. I'll be right over. Is everything OK?'

'No, Emerson,' she said. 'Everything is *not* OK.'

And then the line went dead.

I held the phone away from my face, staring at it.

'What's the matter?' Lulu asked, hopping around on her bare feet, probably getting black nail polish all over the white fake-fur carpeting.

'My mom just hung up on me,' I said in disbelief.

'She did?' Lulu shrugged. 'My mom does that all the time. When she remembers to call me. Which is once a year, on my birthday.'

Aw. I felt so bad for Lulu, I reached out to give her a hug.

'Well, my mom's never done that before,' I said. 'I think something might really be wrong. I mean, aside from the fact that she is supremely annoyed with me for spending the week at a boy's house without his parents being there.'

Lulu looked concerned. 'Like you think Robert Stark might actually be there holding a gun to her head, making her call you, so it's actually a trap, or something?'

'Oh, great,' I said, giving her a sarcastic look. 'I hadn't even thought of that. She says she's at a Starbucks. Why would Robert Stark be holding a gun to her head at a Star-bucks?'

'Oh,' Lulu said. She seemed a little disappointed. 'Yeah. You're right. That's not very likely, is it?'

I gave her another hug. I just couldn't help it, she was so cute. 'I gotta go. I'll see you later.'

'But what about our banana splits?' Lulu called after me as I ran to grab my jacket and hat, as well as a leash and coat for Cosy.

'Save mine,' I yelled. 'I'll be back for it.'

'I hope so,' I heard Lulu shout as I jumped into the elevator.

She had no idea how much I hoped so too.

Eleven

I found my parents sitting at a table in the back of the cafe, huddled over tall cups of coffee, looking extremely serious. Since they were both professors, they looked serious most of the time anyway.

But this was out-of-the-usual serious. Dad had dark circles under his eyes, and it appeared to have been a while since his face had seen the business end of a razor.

Mom's hair could definitely have used some conditioning, and I don't think she was wearing a lick of make-up. Not that she'd ever been a close personal friend of Maybelline's.

But I'd come to find out that a little goes a long way when it comes to mascara and lipgloss, something about which someone might want to remind Nikki.

God, did I, Emerson Watts, just think that? What was happening to me?

Robert Stark, despite what Lulu had worried about, wasn't anywhere nearby. So they weren't being held hostage.

But they didn't say hi or even wave while I got my biscotti and herbal tea (caffeine is a big trigger for Nikki's acid reflux) and then joined them at their table. They acted like we were complete strangers.

Which is totally unfair, because while I may not be

related to them by blood any more, I'm still their daughter. Even if I've shamed the family name by allegedly hooking up with Brandon Stark. Or so every major tabloid in the US and most of the UK claim.

'So, hi!' I said, trying to act all cheerful while I peeled off my leather jacket. Cosabella got to work prancing around and sniffing them excitedly, which Cosabella considers her personal life's work . . . sniffing everyone and everything, and basically making people smile, because she wants only one thing, which is food, and to be petted and admired.

Well, I guess that's two things. Or three.

'Hi,' Mom said finally, while Dad was a little bit friendlier, saying, 'Hi, honey.'

'So,' I said when my jacket was off and so was Cosabella's and we were all settled in and I'd had my first sip of tea and burned my tongue and everything. Why do they do that – make their hot water so hot?

'What's up?' I asked. I thought that sounded nice and non-confrontational.

Mom and Dad looked at each other, and I could see that they were giving each other the old *Go ahead, you start, No, you start* eye signal.

Then Dad was like 'Em, your mother and I wanted to talk to you about something. We chose to do so here in this cafe because it's neutral ground, not our place or yours, and we thought it might be a little less emotionally charged than either of our apartments.'

Whoa. My heart began to thump a little harder than

usual. This sounded serious! Neutral ground? Less emotionally charged?

Wait . . . were they getting divorced?

I knew it. Dad worked most of the week in New Haven, teaching at Yale. I'd wondered when he'd taken the job if their marriage – always volatile, since they were different religions and both attractive (I don't know how they'd managed to have a daughter as plain as me) – could survive the stress of so much separation.

And now the truth was coming out. It couldn't!

Or wait. Maybe it was me. Maybe it was me their marriage couldn't survive the stress of! Because of my accident and subsequent coma and then reawakening in the body of a major teen supermodel!

'The thing is,' Dad went on, 'we've been a little distressed about your behaviour lately—'

Wait, I thought. My *behaviour*? Oh God! It *was* me! They were getting divorced because of me!

'Not just your behaviour,' Mom jumped in. 'Your grades this semester were abysmal.'

'My *grades*?'

When Mom had called to schedule this meeting (and then hung up on me), I had thought a lot of things must be going on:

Robert Stark was breathing down their necks, maybe making threats.

They'd found out their apartment was bugged, the way I'd found out mine was (why else the meeting in a Starbucks, instead of at home?).

124

They'd found out about Frida skipping out on cheer-leading camp and flying to South Carolina to rescue me, and were naturally upset about their under-age daughter jetting all over the place without their permission. This wouldn't be the biggest surprise. Frida had told the camp officials she was going to her grandmother's, and insisted no one was going to be any the wiser. I'd thought the whole thing sounded sketchy, but Frida claimed no one was going to find out. She'd be home in time for the Stark Angel show tomorrow night on New Year's Eve.

Now, of course, I knew better.

Then I'd thought maybe they were getting a divorce.

Or even, God forbid, one of them had cancer.

Or was having an affair (Hey . . . Lulu's mom had left her dad for another man. And I wouldn't put it past Mom to announce she was turning lesbian. She wouldn't even tell her own daughters they were pretty. Why would she care about the sexual orientation of a lover?).

But I'd never expected it to be about my *grades*.

All this neutral-ground chatter for a talk about *my grades*?

I'm sorry, but a corporation was trying to kill my friends. The true owner of my body wanted it back. The love of my life had just unceremoniously dumped me.

And my parents wanted to talk about finals?

'How did you even find out about my grades?' I demanded. 'You're not Nikki Howard's guardians. You're not even supposed to have access to—'

Mom pulled something out of her bag. It was a crumpled-up printout from the website TMZ.com. Someone (probably a reporter from their offices, though of course it didn't say that) had broken into Tribeca Alternative High School's main computer and accessed my (or more accurately, Nikki's) grades, then plastered them all over the Net.

And let's just say I wasn't doing so hot.

America's Top Model Not Quite Top of Her Class, screamed the headline.

I snatched the sheet from my mother's hands and scanned it.

'A C minus?' I was stunned. 'Mr Greer gave me a C minus in Public Speaking? That mall cop!'

Dad made a disapproving noise over his coffee. 'Now, Em,' he said.

'But seriously,' I said. 'It's *Public Speaking*.'

'Exactly what I'm thinking,' Mom said, pulling the sheet from my hands. 'There's no reason why you shouldn't have gotten an A in it. You just have to stand up in front of the room and talk. You've never had difficulty standing in front of people and talking before. In fact, no one ever used to be able to get you to shut up.'

'Now, Karen,' Dad said, exactly the way he'd said *Now, Em* when I'd called Mr Greer a mall cop. 'I'm sure there's more to it than that.'

'Yeah,' I said, coming to my own defence. 'You have to make up reasoned arguments, and—'

'What about all those subjects you formerly always did

well in?' Mom demanded. 'How do you explain the C minus in Advanced Algebra? And the D in English? For God's sake, Emerson, English is your native language!'

I scowled. 'I didn't have time to do the readings,' I said. 'It's not my fault—'

Mom gasped triumphantly and pointed straight at me.

'There!' she said, looking over at Dad. 'She said it! Not me! She said it!'

I looked from Mom to Dad, not knowing what had happened.

'What?' I asked. 'What'd I say?'

'*I . . . didn't . . . have . . . time,*' Mom said, hitting the table with her palm to emphasize each syllable. 'Face it, Emerson. You're letting your schoolwork go because you're spending too much time socializing.'

'Socializing?' I made a face. 'Excuse me, but I never get to socialize. I'm working so much, I never even get to see my friends!'

'Oh, I think you get to spend quite a lot of time with your *friends*,' Mom said, reaching into her bag and pulling out a different sheet of paper. 'Quite a lot of *quality* time.'

She unfolded the page to reveal an *Us Weekly* cover that showed me in a bikini hanging out poolside at Brandon's beach house, and him standing right next to me, holding what looked like a cocktail.

Except put in context, I knew that that cocktail was actually a breakfast shake and that bikini was actually my workout gear after going for a perfectly innocent run on the beach.

But it would still look pretty bad to a parent, considering I had, after all, spent nearly the whole week at Brandon's without her permission.

And the fact that the headline splashed above the picture of us together screamed,

BACK ON!
Nikki and Brandon Rekindle a Love So Hot, They Had to Take It South of the Border (Islands)

I felt myself turning beet red. First of all, Brandon's house was on a barrier island. I didn't even know what a border island was. Could the press just write whatever it wanted and get away with it? Apparently.

And second of all . . .

'Look,' I said, remembering what Lulu had said about telling the truth. 'I can explain.'

'There's nothing to explain,' Mom said, folding the picture back up and putting it away again. 'It's all perfectly clear to us. Isn't it, Daniel?'

Dad looked uncomfortable.

'Um,' he said.

'Look,' I said again. 'It's not what you guys think. Brandon made me go with him to South Carolina. I didn't want to. And nothing happened. He and I aren't, you know, boyfriend and girlfriend. I mean, he and Nikki were. But he just wishes he and I were—'

128

'I don't want to hear it,' Mom said, shaking her head back and forth and not making eye contact with me. Which, to be honest, is basically something she really hadn't done all that often since I'd woken up from my surgery. 'I really don't. All I want – all I've ever wanted – is for all this just to be over, and for things to get back to normal and for me to have my daughter back.'

This kind of stung. Because the thing is, I *am* her daughter. On the inside. I've never stopped being her daughter. Even with the not-so-hot grades, I'm still her daughter.

So . . . what did that mean? She only loved me when I got above-average grades and was average-looking? Was this another thing about *character*?

I didn't get it. I really didn't. I felt like Frida and the 'pretty' thing.

'Well,' I said, 'how do you think I feel? But that's not—'

'And so,' Mom went on, completely ignoring me, 'your father and I have decided to just pay them off.'

I blinked at both of them. It was busy in the Starbucks they'd chosen. There were bloggers and NYU students everywhere, crowding every table with their laptops and expensive film equipment (the Astor Place Starbucks is right down the street from the Tisch School of the Arts, where the NYU film school is), looking all angsty in their hand-knitted woollen hats with the ear flaps, and their facial piercings and their tattoos, which they'd all gotten to show off how individual they were.

Except how individual were they really, if *every single one of them* had facial piercings and tattoos?

I was the only person in there under twenty who *didn't* have a pierced lip or eyebrow or any visible tattoos.

And I was also the one with the modelling contract with a corporation I bet all of them hated.

Not without good reason, of course.

But I'm just asking: who was the biggest conformist there?

'What do you mean,' I asked my mom, trying not to let all the bloggers and Eli Roth wannabes distract me, 'you guys are going to pay them off?'

'Stark,' she said. 'We don't have much in our savings and our 401ks. But we're going to pull together what we do have and pay them off, so that you don't have to do this any more. It won't be enough, we know, but it will be a start. You'll be able to go back to being yourself. Em –' Suddenly, I was back to being Em. Mom even reached out and grabbed my hands, resting on the table top – 'we're going to get you out of the contract.'

I stared at both of them. I really wasn't sure I understood exactly what she was saying. I thought I did.

But it was so insane, I just assumed I was mistaken.

'Wait,' I said, inching my hands out from under hers. 'Are you saying . . . you want to violate the confidentiality agreement you signed about my not really being Nikki Howard, and *pay Stark off*?'

'That's exactly what we're saying,' Mom said, withdrawing her hands into her lap. 'We want to get you out of this, Em. We never should have agreed to it in the first place. We only did it because we were scared and . . . well, we wanted to save your life. But now we see that maybe . . . well, maybe it was the wrong choice.'

The wrong choice? They should have let me *die* rather than be a model?

My shock must have shown on my face, since Dad leaned forward and said quickly, 'That's not what your mother means. She means maybe we made the wrong choice not negotiating more—'

'But –' I tried to think back to what had been said in Dr Holcombe's office that day my parents had told me about all the papers they'd signed when they'd agreed to the surgery that had saved my life – 'you can't. You'll lose everything.'

'Well, not everything,' Dad said in his usual cheerful manner, like we were talking about egg sandwiches or something. 'We'll keep our jobs. And they can't take your mother's apartment, which is through the university. So we'll always have a place to live.'

'But you'll go bankrupt,' I protested. 'That lawyer guy in Doctor Holcombe's office said you could even go to jail!' I didn't mention the part about how Robert Stark would have them both killed before he'd ever allow this to happen. If it was that simple – just paying back the money – I'd have tried to do it myself, out of the money in Nikki Howard's bank accounts.

'Well,' Mom said, after she'd taken a fortifying sip of coffee, 'I'd rather go to jail than see my daughter failing to live up to her potential and gallivanting around half naked with playboys on the covers of gossip magazines.'

I have to admit, my jaw dropped when she said this. My mom's always been a feminist.

But I never thought she was a prude.

'Because you think I had sex with *Brandon Stark*?' I couldn't believe this was happening. 'Mother, I did not have sex with him! That wasn't even a bikini. Those were my jogging clothes. I would never have sex with that ass clown!'

There's a possibility I might have said this a little too loudly, since a lot of the NYU kids turned round in their seats to look at us over their foamy non-fat cappuccinos. Some of them had their pierced eyebrows raised. I could see the bloggers beginning to blog furiously about what they'd just seen and heard. Even though they might have been hipsters, they loved a good scoop as much as the next blogger.

Twitter, I imagined, was probably on fire.

My mom, noticing this, hissed at me, 'Emerson! Would you please lower your voice?'

'No, I won't, *Mother*,' I said. If she was going to give me the full Emerson, I was going to give her the full Mother. Although I did lower my voice a little. I mean, it *was* kind of embarrassing.

'For your information,' I whispered, 'the only reason I went anywhere with Brandon Stark was because he said if I didn't he would tell his dad where he could find the real Nikki Howard.'

Both my parents stared at me blankly. Just as I'd known they would. Lulu's advice, to start telling the truth, was all well and good for her.

But her parents hardly even spoke to her. Her dad, a famous film director, just paid all her bills from whatever exotic movie locale he was working on, and her mom had basically disappeared off the face of the planet with a snowboard instructor who was nearly Lulu's age.

In some ways, Lulu was incredibly lucky. I knew she envied me what she considered my 'normal' family.

But she didn't know how big a pain a 'normal' family could be, how judgey and annoying they were half the time. I'd have given anything right then if my mother had just said that I'd looked pretty in that picture on the cover of *Us Weekly* and dropped the whole thing.

'Yeah,' I said, to their uncomprehending stares, 'that's right. The real Nikki Howard is still alive. I mean her brain is. It's in some other girl's body, obviously.'

I saw my mom and dad exchange glances. It was one of those secret-message glances people who are married or have been living together for a long time have with each other.

I could totally read what it said too.

It said, *This girl is completely bonkers, and we're worried about her.*

Yeah. They didn't believe me.

Well, why should they have, anyway? Like Lulu had said, I should have just been honest with everyone from the beginning, instead of trying to protect them all like I was some kind of mother goddess.

'Em –' my mom started to say carefully – 'you've been under a lot of stress lately. It's obvious with your slipping grades and the people you've been hanging around with – well, you're not exactly being the best example for your little sister now, are you?'

I have to admit, that hurt. Tears stung my eyes. *I* wasn't being a good example for Frida? Frida, who'd only ever aspired to go to cheerleading camp her whole life? At least I had a job!

'We think it might be better if, before Frida gets back from camp, you leave for a rest,' Mom said. 'A long rest somewhere you can be away from all the bad influences that have come into your life since you started working in the fashion business. Dad and I were thinking maybe a nice recovery centre somewhere in—'

Recovery centre? Did she mean *rehab*?

'You know what?' I interrupted her.

Why was I even trying? What did I hope to accomplish? No matter what I said, my mom wasn't going to believe me.

And if I let them in on the whole *Nikki's-brain-was-totally-healthy-Robert-Stark-just-tried-to-have-her-killed-because-she-knew-that-the-new-Stark-Quark-PCs-come-bundled-with-spyware-that-Stark-Enterprises-is-using-to-upload-all-the-users'-information-to-their-mainframe-and-she-was-trying-to-blackmail-him-about-it-so-he-had-her-brain-removed* thing, they would just be two more people I loved put in danger.

That was it. I was done.

By not letting them in on the truth, I wasn't lying to them exactly.

I just wasn't necessarily being as open with them as I could have been.

But had they been as fair with me as they could have been? Believing what gossip sites said about me? Getting all raggy with me about my grades, when they knew the kind of pressure I had been under? It wasn't as if I'd had a *brain transplant* or anything this semester. A C minus grade point average was pretty good, if you took that into consideration.

'I just remembered something,' I said, reaching around behind me for my jacket. 'I have to go.'

'Em,' Mom said, no longer sounding like a crazy Icelandic elf, but more like her normal self when she wasn't completely mad at me. She reached out and grabbed one of my hands again.

The thing is, it was too late. It wasn't her fault, necessarily.

But it was way, way too late.

'I'll see you guys later,' I said. And I got up and started to sail out of there, Cosabella skittering along beside me.

But as I walked along, weaving my way through all the tables, I heard people whispering, 'Omigod . . . it's Nikki Howard.'

And, 'Psst . . . that's *her*!'

And, 'No way! Nikki Howard!'

And I realized I was doing it again. Running away from a problem.

When, really, that wasn't going to solve anything.

So I turned around halfway through the cafe and walked back to my mom and dad's table and stood in front of it.

'I'm not saying I don't appreciate what you're trying to do for me,' I said. 'Because I *am* in a jam – just not the kind you think. It's not drugs. I know you aren't going to believe me, but I'm going to ask you to trust me and believe me when I say I haven't done anything wrong. Please don't do anything like go to Stark and try to pay off my contract . . . not yet. It would be – well, it would be a really, really big mistake.'

Looking up at me, Dad's expression was more concerned than ever.

'Emerson,' he said. He was the one who hardly ever used my full name. When he did, it was a big deal. A really big deal, 'what's going on?'

'I can't tell you,' I said. 'I'm just asking you to give me a few more days. And to trust me. Do you think you can do that?'

Mom opened her mouth – to argue, I'm pretty sure.

But before she could say anything, Dad reached out to take my gloved hand.

'Sure,' he said. He gave my fingers a squeeze and smiled up at me. 'We can do that.'

Mom gave him a bewildered look. But then she too glanced up at me and smiled. It was a tight, nervous smile.

But it was a smile just the same.

'Sure, Em,' she said.

I picked up the *Us Weekly* cover that had been lying on the table between us.

'Mom,' I said, holding it up, 'I know this is stupid, but . . . do you think I look pretty in this picture?'

She stared at it blankly. 'Pretty?'

'Yeah,' I said, 'pretty.'

'You . . .' She seemed flustered. 'You look like Nikki Howard,' she said.

'I know,' I said, gritting my teeth. 'But do you think I look *pretty*?'

'Pretty,' Mom said, looking confused, 'is a patriarchal construct designed to make women feel less worthy unless they live up to certain standards established by the male-dominated fashion and beauty industry. You know that, Em. I tell you and Frida that all the time.'

'Yeah,' I said, putting the picture down again. 'I know. That might be part of the problem.'

And I turned and walked out of the cafe.

Twelve

Seriously, could I be having a more messed-up day?

When I got on to the sidewalk outside the Starbucks, swallowing down big gulps of cold air, that was all I could think about. My sad, sorry, pathetic day. First I'd been dumped by my boyfriend (although technically that had happened in the middle of the night).

Then I'd kidnapped a billionaire's son.

Now my parents thought I was a drug addict or something.

Perfect. Great.

Had that been an intervention or something in there? In a *Starbucks*?

God, my parents were such dorks. They couldn't even do an intervention right. Where was Candy Finnigan?

And why couldn't my mom just say Frida and I were pretty? Was it so hard? What was all this patriarchal construct crap? She always said butterflies were pretty. She said the material she'd picked out to reupholster our living-room couch was pretty.

Why couldn't she say we were pretty too? Why couldn't we be strong, independent, and pretty too?

I was struggling to open my umbrella against the sleet – even my umbrella was broken. Fantastic – when

I saw him. A guy in a black trench, standing across the street from me.

He wasn't directly across the street from me. He was sort of off to one side and, unlike me, beneath an awning, out of the freezing rain.

But I noticed him right away. Because he wasn't moving.

Of course we were in the middle of New York City (or the middle of Greenwich Village, to be more exact). The streets were packed with people. That's what caught my attention about him. The fact that he, like me, was standing perfectly still while everyone else around us was moving in one direction or the other.

And he was staring at me, as if waiting for me to decide which way I was going to walk.

And when I looked his way, he quickly looked back down at the cellphone he'd been tapping into.

At first I didn't think anything of it. I kept on struggling with my umbrella, no big deal.

Then something made me look again.

At his trousers.

And I knew.

I just knew. He wasn't just some guy waiting for someone outside a store. He was waiting for me.

He was following *me*.

And he wasn't a stalker either. I had had those before (or rather, Nikki Howard had). I'd had to call Stark security to get them off my back.

But stalkers were different. They didn't dress as well,

for one thing. This guy's trench was impeccably pressed, as were his trousers. They were creased down the middle, the way only trousers that had been dry-cleaned were. They even had a break in them where they fell over his shoes.

Every stalker I'd ever had wore his trousers so short, the hem rose above his sneakers by at least an inch.

And none of them had bothered to get their trousers dry-cleaned.

The guy standing across the street from me looked way more like Stark security than he did a stalker.

Suddenly I went cold all over, and not because of the weather.

The trousers were what had given him away. They were black, and perfectly tailored. They were, in other words, fancy.

I had a tail. A real, official Stark Enterprises security tail.

And he didn't know I knew.

The two of us stood there on the crowded sidewalk across the street from each other, so no way was I going to be able to go over to Gabriel's to see Steven and his mother and sister now, which was what I'd been considering doing.

It was amazing, but my first impulse was to call Christopher. Christopher, of all people! Who wasn't even speaking to me! Why would I call *him*?

And what good would calling Christopher even do? I

mean, he'd probably only hang up on me. Just because he'd come to my rescue once didn't mean he was going to come flying to my rescue again.

Besides, I didn't even need rescuing. I was a strong, independent woman (according to my mother anyway. And not pretty. Got that? *Not pretty. Pretty is a patriarchal archetype*). I could handle this all on my own.

Except . . . how?

Lulu, I thought suddenly. I needed to call Lulu and tell her not to go over to Gabriel's. Just in case they were following her too.

I successfully finished putting up my umbrella, then centred it so Fancy Pants couldn't see me. Then I whipped out my non-Stark-brand cellphone and swiftly dialled Lulu's number.

She answered on the second ring.

'Hey,' she said. Her mouth was full. Of banana split, I didn't doubt.

'It's me,' I said through suddenly frozen lips. 'Don't go over there.'

'Go where?' she asked.

'To the place where you said you were going to go.'

I was speaking cryptically not because I thought if they were already following me, my phone might be tapped, but because I'd suddenly realized the loft might be. We'd been gone for nearly a week. Who knew who'd had access to it while we'd been away? I had never even thought of that. They might have dismantled the acoustic noise generator Steven had installed. I'd never even checked. Had Lulu or I said anything about where Nikki and her family were hiding? I tried to think.

I was pretty sure we had.

'I'm being followed,' I said.

Even the words sounded frightening. I clutched convulsively at Cosabella's leash. She, oblivious, was prancing along beside me, sniffing the wet ground for abandoned bits of street food, pretzels or hot dogs people might have dropped.

'You are?' Lulu sounded delighted. 'Oh my God! It's like something out of a Bourne movie! And you're like Julia Stiles! She's so pretty. Where are you?'

'Astor Place,' I said. I was moving as rapidly as I could in the opposite direction to the loft and the Starbucks, trying to lead Fancy Pants away from the people I loved. Which was ridiculous, since of course Stark knew where my parents and I lived. 'We need to make sure our friends are safe where we left them.'

'Sure,' Lulu said. 'I can do that.'

'*Subtly*,' I said.

'I can be subtle,' Lulu said, sounding hurt.

'I . . .' I didn't dare look back over my shoulder to see if Fancy Pants was behind me. But I was pretty sure he was. I didn't see him across the street any more. 'I don't know what to do. About the guy, I mean.'

'Ooooh, I do,' Lulu said, sounding even more delighted. This whole thing was a game to her, I swear. 'Call Christopher.'

'*What?*' I said. 'Are you crazy?' I had no idea why I was

142

asking Lulu this, since of course calling Christopher had been my first inclination. 'Why would I do that?'

Lulu sighed deeply into the phone.

'We just talked about this,' she said. 'Remember? You have to give him an opportunity to feel needed, and to help you.'

'I can't do that,' I said. I was walking along so quickly, Cosabella was having trouble keeping up. 'What . . . what if he gets hurt? Then it'll be my fault and I'll blame myself forever and *I*'ll be the one who turns into an evil supervillain.'

I didn't want to tell her the real reason I didn't want to call Christopher was that I was afraid he'd hang up on me and I couldn't face another rejection from him.

'But what if *you* get hurt again?' Lulu wanted to know. Uh, that was exactly what I was worried about . . . only not by the people Lulu meant. 'And he blames himself even more, only this time for your ultimate demise? And then he invents a reverse supernova death ray that sucks up all the sun's energy, and we all slowly freeze to death, and then the earth turns into a hollow husk and humanity ceases to exist and it's all your fault because you didn't call him?'

'Oh my God,' I said, 'you've had way too much whipped cream.'

'It could happen,' Lulu said defensively. 'I saw it on TV once. *Call him.*'

'Fine,' I said. There was no way I was calling him. 'And, Lulu. Be careful what you say in the apartment. I think it might be bugged again.'

'I'm always careful,' Lulu said, sounding both hurt and annoyed now. 'I'm totally good at this spy stuff. I rented a whole plane and came and helped Christopher rescue you without anybody finding out, didn't I?'

Uh, I wasn't so sure about that. But I just told her thanks and hung up.

I walked blindly, not even looking to see where I was going, trying to figure out how this could possibly be happening to me. Keeping my phone out, I did call someone . . . but not Christopher.

'So do you not hate me any more?' Brandon asked when he picked up.

'What?' I was confused.

'You're calling me,' Brandon said. 'So I figure you must not hate me any more. Does this mean you wanna go out? I'm free tonight. I mean, I have plans, but I can break them. For you.'

Oh my God. Brandon was the biggest horn dog in the world. It was totally disgusting.

'Brandon,' I said, 'you kidnapped me. And then you made the only person I'll ever love in my life hate me. I completely despise you.'

'So . . .' Brandon said. 'I take that as a no, you do not want to go out with me tonight.'

I held the phone away from my face to make sure it was working properly and I hadn't heard him wrong.

'No,' I said, bringing it back to my face when I was sure cellular service to my area was fully functional, 'I do not want to go out with you tonight. I called to ask why someone from Stark security is tailing me.'

'How should I know?' Brandon asked. 'Maybe because you're worth a lot to the company, and they want to make sure you don't get harassed by fans or hurt by the paps. Because everyone thinks you're dating me now. Even though you're not. You might want to reconsider. Private security's just one of the many perks of being Brandon Stark's woman. Hey, ow, not there.'

I held the phone away from my face again. 'What are you *doing* right now?' I asked.

'Getting a massage,' Brandon said. 'It kinda hurts to be knocked unconscious and then tied up half the day, you know. You and your friends play rough. Since you don't want to be with me, is there anything else? I really am kinda busy.'

'If his assignment was to keep me from being harassed by paps or fans,' I said, 'he wouldn't be trying to keep me from noticing him, which is what he's doing.'

'Oh,' Brandon said in a different tone. 'That's different. Hey, you don't think my dad—'

'I don't know what to think,' I said.

'But do I think your dad is on to us? You tell me.'

'Don't panic,' he said. 'My dad hasn't said anything to me about any of this. I'm sure he has no idea what's going on. What *is* going on, anyway? I mean, have you and your friends figured out what—'

I just laughed bitterly as I dragged my dog down the street. 'Right,' I said. 'Like I'm going to tell you. When

I'm ready to let you in on what's going on, Brandon, you'll know. That's a lot more courtesy than you ever offered me.'

I hung up on him.

My fingers were trembling inside the gloves I had on as I dialled Christopher's cell. What other choice did I have? I didn't know where to go, and frankly I was scared. Christopher, I told myself, would know what to do.

I had no idea at all whether he'd pick up. After the way we'd left things – he'd barely glanced at me as we'd gone our separate ways from Teterboro, where the plane had dropped us off – I half expected he'd let my call go to voice-mail.

But miraculously I heard him saying, 'Hello?' in my ear.

'Christopher?' I said. I hoped I didn't sound as scared and shaky to him as I did to myself.

'What is it, Em?' he asked. He didn't seem to be surprised to be hearing from me. More like . . . resigned.

Great. My boyfriend – ex-boyfriend – was *resigned* to be hearing from me. Because I was such a drama queen? Like those girls I always overheard in the hallways at school blowing stuff out of proportion so they could get their boyfriends to pay more attention to them? *Oh, Jason, I couldn't get my locker open . . . I know, I tried twisting it right then left, but it wouldn't budge. I guess I'm just not* strong *enough. Could you help me? Please? Oh, great. Oh, Jason, you're so strong . . .*

Seriously? That was me now?

On the other hand, a guy *was* following me. I'd

stooped down to scoop up some of Cosabella's poo with a plastic bag from my pocket and kind of looked over my shoulder in a surreptitious way while I was obeying New York City littering ordinances by tossing it into a nearby rubbish bin, and there he was again, standing by the fence to the churchyard, totally pretending to be texting.

'I'm being followed,' I whispered to Christopher.

'I can't hear you,' he said.

'I'm being followed,' I repeated, more loudly this time.

'Where are you?' he asked right away.

Not, *So what do you expect me to do about it?* Or *I told you I don't want to be involved in this any more.*

Surprised – and more relieved than I wanted to admit – I replied, 'I'm on Broadway and Ninth.'

'I'm not far from there,' Christopher said. 'Walk north on Broadway towards Union Square. I'll meet you.' His voice sounded very soothing on the phone, even though I could tell he, like me, was on the street somewhere. I could hear traffic noises in the background. 'How long's he been tailing you?'

'I don't know,' I said. 'About four blocks? I met my parents for coffee, and I noticed him as soon as I got out. He could have followed me there for all I know.'

'What does the guy look like?'

'Tall,' I said, doing what he'd said and walking swiftly north. 'He stops every time I stop and pretends to be texting someone.'

'What's he got on?'

'A trench coat and black pressed trousers. That's what gave him away actually. That he's someone from Stark.'

'How's that?'

'Because of his trousers. They're very fancy.'

'His trousers are fancy,' Christopher repeated, and I realized I must sound like a mental patient. This was my day, apparently, for people thinking I was nuts.

'Seriously, Christopher,' I said. 'This guy is Stark security, not some Nikki Howard fan. Why would Stark security be following me?'

'That's something you might want to ask your boyfriend, Brandon,' Christopher said.

'Oh, ha ha,' I said, trying to sound like I hadn't just done exactly that . . . and like what he'd said hadn't felt like a knife through my heart. 'I told you, Brandon forced me to—'

'Save it, Watts, I heard it all the first time. OK, I see you,' Christopher said.

'What?' This startled me so much, I nearly dropped my umbrella. 'You see me? How can you—'

But then Christopher turned the corner right in front of me and put an arm around me.

'Hi, honey,' he said, and kissed my cheek. 'Right on time.'

I was completely shocked. His lips were warm against my icy skin. And the arm he'd slipped around me?

It felt like heaven.

Especially since I'd been certain I'd never feel his arm around me again.

148

'I already got the tickets,' he said. He was talking in an inappropriately loud voice.

That's when I realized it was for the benefit of Fancy Pants, not me. Because tickets? What tickets?

'Great,' I said, going along with him. I noticed he was carrying a plastic bag from Forbidden Planet, the comic-book store, which was nearby. I remembered, belatedly, that Christopher had a mailbox there, where they held all the comic books he ordered every month. He must have just been making his weekly pickup when I called.

'So, are you ready?' he wanted to know.

He still had his arm around me. It felt so wonderful, I hoped he'd never let go.

But none of this, I knew, was because Christopher actually cared about me any more.

Lulu had been wrong: making a boy think you needed him didn't do anything.

Except make you want him more.

'Sure,' I said. I didn't see how any of this was going to work. Now Fancy Pants, who was standing over to one side of the sidewalk a few yards away, texting, was just going to follow us both.

Or so I thought.

Because a second later, Christopher dropped his arm from around me and, staring at the guy, shouted, 'You. Hey, *you*!'

Thirteen

The guy who'd been following me looked up from his cellphone, startled. Then he looked behind him to see if Christopher was talking to someone else.

'I'm talking to you,' Christopher cried, going right up to Fancy Pants and shoving him on the shoulder. 'Were you just following my girlfriend?'

That's right. Christopher shoved the Stark security guy on the shoulder.

He also called me his girlfriend.

My heart began slamming behind my ribs, and not from the possible confrontation I knew was about to ensue.

Fancy Pants did *not* like Christopher drawing so much attention to him. Either that or he didn't like being shoved, even though, to be truthful, it was only a little shove. He put his cellphone away and said in a controlled voice, 'I don't know you, son. Please take your hand off me.'

'What do you mean, you don't know me?' Christopher asked, still using a voice loud enough to make everyone on the sidewalk look round at us. 'You're sure acting like you know me. Or at least like you know my girlfriend, Nikki Howard. Because you've been following her for the past four blocks.'

There! He'd said it again! *Girlfriend!* I definitely hadn't mistaken it.

When Christopher said the words *Nikki Howard*, a lot more people started paying attention. They actually slowed down on the sidewalk, or stopped walking altogether and stood there and started to stare. One big burly guy who'd been unloading cans of soda from a truck on the corner actually came over and got in Fancy Pants's face.

'Hey!' Burly Guy said. 'That true? You following Nikki Howard?'

Fancy Pants looked quickly around, as if for an escape route. He actually began reaching inside his coat – and not for a cellphone, which I'd already seen him drop into the trench's wide side pocket.

I was standing at just the right angle to catch a glimpse of exactly what it was inside his coat he was reaching for . . .

. . . a gun. In a shoulder holster, the handle nestled underneath his arm.

I gasped and reached out to grab Christopher's arm, my fingers sinking into the leather of his jacket. I think I stopped breathing for a minute. I couldn't believe it.

A gun! He actually had a gun! He was going to try to shoot us!

But between Christopher, Burly Guy, the gathering crowd and me, there were apparently too many witnesses. Because a second later, Fancy Pants's hand dropped away from the gun, and instead he seemed to be looking for a different way out of his tight situation.

151

I continued to hold on to Christopher's arm, so freaked out I wasn't sure I could have remained upright if I didn't cling to him. A gun! He had a gun! And he'd been going to use it!

'That's not nice!' Burly Guy said, poking Fancy Pants in the chest – quite sharply, I thought. Especially considering the fact that he had a gun. 'We leave celebrities alone round here!'

'True,' Christopher said, shaking his head sadly at Fancy Pants. 'We really do.'

Fancy Pants looked perturbed.

But there was no way he could shoot his way out of this situation. Not unless he was some kind of psychopath. There were way too many people gathered round now, watching.

And I highly doubted Robert Stark would hire any psychopaths as part of his security team.

'I wasn't following her,' he said both to the burly guy and to Christopher. 'We just happened to be walking in the same direction, is all.'

'So keep walking, why don'tcha?' Burly Guy asked him.

'Maybe I will then,' Fancy Pants said, looking injured. 'Maybe I will.'

But of course, he kept standing there.

'So go,' Christopher said. 'If you're in such a hurry.'

'Yeah,' Burly Guy said. 'Go, why don'tcha?'

Fancy Pants, throwing us all a very dirty look, began walking slowly away. My heart continued to pound inside my chest as I watched him go, hoping he wouldn't turn back and start shooting.

'Faster,' Burly Guy commanded.

Fancy Pants picked up the pace, walking off towards Union Square. He didn't look back.

'Thank you so much.' I breathed, my grip loosening a little on Christopher's arm. My fingers felt sore from how tightly I'd been clenching him. I couldn't imagine how his arm must have felt.

But he wasn't complaining, I noticed.

'No problem,' Burly Guy said. 'We can't have people harassing our local celebrities. That's what makes New York different from LA, you know? Here, people can walk down the streets and no one bothers them, ya know? Hey, I gotta say, my niece is about as pretty and as talented as you are, and is going to be a superstar herself some day. Can I bug you for an autograph? You know, to inspire her.'

'Of course,' I said. 'I'd be happy to. What's her name?' And when he told me Helen Thomaides, I scrawled, *For Helen, Reach for the stars. Love, Nikki Howard* on a page of his order form.

This, of course, opened the floodgates, and then everyone who'd been standing on the sidewalk watching our little confrontation with Fancy Pants wanted an autograph. Pens appeared from nowhere, and soon I was signing everything from people's drugstore receipts to the backs of their wrists.

As I signed, I tried to keep track of what was happening

beyond the circle of autograph seekers around me. Where was the guy who'd been following me? Had he really just given up? Where was Christopher? Had he too given up on me? Or was he still there?

Finally I felt a hand wrap around my arm. I looked up, startled. Fortunately, it was Christopher, not Fancy Pants. He'd scooped up Cosabella – thank goodness. Otherwise, she'd have been trampled in the rush towards me for my signature – and now he was saying, in a serious voice, 'Nikki? I think it's time to go.'

I looked over at the street and saw that he'd hailed a cab and that it sat with one of the rear doors open.

Christopher was helping me to escape? After telling me he wanted nothing to do with any of this?

I felt a rush of warmth towards him that was even greater than when he'd put his arm round me.

'Oh,' I said to all the autograph seekers, 'I'm sorry, I have to go.'

'To a fitting?' one of the girls who'd asked me to sign her wrist wanted to know.

'To a photo shoot?' another one asked.

'Yes,' I called to them all. What was the point in telling the truth? It would only disappoint them. 'Sorry! Thanks so much! I love you all!' I blew them kisses just like I'd seen movie stars do on TV and ran to the taxi, ducking inside it, then scooting all the way across the seat to make room for Christopher, who was leaning inside to hand Cosabella to me.

'Come with me,' I all but begged him. I could tell he was

getting ready to bail, even though he'd done all those nice things for me already.

'Em,' he said. His face had closed down, his blue eyes shuttered as if no one was home.

'Christopher,' I said, 'he had a gun . . .'

'I know,' Christopher insisted, glancing over his shoulder. 'That's why you've got to get out of here *now*.'

He knew? All that time, he'd acted so calm! He'd shoved the guy, knowing he had a gun? I couldn't believe it. He'd done it for me. Even though he claimed not to feel anything for me any more. Anything but contempt. Maybe what he claimed and what he actually felt were two different things. I hardly dared to let myself hope . . .

'I'm worried about *you*,' I said. People who hadn't gotten my autograph, but had seen the crowd, were starting to drift over to the taxi, curious about who was inside it.

'Would you just go?' Christopher said. 'He's probably found a cab and is on his way back—'

'Please get in.' Now I was begging. 'I *need* you.'

I don't care, Christopher could have said. *You're the one with a problem. Not me.*

But he didn't.

Lulu was right: maybe guys just do want to feel needed sometimes. Not all the time. Because then you come off as a Whitney Robertson, all whiny and completely helpless.

But every once in a while, maybe you needed to stop running and tell other people you needed them, and let them help you.

Including the guy you like.

155

Christopher got into the taxi beside me and shut the door.

He didn't act like he was too unhappy about it either.

'Where are we going?' he asked.

'I *was* going to Gabriel's,' I said. 'I think . . . well, I don't know. But I'm worried Nikki might have said something to someone.'

Just saying it out loud caused my mouth go dry and my pulse to speed up. I couldn't look Christopher in the eye. Not so much because I was genuinely worried about Nikki and her family, which I was.

But because I was aware that we were alone in a nice, cosy cab together.

It was the first time we'd been alone together since he'd woken me up in my bed . . .

. . . and dumped me. Basically.

But now he'd just saved my life.

'You could be right about that,' was all he said though. 'Considering the new friend you picked up back there. But I don't know how good an idea it is to head over there with Stark security on your tail.'

'Where we headed?' the cab-driver wanted to know. He had to yell to be heard through the bulletproof glass between the front seat and the back seat. He'd released the brake and we were cruising down Broadway, going the opposite direction to the way Fancy Pants had walked off.

If he hadn't jumped into a taxi of his own, and was following us that way.

'Just keep driving,' Christopher yelled up to the driver.

He was evidently thinking the same thing I was. 'We'll tell you when to turn.'

'Do you think he's following us?' I asked Christopher, turning around in the seat to look.

All I could see, however, was the usual vast ocean of taxis behind us. There was no way to tell which if any of them held Fancy Pants.

'Absolutely,' Christopher said. 'He's in that third cab to the left, next to the bus.'

I gasped, turning quickly back around in my seat. 'How do you know?'

'I saw him ditch the trench in a trash can up the street,' Christopher said. 'It's an old trick. He thought we wouldn't recognize him without it. I saw him while you were doing the autograph thing.'

'What do we do?' I asked anxiously.

'I say we go for a nice drive downtown,' Christopher said, 'and try to lose him, then get out and jump on to the subway back uptown when it seems safe.'

I couldn't believe Christopher was being so calm. This was obviously the new, supervillain Christopher, who was used to being in high-speed car chases.

Although we weren't really going high speed, considering we were stuck at a red light.

I looked down at Cosabella, who'd jumped on to my lap to peer out of the window. Cosy loved being in any moving vehicle. Looking down at her was easier than looking into Christopher's face, which always just reminded me of how much I wanted him.

And how much he, in return, did not want me.

At least, up until a few minutes ago. I still wasn't sure if I should allow recent developments to give me hope that things were changing.

'What makes you think Nikki would rat us out?' Christopher wanted to know.

'She's mad,' I said. 'About this whole thing. The fact that she can't have her old body back. It's what she asked Brandon for, you know.' I turned my head to look at him, feeling suddenly shy. 'In exchange for telling him why his dad tried to have her killed.'

Christopher stared back at me blankly. 'She asked him for what?'

'Her old body back,' I said.

His eyes widened. 'Wait . . . she wanted you to—'

'Yeah,' I said glumly. 'She really hates the body she ended up with.'

Christopher bristled.

'Did it ever occur to her that that's what happens,' he said, 'when you try to blackmail your boss? What did she expect?'

I goggled at him. 'Well, not to have him try to murder her.'

'Blackmail's against the law, you know,' Christopher said. 'It tends to make people angry.'

'Well, whatever Robert Stark is doing is against the law too,' I pointed out. 'I know two wrongs don't make a right, but it's not like Nikki knew any better.'

'Uh, she's a member of the human race, isn't she?' he

asked. 'Plus, I thought she was an emancipated minor. So you can't say she didn't know better. She claims to be an adult.'

'I'm just saying,' I said, starting to feel a little less warmly towards him than I had when he had just saved me from Fancy Pants, because I was having such a hard time making him see how important losing her looks would be to a girl like Nikki. 'I know how she feels. It's horrible to have to give up your whole life because you made one stupid mistake.'

'What was your mistake?' Christopher asked. 'Pushing your little sister out of the way when that TV came loose so it fell on you and not her? Being in the wrong place at the wrong time? You didn't make any mistakes. And neither did Nikki.'

The vehemence with which Christopher spoke surprised me. I hadn't known he felt that strongly . . . about anything other than avenging my death, which now was a moot point, since he knew I wasn't dead.

'I – I guess I never thought of it that way,' I said, absently stroking Cosabella's woolly little head.

'So she lost her body,' Christopher said. 'She's still got her mind. Just because her former career was entirely based on her looks, that doesn't mean she can't have a new career, this time using her brains instead. Has she even considered that? It's not like she doesn't have good business sense. As you might have noticed, considering the fact that she scared the owner of a multinational corporation into trying to have her murdered.'

I blinked at him. It was true. Nikki had a lot more going for her than just her face.

But how was anyone going to convince her of that?

'If we could only figure out what Robert Stark was so scared of her revealing to everyone,' I said slowly. The embryo of an idea was forming in my mind. 'The thing with the Quarks, I mean. The fact that she was instrumental in discovering it . . . if we could uncover it and make it public, that might be enough to boost her self-esteem into not wanting someone to hack into my head and scoop my brain out of it again.'

Christopher yelled at the cab-driver, 'Turn right here!'

The cab-driver yelled back, 'You are crazy! I'm in the wrong lane!'

'Just do it,' Christopher yelled back. 'There's an extra twenty in it for you.'

Cursing, the cab-driver made a right turn so suddenly, Cosabella and I lurched over into Christopher. He threw an arm across my shoulders as, all around us, cars and trucks honked. Cosabella scrambled to find footing on the seat, which mainly involved stabbing her paws into my thighs.

'Sorry,' I said, mortified that parts of my own body had gone flying into Christopher's. 'I'm sorry.'

'It's OK,' he said. He was craning his neck to look behind us. 'We lost him.'

'We did?' I tried to straighten up, conscious that Christopher hadn't moved his arm. It was horrible to be so hyper-aware of these things, when I was sure he didn't care at all. 'Well, that's good.'

160

'And I get what you're saying,' he said. 'About Nikki. She has good instincts. They just need to be guided in the proper direction. She was right to do something about what she overheard regarding the Quarks. She just didn't do the right thing. Blackmailing her boss instead of trying to stop him does nothing for the greater good . . . which is what you want to do.'

'Robert Stark isn't collecting all that data for no reason, Christopher,' I said, looking into his eyes. He still had his arm around me, so it was kind of hard not to. Also not to notice his lips, which were looking highly kissable. But I tried to turn my mind to higher things, such as saving Nikki and her family. 'I was paying attention to your speech about him in Public Speaking. You don't get to be the fourth-richest man in the world by doing things for no reason. Tomorrow night I have to go to a party at his house. If there's going to be any chance of my finding out what it is he's doing, it's going to be then—'

'Whoa,' Christopher said, his arm tightening. 'You're going to confront him yourself?'

'Well,' I said, 'I think it's going to be our only chance of ending this. Otherwise . . . well, my parents are threatening to bankrupt themselves because they think they can just waltz into Stark Corporate, pay off my contract and be done with this. Which is so never going to happen. Steven and his mom are going to have to live in hiding forever, for fear of what Robert Stark and his cronies are going to do to them. And Nikki's going to get herself killed – or kill herself – trying to be who she used to be. So . . . yeah. I'm going to confront him myself. With your help, if you're willing. What do you think? Are you willing?'

Christopher didn't say anything right away. The cab rumbled along Houston Street, taking us God only knew where. I held my breath, waiting for his answer. I knew I couldn't do any of this without his help. I needed him – and his cousin Felix – to break back into Stark's mainframe and see what they could find out. I didn't think I'd be able to just walk up to Robert Stark and go, 'Tell me everything.' I needed to arm myself with some information first.

Information only they could get. If they looked in the right place. And it wasn't encrypted. Which it probably would be.

Still. The least they could do was try . . .

'You're crazy,' Christopher said. He seemed angry. At me. At himself. At the whole situation. For which I couldn't exactly blame him. 'This whole thing has been completely crazy.'

'I know,' I said with a shrug. Secretly, though, I was encouraged. A *You're crazy* wasn't a *No*.

'That guy back there had a *gun*,' Christopher went on. 'Brandon Stark didn't even have a gun, and he managed to kidnap you just by threatening to do mean things to your friends. How do you think you're going to cope with his dad, who's a *real* gangster?'

'Well,' I said. Suddenly I didn't feel quite so encouraged. There were actual tears in my eyes, 'that's why this time

I'm asking you for help. I know I can't do it alone any more. I need you, Christopher.'

'You're damn right you do,' he said. 'It's about time you realized it.'

Then he pulled me roughly towards him and kissed me on the mouth.

Fourteen

'Where have *you* been?'

That's what Felix wanted to know when we showed up in his basement an hour later.

It was obvious from his tone that he didn't mean where had we *just* been – escaping from Stark security goons and making out (well, a little) in the back of a cab.

He meant where had we been since he'd last seen us.

In fact, I wasn't sure he'd moved from in front of his multiscreened computer command centre since the first time I'd met him. He still seemed to have on the same clothes – baggy jeans, green velour shirt and a lot of gold chains.

The only difference really was that there were a lot more empty plates piled up around him. His mom had evidently been bringing his meals down to him.

Well, it was hard being a computer hacker under house arrest . . . though I guess there were some perks. Like sandwiches and brownies from Mom upstairs.

'We just outran a guy from Stark security,' Christopher informed him. 'He was following Em. He had a gun.'

'Em?' Felix spun round in his overpadded computer chair to look at me with narrowed eyes. Then he nodded. 'Oh, that's right. I read the medical file. You're just borrowing Nikki Howard's body. Your real name's Emerson . . . Watts, right?'

'Uh, I get to have the body for keeps, I'm hoping,' I said. 'Getting your brain swapped into someone else's body is no picnic, you know.'

'Especially if it's Nikki Howard's body,' Felix said, and he made a growling noise. 'Mamacita, I'd like to get me some of that!'

Christopher walked over to his cousin and slapped him on the back of the head.

'Hey,' he said severely, 'show some manners. Just because you live in a basement doesn't mean you don't have to act like a gentleman around ladies.'

'Ow,' Felix said, reaching up to clutch his head. 'Stop. I was only playing.'

'It's OK,' I said to Christopher. I actually felt a little sorry for his cousin. It had to be hard to be so smart and yet not to have any outlets – positive ones, anyway – for all that intelligence.

'No,' Christopher said, shaking his head at me. Felix might have been playing, but Christopher definitely wasn't. 'It's not.'

I blushed. Christopher was being chivalrous towards me now . . .

. . . but back in the cab, after he'd pulled me so roughly towards him and kissed me, he'd pushed me away just as roughly and muttered, 'Sorry. I didn't mean to do that.'

I'd stared at him in astonishment, my lips still tingling from where his mouth had bruised mine, and said, 'Christopher. It's all right.' Believe me. It was *more* than all right.

'No,' he'd said. 'It's not.'

So. I still wasn't forgiven. Not yet. It was just that he couldn't help kissing me from time to time.

Boys are so weird.

Now he pointed at one of the computer monitors in front of Felix, which was streaming information.

'We're still on Stark's mainframe?' he asked.

'Yeah,' Felix said. He sounded sulky. He leaned back in his computer chair so that he could rest his gigantic feet on one of the milk crates that made up his jerry-rigged command centre, near some of the empty plates. 'Not that they're doing anything interesting. I'm more bored with this hack than with all the Stargates combined.'

'They're actually doing a lot interesting,' Christopher said. 'They're storing all the data people who bought the new Quarks are uploading.'

This information startled Felix so much that he jumped, bringing his feet down from the milk crate and accidentally taking all the plates down too, causing them to fall to the floor with a crash.

He didn't seem to care or even notice, however. His fingers began flying over the keyboard in front of the Stark monitor.

'Holy crap,' he said, looking – for the first time – actually wide awake and excited. 'Why didn't you say so in the

166

first place? What would they care about a bunch of data from some pissant plastic student laptops? It doesn't make any sense. Where are they storing it? I'm not seeing it.' He took a slurp from one of the Cokes his mom had brought down to us (Aunt Jackie was super happy to see me. She'd gotten the complete Nikki Howard fragrance collection for Christmas from her husband, and wanted me to sign the box, with Nikki's face smiling alluringly up from it). 'Where are they putting it?'

'What do you mean, you're not seeing it?' Christopher demanded. 'Can you find the data or not?'

'Oh, it's on here,' Felix said, slurping a Coke. 'Their encryption is a joke. I've never seen a corporation so full of itself. It's like they think no one can touch them. And maybe that's because no one's ever cared enough before to try. But, I mean, I can't tell what they want all this crap for. They've got kids' Facebook and Flickr pages, even their damned *dental* records. What would they want *that* for? And here's a bunch of online budget travel reservations. Priceline and cruise ships and spring-break school trips . . .'

'Maybe they want to get into the travel business?' I ventured with a shrug. 'Stark doesn't have a commercial airline.'

'Phoenix,' Felix said.

'They want to base their travel hub out of Phoenix?' Christopher asked, confused.

'No,' Felix said. His straw hit the bottom of his Coke can. 'That's what they're calling the database where they're keeping all these files. Project Phoenix.'

Christopher looked at me blankly. 'What's in Phoenix?

I shrugged again. 'Desert?'

'Senior citizens,' Felix said, when Christopher looked at him. 'Old people who drive golf carts. In pastels.'

'Look it up,' Christopher said to Felix.

Felix sighed, and typed the word *phoenix* into a search engine.

'*Phoenix*,' he read, when the definition came up. 'A mythical sacred fire bird with a thousand-year life cycle, near the end of which it builds a nest of myrrh twigs, then self-ignites, then is born anew from the ashes.'

We all looked at one another blankly.

'Maybe it's a new video game,' I suggested. 'And the people whose data they've collected all have high scores on *Journeyquest* or something. And they want to send the game to them as testers.'

'Then they should have sent it to me,' Christopher said, looking (justifiably) offended.

'Yeah,' Felix said, clicking on the Facebook page of one of the new Quark owners. 'And no way does this loser play *Journeyquest*. Look at him. *Hi, I'm Curt. I like the Dave Matthews Band. I only drink organically grown coffee. I'm going hiking with my dog in Seattle at the end of the month. I suck.*'

I looked at Curt's profile. He definitely wasn't a gamer. He listed running and biking as his hobbies. He was attractive, without an ounce of body fat on him. He liked dogs and his nephews and wanted to save the whales.

All of which were admirable qualities and it was mean of Felix to be making fun of him.

'Show me another one,' I said.

'*Hi*,' Felix said, clicking on another profile. '*I'm Kerry*. Ooooh, Kerry's hot. She likes writing and sunsets. I like writing and sunsets too, Kerry. Look at that, Kerry's going to Guatemala to help teach children to read next month. That's nice of her. What else does Stark know about Kerry? Let's check her medical records. She had to email them to the programme she's going to Guatemala with. Oh, look at that. Perfect health. Not even a cavity. Surprise. Those Quark buyers are way too healthy. Eat a cheeseburger, Kerry, swimming in grease!' Felix was yelling at his monitors.

Felix got excited way too easily. Maybe it was all the caffeine and sugar in the Cokes he drank.

'It's weird,' I said, 'that they're all so crunchy granola.'

'Or,' Christopher said, looking at me, 'someone at Stark is purposefully weeding through this data.'

'And only saving the files on the healthy, attractive ones?' I squinted at Kerry's Facebook picture. She was standing in the sun on a hiking trail, wearing a T-shirt and shorts. She looked slim, fresh-faced and happy.

'But why?' Felix asked, reaching for the Coke I hadn't touched (Nikki's body couldn't handle caffeine or high-fructose corn syrup). 'I hate healthy people.'

'I don't know,' Christopher said. 'But what else do they all have in common?'

'They take good care of their bodies,' I ventured.

'They're all hot,' Felix said.

'And they're all going places,' Christopher said, 'with their lives.'

'Robert Stark is forming an army,' I said with wonder.

'Yeah,' Felix said sarcastically. 'Of really boring people.'

Fifteen

'Oh, thank God you're here,' Gabriel said, opening the door to his apartment.

I couldn't figure out why he was so happy to see us. Not at first.

I'd offered to come over to his apartment with a take-away, having realized I was going to be no help whatsoever in solving the mystery of Project Phoenix . . .

. . . at least, not by sitting round reading over file after file of incredibly attractive Stark Quark owners. That was something Christopher and Felix could do on their own.

So you could imagine my surprise when Christopher said he would come with me to Gabriel's. Don't ask me why. He hadn't grabbed and kissed me again, or supplied an explanation for why he'd done so in the cab that afternoon. As far as I could tell, he still hated my guts and planned on continuing to do so indefinitely.

I couldn't help wishing I could be more like Nikki. I'm sure she'd had plenty of guys play weird mind games with her. She wouldn't put up with Christopher's guff for more than five minutes. I'd love to have asked her how she dealt with guys like him. I would have done so, in fact . . .

. . . if I thought I could get away with it without her

punching me in the mouth and demanding again that I give her back her body.

Inside the Thai restaurant where we'd gone to pick up the takeaway, it had been warm and dry and had smelt insanely good. I'd ordered one of almost everything to go, then sat waiting for the food on a red vinyl padded chair with Cosy on my lap while Christopher sat beside us, texting Felix on his cell.

After a little while of trying to ignore Christopher's presence – his highly kissable lips and big, raw-looking hands – it occurred to me: wait a minute. I didn't have to ask Nikki for her advice. I could just come right out and demand an explanation from Christopher himself about where we stood as a couple. I deserved that, at the very least. I mean, we'd been friends for years before we'd ever been boyfriend-girlfriend (if we were even that).

What was I so scared of anyway? He was just a high-school boy. I was freaking *Nikki Howard*, supermodel.

Even if I wasn't really.

Why was I so scared of what he was going to say anyway? We'd already hurt each other as much as we possibly could. What more could we possibly do?

And Lulu had said we needed to communicate more. Right?

'Christopher,' I'd begun, after taking a deep breath and telling myself to be brave. After all, *he'd* kissed *me*? That had to mean he still liked me, at least a little. 'What exactly—'

'Don't,' he said. He didn't even look up from his cellphone.

'Don't what?' I asked, offended. I mean, really! The least he could have done was look at me!

'Don't start talking about our relationship,' he said.

How had he known? How do they always know? What do they have, some kind of radar?

'Uh,' I said.

Now I wasn't just offended. I was mad. I wasn't one of those whiny *I want to know where our relationship is going* kind of girls. I'd never brought it up once, not in the whole time we were going out.

Which, OK, had only been for, like, two weeks. And for a large part of that time I'd been shacked up with Brandon Stark . . . against my will.

But still.

'I think I have a right to know where our relationship currently stands,' I said indignantly. 'Because I'll be honest: if you're going to keep playing these head games, I'm just going to start seeing other people.'

Yeah! That sounded good. Like something Lauren Conrad or someone would say. Not that Lauren Conrad is this huge role model or anything.

But who else do we single girls have to guide us during these complex modern times? Seriously, everyone else is divorced.

Christopher lowered his cellphone and stared at me with an expression of utter disbelief.

'*What?*' he said. His voice cracked.

'I mean it,' I said.

I didn't want to get into a huge fight in a Thai takeaway place in Queens.

But come on. A girl has to have standards.

'You can't just come rescue me – twice – kiss me a bunch of times, and then act like you don't even care about me.' I tossed some of my hair. 'I don't have time for this kind of game playing. I need to know. Either you're into me or you're not. If you are, great. If you're not, quit kissing me. It's only fair.'

This was good. I had no idea where this stuff was coming from or anything. But I liked it.

'Well,' Christopher said, 'to tell you the truth, right now, I'm really not that into you. Because you're acting like someone I don't even know. And it's not that cute.'

Stung, I tried to pass off the tears in my eyes as a reaction to all the hot grease in the air from the frying. Maybe Lauren Conrad wasn't that great a role model after all.

'I'm not acting like anyone,' I said, 'except myself. You said I needed to grow up, and that's exactly what I'm doing. I'm just requsting some honesty from you. I really love you, and I want to know if you—'

'Jesus,' Christopher said. He lifted his cellphone into the air again. I couldn't help noticing he was blushing. 'Would you stop saying that?'

'Stop saying what? That I love you?'

I had to admit, torturing him was kind of fun.

'Yes,' he said, looking extremely uncomfortable. 'You keep saying it, but then you don't act like it.'

'How do I not act like it?' I demanded. Now *I* was blushing. I really hoped the cashier seated a few feet away who was staring into space didn't speak good enough English to tell what we were saying.

'By flying off to Brandon Stark's beach house, for one thing,' he pointed out. 'And letting the whole world think you're in love with him and not me, for another. Then, when I came to rescue you, you wouldn't even come with me—'

'Oh, would you let that go?' I demanded. 'I already explained that!'

'You can't just say you're sorry for something and have it all be better,' Christopher said. 'You may love me, but you don't act like it. You don't trust me.'

'I called you today when I was being followed!' I reminded him.

'Was I the *first* person you called?' he asked.

I felt myself blushing harder. How had he known I'd called Lulu first?

'You were the first person I *thought* of calling,' I said. 'But you were so mean to me on the plane. You have this whole evil supervillain thing going. It's not very attractive, you know.'

Actually it *was* quite attractive, but I didn't want him to know that. It would only encourage his bad behaviour.

Like now. He rolled his eyes and turned back to his cellphone.

It was at that point that *my* cellphone rang. It was

Gabriel, calling to ask how soon I thought we'd get there.

'Uh,' I said. 'Pretty soon.'

'It's just,' he said, 'the sooner you get here the better, actually.'

'Oh, why?' I asked.

'You'll see when you arrive,' was all Gabriel would say in a slightly agitated voice.

This had seemed very mysterious, but he wouldn't say anything more. We were going to take the subway to Gabriel's place to further throw off anyone from Stark who might be following us. But we ended up with so many bags of food that another cab seemed like the best idea, so Christopher finally flagged one down – our argument on hold indefinitely – and we made it to Gabriel's place without anyone seeming to tag along behind us. Nor, when we looked up and down Avenue A and Sixth, where Gabriel lived, did we see anyone who looked out of place – in pressed trousers and black shoes – lurking around.

When he opened the door to his apartment, I figured out everything about Gabriel's mysterious comment, however. He wasn't concerned about Stark security showing up unexpectedly. His anxiety was because his bachelor pad had been turned into an impromptu beauty salon.

Lulu was there, working her magic. Or trying to, anyway.

'Look,' she was saying to Nikki. 'You're just not cut out to be a blonde any more, Nikki. Face facts.'

176

Nikki, sitting on a stool in the middle of Gabriel's living room – his taste seemed to lean towards mid-century modern. He had a very fifties vibe going on, with low couches and a coffee table cut out like a kidney-shaped pool, and deep shag-pile rugs, modern art, the works. It was super old school – was sulking.

'No,' Nikki was seething. 'I've always been a blonde. I'll always be a blonde. I want to stay a blonde!'

Nikki had foil packets sticking up all over her head, indicating something of a chemical nature was already going on with her hair. It just didn't appear to be what she wanted.

'Trust me,' Lulu was saying. 'You're going to look adorable. For once your insides are going to match your outsides.'

This sounded ominous.

'Just give it a chance,' Lulu said. 'Like that purple eyeshadow I was trying out on you. It's going to bring out the green in your eyes.'

'I told you,' Nikki seethed some more. 'I want to be *blonde*.' She stabbed a finger in my direction as Christopher and I came in with the bags from the Thai restaurant. 'Like *her*! Like I used to be!'

Steven, sitting at Gabriel's kitchen counter thumbing through a magazine on architecture – Gabriel had dozens of them lying around – had leaped up as soon as he saw us.

'That smells incredible,' he said, relieving us of all the bags we carried. 'You two are lifesavers.'

It felt good to be called a lifesaver, even if all we'd done was brought dinner.

Mrs Howard had locked herself into one of the bedrooms with a migraine and wouldn't come out. I could totally see why. It looked like a tornado had struck Gabriel's apartment. There were shopping bags from stores like Intermix and Scoop scattered everywhere. How Lulu had managed to buy so much for Nikki in so little time, I'd never know.

'I don't even know why we're doing this,' Nikki complained as Lulu sponged foundation on to her face, 'since I'm just going to get my old body back soon. It's all a mute point.'

'Moot,' Gabriel corrected her, as he pulled plates down from a kitchen cabinet. 'Moot point.'

'That's what I said.' Nikki glared at him. It was weird, but even with the foil packets popping up out of her head like alien antennae, she was already looking better. Lulu had put her in some kind of black halter top that accentuated her creamy shoulders, and a pair of jeans that weren't hand-me-downs from me and actually fitted the curve of her hips. She was starting to look . . . well, cute. Alien cute. But cute. 'And nobody asked you, Prince William.'

'Oh, that's very nice,' Gabriel said. He was practically snarling at her. I'd never seen him looking so frazzled. 'I give you shelter in my home, risking my life in doing so, and you make fun of my accent. You're extremely pleasant to have around, did you know that, Nikki?'

'Bite me, Harry Potter,' she said with a sneer.

178

He looked at me helplessly. 'Do you see?' he asked. 'Do you see what I have to put up with?'

I felt bad for having dragged Gabriel, who really had been an innocent bystander, in on all this.

'Have some pad see ew,' I said, handing him a container. It was the only thing I could think of as a way to make it all up to him.

'Oh, thanks ever so much,' he said. I was pretty sure he was being sarcastic.

An alarm went off. Lulu looked at her cellphone and squealed. 'It's time to rinse,' she said, and grabbed Nikki to pull her off the stool and into the bathroom. Nikki went with her, but not without grumbling. When the door shut, Steven turned to us and said, 'If we don't find a way out of this mess soon, I think we're all going to go insane.'

'I'll put a bullet through my own brain.' Gabriel sounded grim. 'Let alone wait for Stark to do it. Your sister will drive me to it, Howard. No offence.'

'I know what you mean,' Steven said as he took a seat at the kitchen counter and dug into a container of panang curry without waiting to put any of it on one of the plates Gabriel had provided. 'She's always been like that, if she doesn't get what she wants.'

'That's how she got where she is today,' I said. When everyone looked at me, I added, 'Well, I mean, one of the highest-paid fashion models in the world.'

'And also somebody one of the richest men in the world wants dead,' Steven pointed out.

'Well, she's not getting her old body back,' Christopher

said, shovelling some pad thai into his mouth. 'However much she might think otherwise.'

I blinked at him. He claimed to hate me, then kissed me and came to my defence at every possible moment, while insisting we couldn't get back together because of my trust issues. What was going on with him?

'I know,' Steven said. 'But we can't go on living in hiding for much longer. And Gabriel can't be asked to put up with us for long.'

The sound of shrieking came out of the bathroom. There was a bang, and the sound of water spraying.

Then Nikki's voice screamed, 'Lulu! *What did you do?*' Her voice was drowned out by the sound of a blow-dryer.

Gabriel looked towards the ceiling, as if praying for patience.

'Have either of you heard of something called Project Phoenix?' Christopher wanted to know.

'I went to Phoenix once,' Steven said, chewing. 'Nice weather.'

'Is it a band?' Gabriel asked. 'I think I caught them once in Wales.'

'I'm fairly certain it's not a band,' Christopher said. 'It's something Robert Stark is working on.'

'No idea, then,' Gabriel said.

'What is it?' Steven asked.

Christopher filled them in on what little we knew so far about Project Phoenix. The explanation took us through most of the carton of pad thai and the remains of the pad see ew.

'It makes no sense,' Steven said when Christopher finished.

'It does,' Christopher said. 'We just can't see it.'

'I saw on the news today,' Gabriel said, 'that they're building an elevator to space.'

We all turned to look at him.

'Well, they are,' he said, swallowing. 'An American company. Rather than launching a shuttle every time we have to send something up to the space station, we'll just send it up in an elevator they're building from a mobile seagoing platform that will reach all the way up to space. It makes sense, don't you think? Anyway, maybe that's what Project Phoenix is. Robert Stark's own space elevator.'

Christopher shrugged. 'It makes more sense than anything else.'

It was just then that the door to the bathroom opened and Lulu and Nikki came out.

Or at least, it had to have been Nikki. Because that's who Lulu had gone into the bathroom with.

But the girl with whom she emerged looked completely different. She had wavy dark hair, instead of Nikki's flat auburn hair, and a glowing complexion instead of Nikki's dead-looking, over-foundationed skin.

And there was a bounce to her step I'd never noticed in Nikki's before. She had on a flowing black empire-waist top and a pair of leggings that suited her figure perfectly.

Her step wasn't the only place where there was bounce, either.

'Jeez,' the girl said rudely when she saw us staring at her. And by us, I mean mostly Christopher and Gabriel, though Steven and I were a bit slack-jawed as well. 'Take a picture, why don'tcha. It'll last longer.'

OK. So it *was* Nikki after all.

'Nikki,' I said, feeling slightly dumbfounded. 'You look . . . great.'

'Chokers are so two thousand and five,' Nikki said, fingering the silver skull and crossbones on a black velvet ribbon at her throat. Did she really think we were only looking at the choker? 'Which is what I told Lulu. But for some reason, this one works.'

'The whole thing works,' Gabriel said. I noticed he was holding a forkful of pad see ew frozen halfway to his mouth. He sounded slightly out of breath.

'I figure no one from her past life will recognize her,' Lulu said, giving one of Nikki's new curls a pat, 'in her new body like this.'

'You can say that again,' Christopher said.

I elbowed him, hard. 'Oof,' he said, and quickly closed his mouth after giving me a slightly devilish grin.

Gabriel, however, continued to stare.

'It's very retro,' he ventured.

'Yes,' Lulu said, glancing meaningfully around at Gabriel's decor. 'Isn't it?'

Sixteen

When I woke up the next morning, I wasn't in bed alone.

I don't mean just Cosabella either.

Or, unfortunately, Christopher.

There was a five-foot-nine agent in a silk aubergine-coloured jacket and skirt sitting on the edge of my mattress, texting madly, her hosed legs crossed and one Jimmy Choo bouncing up and down on the end of her toes.

When she noticed my eyes were open, Rebecca paused, her thumbs hovering over her BlackBerry, and said, 'Finally. I thought you were never going to wake up. Did you take a full ten mills of Ambien or something? You should really cut back to the fives. Well, are you going to get out of bed or what? We have loads to do, Nikki, and we don't really have all day. Get a move on.'

Then she went back to texting.

This really wasn't how I'd dreamed of starting the morning. In my fantasies, I'd planned on waking with a hunky – albeit slightly villainous – eleventh-grader between my sheets.

But I'd been unable to lure Christopher up to my apartment after we'd stopped at Gabriel's, since he'd decided to go back to his cousin Felix's to continue working on the Project Phoenix conundrum.

There was also the small matter of his continued disgust over my 'trust issues'.

You know if a teenage boy turns down an invitation to a single girl's apartment, it's bad. Really bad. The guy really must hate my guts. What was I going to do to convince him that I trusted him?

My relationship problems weren't exactly putting me in the mood for an early morning visitation from my agent.

'What are you doing here?' I asked Rebecca as I dragged a pillow over my head, disturbing Cosabella, who'd been sleeping soundly until I did this. Some watchdog she was. Robert Stark could have sent twenty of his henchmen in to kill me in my sleep, and she wouldn't have done anything more than snort and roll over to make herself more comfortable.

'You have a big day today,' Rebecca said, still punching her tiny keyboard. 'The party at Robert Stark's. And then the Stark Angel lingerie show tonight. *Live*, in case you don't remember. It's New Year's Eve. The diamond bra? Your big television debut? A billion potential viewers? And let's just say you haven't been among my most *reliable* clients lately. All this running away to pop off on to private jets and to people's beachside compounds. I wanted to make sure you got up on time to get your hair and make-up and fittings done.' She flicked a glance down at me. 'Your roots are showing. And how long has it been since you had your cuticles trimmed? Your nails are a mess. And when is the last time you waxed *down there*? Need I remind you that you're practically wearing a thong on national television tonight? Really, what was that thing with Brandon Stark down in South Carolina? Not that I don't applaud your initiative. He's a wealthy boy. But can't you get him to buy a house somewhere close by? The Hamptons? All your *people* are up here, darling.'

I knew what she meant by *people*. My hair people. My nail people. My waxer. My facialist. My stylist. My nutritionist. My trainer. My publicist. My agent. It takes a village to make someone look as good as Nikki Howard. It would be wrong to think she looked as good as she did *naturally*. I mean, there were some genetics involved, but teamwork (and photoshop) had a lot to do with it too.

The one part of being at Brandon's that had been kind of nice was that, for once, I hadn't been surrounded by all those people. I'd just been . . . well, me again.

For a change.

I lay there not moving. Who had let Rebecca in? Karl, the doorman? Because he knew her so well? Well, Karl and I were going to have words. Because this was unacceptable.

Lulu? I highly doubted it. Why wouldn't she have woken me up to tell me Rebecca was lurking around? This was so not like Lulu . . . and so not how I'd wanted to begin my day. I'd wanted to lie around, hugging the memory of Christopher kissing me so roughly in the cab. (Why couldn't I rewind time and go back to that moment and do it all again, only right, so we didn't fight afterwards?)

Except I couldn't. Because Rebecca was leaning over and smacking my butt.

'Get up! And be sure to eat a big breakfast. And lunch. I don't care if you show a little tum on TV tonight, I can't have you passing out on me again, like you did at the Megastore opening. No hypoglycaemia today. Work! Work, work, work!'

Rebecca got up and teetered out of my room in her insanely high heels.

'The car's coming to pick you up for the Stark party at seven,' she bellowed. 'Be here, or I'll chop you into little bits and feed you to the other models I represent. Believe me, they're hungry enough to eat up every little bite.'

She clip-clopped out of the room. A few seconds later, I heard the elevator doors opening, and her stepping into it, talking loudly on her cellphone.

'What?' she was saying. 'No, not the python. I said the lizard skin. Can't anyone follow simple instructions any more? What is wrong with the world?'

Sighing, I got out of bed, Cosabella darting quickly after me because morning is when she gets her first bowl of food for the day (I have no idea how Cosabella eats so much and stays so thin. Possibly it's because she never stops moving, except when she drops off into an exhausted sleep on my neck at night).

As I opened Cosabella's can in the kitchen, I wondered if Christopher and Felix had made any progress trying to figure out what Project Phoenix was. Obviously I was going to do as much snooping as I could when I got to Robert Stark's Upper East Side town house. But it would have been nice to have some clue what I was supposed to be snooping for.

I was scooping some of Cosy's nasty-smelling food into her bowl when I heard a sound and straightened up, only to see a very large, almost naked male figure sneaking out of Lulu's room.

I screamed as loudly as I could, causing Cosy to jump about a foot in the air, and the male to shriek almost as loudly as I had.

'Em, it's me!' the male cried, and when my eyes had had time to focus after they were done spinning around in circles of shock, I saw that it was, indeed, someone I knew.

Someone who was, in fact, Steven Howard, Nikki Howard's brother.

In an undershirt, boxer shorts and a pair of socks.

Coming out of Lulu's bedroom! With his blond hair sticking up all wild, like he'd just woken up!

And now Lulu was coming out of her room right after him, wearing one of her fancy negligees and rubbing her eyes all sleepily, going, 'Stevie? Is something wrong? I thought I heard screaming.'

Oh no. No, I could not handle this. Not first thing in the morning (even though a glance at the clock on the microwave told me it was closer to noon than morning).

Steven and Lulu? I mean, I'd known she'd *wanted* it to happen – wanted it to happen more than anything – but . . .

'Oh, hi, Em,' Lulu said, giving me a drowsy smile. 'I didn't know you were home.'

But Steven was . . . well, he was . . . he was my *brother*!

Wasn't he? Maybe not technically, but –

Actually, yes, he was. Technically. This was so . . . so wrong. So gross. So . . .

. . . so typically Lulu.

'Steven spent the night,' Lulu said, like it was the most natural thing in the world, going over to the refrigerator and pulling it open. 'We're a couple now. What do you guys want for breakfast? Scrambled eggs? Steven likes his eggs scrambled, don't you, Steven?'

Steven was standing there in his socks and underwear turning bright, bright red.

But not as red as *I* could feel myself turning.

'Uh, hi, Em,' Steven was saying. He'd gone to sit behind the kitchen counter on one of the stools, so the fact that he was in his underwear wasn't *quite* so apparent. 'I'm really sorry about this. We didn't know you were home. I, uh, checked the acoustic noise generator. It's still working. There are no bugs in the loft. So we're safe here.'

'Well, that's good, I guess,' I said. I was glad I had on my flannel rainbow pyjamas. They covered me from neck to foot.

'Steven and I are so in love,' Lulu said, smiling ecstatically as she piled eggs, butter, cheese and cream next to the stove. 'He told me he loved me after I gave Nikki her makeover yesterday. She looks so good now. She was so happy. She was really happy, wasn't she, Stevie?'

'She was,' Steven said. He was still blushing. It was weird to see his cheeks turning the same colour pink as my pyjamas. 'It was weird to see Nikki happy for once.'

'She says she's going to go to college,' Lulu said. 'Business school. That was Gabriel's idea. She and Gabriel get along weirdly well. When she isn't calling him names. I wish she wasn't quite so abusive towards him. It's not very nice. But I guess we can't expect miracles. Oh, Em, are you all right?'

I think I was staring at them so hard I'd forgotten to breathe. I closed my mouth shut with an audible snapping sound.

'Uh-huh,' I said, and nodded.

'Is it Steven and me?' Lulu asked, glancing over at Nikki's brother like she couldn't understand why I was so surprised. 'He said he was sorry for blurting out that he loved me, that it had just slipped out,' Lulu went on, cracking some of the eggs into a bowl. 'But I wouldn't let him take it back. Would I?'

Steven shook his head. 'She wouldn't,' he said.

'I knew he really meant it, and that we were meant to be together forever. Because I'm the future Mrs Captain Steven Howard.' Lulu looked thoughtful as she switched on the coffee-maker. 'Wow. Is it just me, or does that sound really hot? Mrs Captain Steven Howard.' She glanced over at me and Steven. 'I'm going to keep my maiden name for my albums, though, of course.'

I widened my eyes at Steven. Did he even know what he'd gotten himself into? I wondered.

He gave me a sheepish smile.

'What can I say?' He shrugged his broad, bare shoulders. 'I love her.'

I shook my head in wonder. Stick a fork in him. Steven was *done*. Lulu had caught him, reeled him in, stuffed him, and served him up with a nice lemon and garlic sauce.

And he looked really happy about it, apart from the blushing thing.

'Wow, you guys, that's so sweet,' I said, meaning it.

I wandered out of the kitchen and back into the living room, because I had a lot to do. Rebecca had left a list. Apparently there was a stylist coming over with a selection of gowns for me to choose from to wear to Robert Stark's party, not to mention my waxer – Katerina, who normally performed this service for Lulu and me, had apparently been dismissed . . . at least in the waxing department. Which was just as well. It was a bit odd to have the person who cleaned your toilet also waxing you – hair stylist, and nail people . . .

'You know what?' Lulu went on, making Steven a cup of coffee. 'I never noticed before, but you two have the same colour eyes. Robin's-egg blue. That's my favourite colour. Both of you.' She turned from me to Steven with the dopiest smile I'd ever seen. 'It's like the sky is in your faces!'

Oh, wow. And I'd thought Steven had it bad? Lulu was done too.

Was this what people who were in love were like? Maybe it was just as well Christopher and I couldn't work things out. I didn't want to become a zombified dope like those two.

The buzzer on the intercom went off. Still feeling a little dazed from my discovery, I wandered over to it and picked up the receiver. It was Karl, letting me know my first appointment had arrived . . . Salvatore, with the clothes.

I thanked him and said to send him up.

'Uh, guys,' I said to Lulu and Steven. 'My clothes guy is here.'

'Oooh,' Lulu said, going over to Steven and putting her arms around him. 'Fashion show. Fun.'

I guess Steven really *was* my brother, because the sight of him snuggling with a girl – even a girl I really liked, such as Lulu – skeeved me as much as it would have skeeved me to see Frida making out with someone.

'Yeah,' I said, 'OK. If you two could just hold off doing that until after I've had breakfast, that would be great.'

'Sorry,' Steven said, looking like he meant it.

'Oh, I'm sorry, Em,' Lulu said, pulling her arms away from Steven like he'd electrocuted her. 'I forgot you still haven't found love like we have. I shouldn't rub it in.'

'No,' I said. 'I've found love and everything. Christopher and I just still need to work out a few things.'

'Oh,' Lulu looked sad. 'I feel so badly for you.'

'Yeah,' Steven said. 'Do you want me to, I don't know, put him in a chokehold or anything?'

I couldn't help smiling at that.

'I don't think that's going to help anything,' I said. 'But thanks. Maybe if you two went and put some more clothes on for when the guy comes? Because he's going to be here any minute.'

They scooted out of the room – well, Steven stomped more than scooted, on account of his size – just as the elevator doors opened to reveal Salvatore, carting a wheeled rack of dresses and gowns for Robert Stark's party.

'Ciao, bella,' he said, kissing me on both cheeks. His assistant, a stick-thin woman with dark hair, began unzipping the garment bags to show me what was inside them.

'Very chic, this,' Salvatore said, fingering the sleeve of my pyjamas. 'I have seen in this month's *Vogue*, yes?'

'Very funny,' I said. 'Thanks for coming over. Would you like some coffee?'

Salvatore and his assistant did want coffee. And so, later, did the waxer, hair stylist, and their assistants when they showed up. And the nail tech and her assistant. I seemed to spend my entire day making cups of coffee – and sandwiches – for people, in between getting primped and styled for the evening's command performance, and trying to avoid seeing Lulu and Steven with their tongues down each other's throats.

This, however, proved harder to do than I thought, since they were kind of all over each other, and Steven wouldn't go back to Gabriel's place. Lulu made him stay to help pick out what I was wearing to Robert Stark's party – a short black spangled dress by Dolce & Gabbana. Then she made him stay because she decided she wanted him to come to Robert Stark's party as her escort.

'I think that would be a really bad idea,' I said. And not just because I didn't want to be distracted from my snooping by her and Steven making out all night. 'What if someone recognizes him?'

'Oh, baby,' Lulu said, holding Steven's face between both her hands, then giving him a big kiss. 'I didn't think about that.'

Gag.

'It's better that I stay with my mom and Nikki, anyway,' Steven said. 'I haven't seen them since yesterday.'

Yes, I thought. Go back to Gabriel's now.

The buzzer on our intercom went off. I went to the receiver to pick it up just as my cellphone vibrated.

'Yes?' I said, lifting the receiver to the intercom. I checked my cell. It was Christopher.

'Brandon Stark is here, Miss Howard,' Karl said, 'to take you to his father's party.'

Perfect, I thought, rolling my eyes. Brandon had been completely ignoring me since my phone call to him yesterday. It was so like him to think his reward for that would be that it would be all right to show up at my apartment to escort me to his dad's party without even asking.

'Tell him I'll be right down,' I said, and hung up the intercom to answer my cell.

'Christopher?' I said.

'Em,' he said, 'you can't go to that party tonight.'

'Uh,' I said, 'I have no choice. The million-dollar bra has been taken out of the vault. I've been waxed and buffed and shined. I'm in my borrowed dress. The car is here.'

I didn't mention the part about Brandon being in it. Christopher and I were fighting enough as it was.

'Em,' he said, 'you don't understand. *You're* Project Phoenix.'

Seventeen

'Wait,' I said, gripping the phone more tightly to my ear. A chill had passed over my body.

But that was surely only because I was standing there in a too-short sleeveless dress on a chilly 31 December evening in downtown Manhattan.

'What are you talking about?' I asked. 'How can I be Project Phoenix?'

'I don't know,' Christopher said. 'I don't – we don't – still even know exactly what Project Phoenix is. But we've found a link from it to the Stark Institute for Neurology and Neurosurgery. And your name.'

'*My* name?' I echoed. 'Emerson Watts? Or—'

'No. Nikki Howard. Em, think about it. Think about what all these people have in common. They're young. They're healthy. They're attractive.'

'So?'

'Just like Nikki Howard.'

'What are you guys talking about?' Lulu asked me curiously, adjusting one of her fishnets, which had gotten twisted around her leg.

'Nothing,' I said to her. 'Go on down to the car and let Brandon know I'll be right there, will you?'

Lulu shrugged. 'OK.'

'No!' Christopher cried, overhearing me. 'Em, you can't go to that party!'

'Christopher, I have to,' I said. 'If I don't go, Robert Stark will know something is up.' And a billion fans would be tragically disappointed. Not to mention the show's sponsor, De Beers. 'And anyway, I don't see what the connection is between the Stark Institute and all those other people and me.'

'You don't?' Christopher sounded slightly hysterical. 'Em, don't you get it? Curt? He's just going on a hiking trip in the Cascades. By himself. He goes missing, who's going to know what really happened to him? Kerry, going to Guatemala to teach children to read? She disappears along the way? She's one of thousands who goes missing every year. Same with all these other people. It's freaking genius, Em. Young, healthy kids . . . and Stark has its pick. They may have been doing this for years. All these pretty missing girls we hear about on CNN every day . . . for all we know, Stark may have been behind it all along.'

'Christopher . . .' I shook my head. I loved my boyfriend. I really did.

But his hatred for Stark – because of what he'd seen them do to me – may have caused him to go round the bend.

I guess I could understand it. He'd seen me get crushed to death right in front of him. The post-traumatic stress this had inevitably caused him had to have been severe. I loved him, but he was one messed-up dude.

And then he'd found out the accident had been no

accident at all, but had been caused by Stark. And that I wasn't dead, but was living in some other girl's body.

No wonder he'd lost his mind and morphed into Iron Man.

Only without the super suit and in teenage form.

'Em,' Christopher said. He was still speaking fast and still panting a little, 'listen to me. Robert Stark is a marketing genius. He's dedicated his life to finding a demand, then supplying the product for that demand at a price that drives all other competitors out of business. The question isn't *whether* he's doing this. It's *Why hasn't anyone caught him before now?*'

The buzzer to my intercom went off again. It was Brandon's driver, I knew, wanting to know where I was. Lulu had already gone down.

'Look,' I said. 'You're probably right.'

What else was I going to say? I had to just play along with him. Was this what it was like, I wondered? To be Lois Lane or Lana Lang or Mary Jane Watson or any of those other women who were the girlfriends of superheroes? I mean, those guys were crazy, right? The men who thought they were superheroes. How were you supposed to deal with them? You didn't want to upset them or get them riled up, or they'd just go and put on their capes and jump out of the window to get shot at.

So you just went along with their craziness, trying to soothe them as best you could in the hopes that they'd stay home, where it was safe.

Then you went out and did whatever you wanted behind their back.

'We'll talk about it when I get home,' I said in the most soothing voice I could summon. 'We'll figure out the best thing to do then.'

'What?' Christopher cried. 'Em, *no*—'

'You can't do anything about it now anyway,' I said. 'I mean, what are you going to do? Call the cops? You don't have any proof. Are any of those people missing yet?'

'Well,' he said, 'no. And technically there's no proof except what happened to you. Which wasn't an accident either. But—'

The buzzer went off again, for a much longer time.

'Right,' I said. 'Look, I've got to run. Everything's going to be all right. I'll call you from Robert Stark's to prove it.'

'Don't go to that house, Em.' Christopher sounded mad. He sounded more than mad. He sounded furious. And also scared. 'I'm warning you, Em. Don't you even think about—'

'Love you,' I said, grabbing my bag and faux fur and running for the elevator. 'Bye.'

'Don't you hang up,' Christopher said. 'I mean it. Don't you dare—'

'Oh, I'm in the elevator,' I said as I pressed the button. 'You're breaking up. I'm losing you . . .'

'You are not losing me,' Christopher said. 'Em, don't be stupid. I—'

I hung up.

Really, I wasn't trying to be mean. It was just that I didn't have time for Christopher's supervillain stuff right then. Rebecca's warnings from that morning were still sounding in my ears. I had to get to Robert Stark's party, and then to the studio where the lingerie show was being broadcast, or my butt was toast. I completely valued my relationship with Christopher, and I totally thought something was up with Robert Stark.

But I had my professional obligations to fulfil.

And besides. What was Robert Stark going to do to me?

That he hadn't done already, I mean.

'Where *were* you?' Lulu wanted to know when I finally fell into the back of the limo.

'Sorry,' I muttered, climbing over Brandon's out-stretched legs. 'Important call. Would you *move*?' This last was directed at Brandon.

'My bad.' Brandon was clearly already drunk. Since this was how he was any time he had to see his father, this was no surprise.

'But really,' Lulu said. 'What did Christopher want?'

'I have no idea,' I said truthfully.

'He wanted to come,' Lulu said sympathetically. 'Didn't he? As your date?'

Brandon looked up from his highball glass at this. 'You're back together with that guy? Leather-jacket guy?' He looked disappointed.

'None of your business,' I said, wagging a finger at him. 'Go back to your drink.'

Brandon glared dopily down at his whisky.

'Guys who wear leather jackets always get the girl,' he muttered.

If only he knew the truth.

Robert Stark's huge ten-bedroomed four-storey grey town house, with its subdued black trim, private garage, indoor pool, ballroom and vast private back garden, was about as far uptown as you could get from my place and still be on the Upper East Side. Just off Fifth Avenue, it was steps from Central Park and the Metropolitan Museum of Art.

His annual New Year's Eve party was so popular, and attended by so many celebrities and wealthy politicians and Stark shareholders, that there was already a traffic jam just to get to his place. Lulu and Brandon and I had to get out and walk the last block, and then fight the crowd of paps that had gathered outside.

The whole time – well, during the walk to his dad's house anyway – I quizzed Brandon, trying to see if he knew anything about Project Phoenix.

'What is that?' he'd asked, still slurping scotch from the glass he'd brought along during the stroll from the limo. 'A new stadium someone is building in Arizona?'

Seriously. A band? A space elevator? And now a stadium?

'No,' I'd said. 'It's something your dad is doing using data from people who bought his new Quarks.'

'How's that going to work?' Brandon wanted to know.

'That's what I'm asking you,' I said, frustrated.

'Well, if I knew that, would I be here with you?' Brandon asked. 'No, I'd be in my dad's office, telling him I knew and to get the hell out. Right? So, try again.'

I hunched along beside him, defeated. Christopher and Felix had to be on to something . . . but that *I* was Project Phoenix? It was all just too crazy.

Still, at least Christopher was trying.

Which was more than could be said for me. I was at a *party*. Worse, a boring party for celebrities. I saw Madonna getting out of a limo right in front of the red carpet leading up the steps to the wide-open front door (which was a bit weird, because she lived just around the corner. She could almost have walked. Although not in those heels, I realized when I looked at her gladiator platforms). The governor of New York was going inside just ahead of her.

'There's Nikki Howard!' the paps gathered on either side of the gold security ropes cried when they saw me with Brandon. 'Nikki! Is it true you and Brandon Stark are engaged?'

'Absolutely,' Brandon said drunkenly into the first microphone thrust in his direction. 'Hey, watch the drink.'

'No,' I said. 'We're just friends.'

'I'm engaged,' Lulu said to a reporter who had asked her whether her album was ever going to drop. 'Well, OK, engaged to be engaged some day. I'm a bit busy at the moment to be thinking about getting married. I'm recording my new album.'

'Lulu,' I hissed at her. 'Can it on the engagement stuff. No one's supposed to know about you know who.'

'Oh, the identity of my husband-to-be is a secret,' Lulu squealed as I dragged her past the uniformed security guards posted on either side of the door and into the town house. 'He's very shy. *You* know. Not used to life in the spotlight yet.'

Inside the Stark mansion, there were models in Stark Angel bra-and-panty sets, complete with wings – not any of the models from the show I was going to do later though, and their wings were smaller, for better manoeuvrability – offering glasses of champagne to everyone and taking people's coats as soon as they entered. Further into the house, which was sumptuously decorated and made up entirely of marble and black wood panelling, were magicians, jugglers, fire-eaters, and acrobats from Cirque du Soleil.

Lulu took one look at the fire-eater, who had quite a circle of admirers, and said, stomping her foot, 'I *knew* I should have had a fire-eater at my party.'

Brandon, who'd traded his empty glass from the limo for a flute of champagne from a passing Stark Angel's silver tray, made a face.

'Fire-eaters suck,' he said. 'Your trapeze girl was great.'

'Really?' Lulu looked sceptical. 'I don't think anyone even noticed her. She was hanging way above everybody's heads.'

I stood there holding my champagne, which of course I wasn't drinking, wondering what I was even doing there. We'd wandered into Robert Stark's cavernous ballroom – the ceiling was twenty feet high at least, and painted with cherubs that looked like chubby versions of the Stark Angels who were wondering around (minus the bras), and dotted all over with humongous crystal chandeliers that glittered like the drop earrings I was wearing. All around us were celebrities who were drinking and chatting and crowding the impressive buffet, where paper-thin curls of roast beef, fat ruby-red strawberries, caviar in gold bowls with pearl spoons and huge pink shrimp curled in chilled bowls were being served on fine china plates by caterers in white suits. I saw Madonna again, this time talking to Gwyneth Paltrow, and Jay-Z hanging out with Bono. Everyone was there, at least for a little while. It didn't seem like the kind of party you stayed at for a long time . . . just one of those parties you stopped by, said hello, and left . . .

Part of that might have been because the French doors leading from the ballroom out to the back garden were wide open, and a chilly breeze was coming in. Then again, the room was roastingly hot because of all the bodies in it. People were milling in and out of it, not even bothering to get their coats to go outside.

'Oh, look,' Lulu said, pointing at someone over by the buffet, 'there's Taylor Swift. I'm going to go tell her about Steven. She's going to be so happy for me.'

I grabbed Lulu's arm before she got more than two inches away.

'Would you stop?' I whispered. 'No one's supposed to know about Steven.'

'I won't tell her his last name, silly,' Lulu said. 'But I'm just so happy. I'm busting to tell everyone I know!'

She wrenched her arm out of my hand and hurried off. There really wasn't anything I could do to stop her, beyond tackling her and sitting on her, which I was pretty sure wouldn't go unnoticed.

Brandon, who'd disappeared for a minute or two, reappeared holding a plate of shrimp, which he chewed noisily in my ear.

'Have you tried this shrimp?' he asked. 'It's freaking amazing.'

'Would you get away from me?' I said irritably. 'I hate you.'

'You're so moody,' Brandon remarked, chewing loudly. 'Just because I kidnapped you and tried to force you to be my girlfriend. I thought you'd be over that by now. Here, just try a bite.' He waved a shrimp in my face. 'The cocktail sauce is really good.'

'Stop,' I said, and stepped away from him . . .

. . . right into the path of Rebecca, wearing a long black evening gown, which fitted her body like a second skin and had a slit up to her pelvic bone, practically.

'Oh good, there you are.' She grabbed my arm. 'I've been looking everywhere for you. What are you doing, hiding in this corner with Brandon? Why aren't you mingling? You're here to mingle. You're the Million Dollar Bra Girl.'

Brandon let out a giant horse laugh at that.

'Million Dollar Brawr Girl!' he said, doing a pretty good imitation of Rebecca. 'Better get cher brawron!'

Rebecca sent him a withering look.

'Brandon,' she said severely, 'are you drunk?'

'Of course,' he replied, licking a shrimp.

'Get out of my sight then,' Rebecca said. She began steering me away from Brandon towards the centre of the room. 'Mr Stark Senior has been asking for you all night. He wants to introduce you to some of his shareholders.'

I hurried along beside her, practically having to jog. I had no idea how she walked so fast in such high heels. We were approaching a group of tuxedoed men and women in evening gowns. I could tell they were older because the men all had grey hair.

'Found her,' Rebecca called, in her Brooklynese.

The people turned and the group broke apart a little. I saw that at the centre of it was Robert Stark, looking as absurdly handsome – only older, of course – as his son. He smiled at me, his teeth startlingly white against his tanned, weather-beaten face. He'd been using his own Stark-brand teeth-whitening strips, I saw.

'Ah, there she is,' he said, and put his hand on my bare back. 'Nikki Howard, everyone, the star of this evening's performance.'

All the old people smiled at me. They looked kind and attractive and rich. Very, very rich. The ladies had a lot of diamonds dripping from around their necks, and the men's faces were very puffy and red, like they'd had too much to drink already.

'So nice to finally meet you, dear,' one lady in a long beige dress that was tastefully decorated in sparkles at the bottom said, reaching out to shake my hand. She said her name, but I instantly forgot it.

'Nice to meet you too,' I said.

She seemed to hold on to my hand for way too long. It was creepy. I wanted to get away from her, and from Robert Stark and the rest of his friends. Or shareholders, I guess they were.

Except that two things happened at once.

One was that I glanced down at our clenched hands and noticed that around her slender, blue-veined wrist was a black velvet cord, and that from the cord dangled something that looked to me like a gold bird that was on fire.

Or, you know. A phoenix.

And when I looked up, wondering if I was interpreting what I was seeing correctly, I noticed someone over her shoulder, just coming into the ballroom.

And that was Gabriel.

Who, like me, was undoubtedly being forced to come to this party by his agent.

Except that he was with someone. A pretty brunette of about average height, who was wearing a purple dress with a black corset laced up *tight* to flatter her cute figure, and matching purple eyeshadow. It took me a second to recognize who she was, Lulu's makeover had been so complete:

None other than Nikki Howard.

Eighteen

'Excuse me,' I said to the woman, who was still holding my hand. 'I actually have to go make a phone call.'

I didn't want to say I had to go say hi to someone I knew, because I didn't want to draw Robert Stark's attention to Gabriel's date. I had no idea whether or not he'd been alerted to the fact that Nikki was still alive, or if he knew whose body she'd been put into or what she looked like.

I figured the less attention I drew to Nikki, the better.

But Robert Stark, it turned out, wasn't done with me.

'Oh, I'm sure your call can wait,' he said, putting his arm around me and turning me so I couldn't even see Gabriel or Nikki any more. 'There are some more people I'd like you to meet. This is Bill and Ellen Anderson, also Stark shareholders, as I'm sure you know.'

I found myself shaking the hands of more old people in evening wear . . . again dripping in diamonds and rosacea . . . and again with black cords around their wrists with what looked to me like a gold phoenix dangling from each of them.

Hey, I was no expert on mythological birds. But if it had fire shooting out of its wings, was it not a phoenix?

It seemed like everyone Robert Stark dragged me round the room to introduce me to that evening had a phoenix hanging from their wrist. It was so bizarre!

I hadn't seen any gift bags being given out at the door. But maybe I'd just missed them. Maybe Christopher was completely wrong, and Project Phoenix was some kind of charity and all the Stark shareholders were donors.

It seemed kind of rude to ask, especially when they were being so gracious to me, taking so much time to ask how I was and saying how nice it was to meet me and all that. My mom had always told me to be kind to the elderly. I couldn't exactly run away, even though I really wanted to. I was dying to ask Gabriel what he was thinking, bringing Nikki here.

Was she going to cause a scene? Confront Robert Stark about what he'd done to her? Didn't she know he'd just have his security staff drag her out? No one would believe her anyway.

Finally Robert Stark seemed to be satisfied that I'd met enough of his shareholders, and he said, glancing at his platinum watch, 'Well, I'm sure you'll be needing to leave for the studio to get ready for tonight's show.'

He wasn't kidding. I saw that the hands of his watch said it was close to eight thirty.

'I do have to go,' I said. 'It was really nice meeting your friends.'

'Shareholders,' he corrected me. 'Never mix business with friendship, Nikki. That's something you never could keep straight, isn't it?'

I stared at him. Was he kidding me? Did he really think I was Nikki? I mean, the real Nikki? Did he really not remember?

'Uh,' I said. 'I'm not Nikki. You know that, right? You know I'm really Emerson Watts?'

You killed me, I wanted to add. *You killed me and put my brain in Nikki Howard's body because she was blackmailing you. The real Nikki's here in this room, you know. She can back this whole story up. Do you want me to get her?*

But my heart was thumping so hard just from the few words I had said, waiting for some response from him, some acknowledgement. I couldn't get further than *You know I'm really Emerson Watts?* before Robert Stark lowered his sleeve over his watch, looked over my shoulder and smiled broadly.

'Ah, Gabriel,' he said. 'So good to see you. Thank you for coming. Can't wait to see your performance tonight. And who is this lovely creature you've brought with you?'

I spun round slowly, hardly daring to believe any of this was happening. Robert Stark. Robert Stark, the man who had ruined my life, was actually about to speak to Nikki Howard – the *real* Nikki Howard, the one he'd tried to have murdered.

And he didn't even know it.

Nikki looked even more amazing up close than she had from across the room. It wasn't that she appeared so different than she had before. (She did, obviously, because she'd gone from looking like a washed-out rag to a punk-rock princess.

Her hair, now dyed almost jet black, had been scrunched dry, rather than straightened, so the natural waves framed her heart-shaped face in a more flattering way.

And her make-up, rather than being a carbon copy of how she used to do it when she was in her old body, had been done for her new face, so that the tones played up her new eye colour and emphasized the curve of her lips and cheeks.)

It was more like she was carrying herself differently. She seemed . . . proud. And playful. And, yes . . . hot.

Suddenly I could see why all those guys – even other girls' boyfriends – had gravitated to Nikki. It was totally obvious to me now that it had never just been about her looks. It was about something more. Something I knew I didn't have. Something that was essentially, irrevocably . . . Nikki.

'Why, hello,' Nikki said, extending her hand towards Robert Stark. Not in a handshake. So that he could kiss it. 'You can call me Diana Prince.'

Diana Prince? *Diana Prince?* How did I know that name? Oh my God.

Diana Prince? That was Wonder Woman's alter ego.

Nikki Howard had named herself after Wonder Woman.

'So nice to meet you, Miss Prince,' Robert Stark said. And he actually raised her fingers to his lips, and kissed them. 'Have we met somewhere before? You seem familiar.'

'Oh,' Nikki said, with a kittenish smile, 'I think you would remember having met me.'

'I certainly would,' Robert Stark said, smiling back. 'Well, Gabriel, like I said . . . good luck tonight. Miss

Prince . . . Miss Howard . . . good evening to you both.'

And he walked away, towards a set of his guests who were waiting for him by the ballroom doors.

It was only after he was out of earshot that I realized I'd been holding my breath the whole time, and released it.

'Oh my God,' I cried. 'You guys. I nearly had a heart attack just then. Nikki – I mean, Diana. What are you *doing* here?'

'Oh,' Nikki said, looking after Robert Stark, her purple-lined eyes narrowed. 'I just wanted to see his face one last time. Before it's behind bars.'

'I tried to keep her from coming,' Gabriel said. It was only then that I realized how highly frustrated he looked. 'But she insisted. Loudly. I think my eardrums are broken.'

And now I was beginning to suspect his frustration had nothing to do with disliking Nikki. The opposite, in fact.

Nikki rolled her eyes dismissively in Gabriel's direction. Turning to me, she said, 'Please tell me your friend with the leather jacket came up with something we can use to put that scumbag in jail. Other than our word that what happened is true.'

'He has –' I said – 'Some kind of theory, anyway.' I didn't want to tell her that Christopher's theory was totally insane, and that it revolved around . . . well, the two of us. 'But he has no proof . . .' I let my voice trail off as I stared towards the ballroom doors, having just noticed something.

'Or maybe he has,' I added thoughtfully.

Nikki and Gabriel turned to look in the direction I was staring.

'Oh,' Nikki said, still bored, 'that's nothing. The old people are all leaving. They always do that. Because it's after eight. Way past their bedtime.'

'It's not all the old people,' I said. 'It's only the old people I just met. The Stark shareholders. Where are they going? They aren't getting their coats.'

I started walking swiftly towards the doors myself.

'Uh, Nikki,' Gabriel said, conscious that, despite the mass exodus of the shareholders, the ballroom was still crowded with people who might think it strange if they overheard him calling me Em. 'Where are you going?'

'I'll be right back,' I said to him. I was jogging now. Which wasn't easy in heels.

But when I got to the hallway the shareholders had disappeared into, it was empty. Well, except for a staircase cordoned off by a velvet rope and manned by a Stark security guard.

'Excuse me,' I said, going up to him. 'Did you see Robert Stark go by here?'

'Yes, ma'am,' he said. 'He's upstairs.'

'Oh, great,' I said, finger combing some of my hair out of my eyes in a manner I hoped he'd find irresistibly fetching. 'Can you let me up to see him for a minute? I'm Nikki Howard. I just have to tell him something about the show tonight. It'll only take a second.'

'I know who you are, Miss Howard,' the security guard said with a polite smile. 'Unfortunately, I can't let you up. Authorized personnel only.'

As he said this, Mrs Whatever Her Name Was, with the blue veins and the sparkles around the bottom of her dress, came hurrying up.

'Oh, hello again,' she said to me with a vague smile.

'Hi,' I said, smiling back.

Then, to the security guard, she said, 'I'm so sorry I'm late. I had to go to the little girls' room.'

She actually said that. The little girls' room.

Then she did something extraordinary. She held up her bracelet. The one with the phoenix – or what I thought was a phoenix, anyway – dangling down from it.

And the security guard said, 'Of course, madam.'

And he undid the velvet rope and let her up the stairs.

Now of course I was bursting with curiosity to get up those stairs and find out what was going on up there.

Because it seemed like, without a doubt, those bracelets or whatever they were had some kind of significance.

I turned round and, ignoring the guard who'd snubbed me, hurried back over to Gabriel and Nikki, who'd been waiting for me back at the doors to the ballroom.

'What was that all about?' Gabriel asked.

'There's something going on upstairs,' I said. 'We need to get up there.'

'Em,' Gabriel said, pulling out his cellphone. 'We're needed onstage for the Stark Angel show, which is going on live in approximately . . . one hour.'

'Where's Brandon?' I asked. I looked around the ball-room and finally saw him, slow-dancing with someone who looked a lot like Rebecca. I was halfway across the room before I realized it *was* Rebecca.

When she lifted her head from his shoulder after I poked it, her shrug was eloquent.

'What can I say?' she asked. 'I've still got it. He thinks I'm hot. And anyway, what do you care? You don't want him.'

'I didn't say anything,' I said. 'I just need to borrow him for a minute.

'Well, make it snappy,' Rebecca said. 'And you better not be having second thoughts about his three hundred million. You let them slip through your fingers, missy. You can't blame me for scooping up your leftovers.'

I knew she was referring to Brandon's money, which she'd always encouraged me to try to snatch up by getting myself engaged to him. I guess she figured if I wasn't going to go for it, she would.

'You're entirely welcome to him,' I assured her. I'd take penniless supervillain Christopher, who I wasn't even sure wanted me, over multimillionaire Brandon any day.

I only wished Christopher would realize it.

'Fine,' Rebecca said. 'Brandon, Nikki's here. She wants to ask you something.'

Brandon looked scared. 'Oh no, not Nikki. She's a bitch.' Then, when he saw me, he smiled. 'Oh, *that* Nikki. OK. Hi! Have you got your brawron?'

'Oh for God's sake.' I grabbed Brandon by the arm and steered him a few feet away from Rebecca so we couldn't be overheard. 'Brandon, I need you to get me upstairs. Your dad's having some kind of meeting up there, and I want to see what it's about without him knowing I'm there. Is there some way I can get up there other than the main staircase? He's got a guard there, and the guard won't let me by.'

'Sure,' Brandon said. 'Servants' staircase, in the back. This way.'

He slipped an arm round my shoulders and led me towards the French doors out to the back garden. I'm sure everyone who saw us must have thought we were leaving the party to go hook up. Even the people who were in the garden with the fountains and the architecturally sculpted bushes would have seen Brandon lead me from the ballroom, down the paved path and up to a door the caterers were using to bring the food in and out . . . it led straight into the massive industrial-sized kitchen. Everyone in there working stared at us as we walked by the chilled trays of shrimp and tiny goat's-cheese-filled canapés in our evening wear.

'Hey,' Brandon said, spying these, 'I didn't see those.' He plucked up a few and popped them into his mouth while I rolled my eyes.

Then Brandon opened a door and we were in a dingy hallway, with a narrow stairway that curved upward.

'See?' he said. 'Servants' staircase. I used to spend hours playing in here when I was a kid. I pretended I was an orphan and some loving parents were going to come and adopt me and take me away from this terrible place. *Ha!*'

His bitter *ha!* echoed up and down the staircase.

'Thanks, Brandon,' I said. 'Would you let Gabriel and Nikki know I'll be back as soon as I can? And that if I'm not . . . they should call the police?'

'Sure,' Brandon said affably. 'That's Nikki back there, with the black hair?'

'Yeah,' I said, not sure I wanted to hear what he had to say about that.

'She looks kinda hot now,' Brandon said. 'But you know who's really hot. Your agent. What's up with that?'

'Yeah,' I said, *really* sure I didn't want to hear about that. 'I don't know, Brandon. I have to go now.'

'OK,' he said. 'You'll let me know if you find out anything I can, you know, use to send old Robert to the big house. Because I really hate that guy.'

'Consider it done,' I assured him.

Then I started climbing the twisted staircase . . .

I wasn't quite sure what I expected to find when I got upstairs. Certainly not what I found.

Which was a maid in a black uniform and a white apron opening the first door just as I was about to. She was so startled to see me, she nearly dropped the entire tray of empty champagne glasses she was holding.

'Oh my goodness!' she cried. 'Can I help you?'

I had no idea if she'd recognized me, let alone what I should do. I didn't want her to turn me in to the security guard.

216

But I wasn't sure that she didn't know I had no right to be on that floor.

'I – I think I made a wrong turn,' I stammered. When all else fails, and you're a blonde supermodel, acting like an airhead never fails to work wonders. People pretty much expect it of you anyway, and invariably find it charming. It's stupid and sexist, but it works.

Even on other women, especially if they're older than you. It brings out their maternal instinct or something.

Well, it probably wouldn't work on my mother. But it works on almost everyone else.

'I – I was looking for – for the little girls' room,' I stammered.

Thank you, Lady Whose Name I Forget.

'Oh,' the maid said with a laugh. 'It's two more doors down, honey.'

'Oh, sorry,' I said, giggling. 'I'm such a ditz. Thanks very much.'

'You're so welcome,' she said warmly.

It had worked. Thank you, God.

I slipped past her along the hallway. Unlike the scene downstairs, it was hushed and quiet. There was deeply piled carpeting on the floor – grey, of course – and stark seascapes hanging on the walls, each lit with its own individual painting light . . . the only lighting to see by. I waited until I couldn't hear the maid any more on the stairs, then listened to hear if I could detect any other sounds.

And soon enough, I heard it: the drone of a human voice coming from a room a few doors down from where I stood. I padded towards it, my stilettos silent on the plush carpeting.

Pressing my ear to the thick door, I listened as closely as I could. It was a woman's voice. It sounded nice.

But I couldn't tell what she was saying. I could hear no other sounds.

What should I do? Open the door and go in? Who knew what lay on the other side. What if I walked into some kind of Stark shareholder business meeting or something, and everyone turned and looked at me?

And Robert Stark – who had to be in there – had one of his security goons shoot me?

Or worse, drag me out in front of everyone? I'd be so embarrassed. Getting shot would be preferable. Then I'd just be dead, not mortified.

What if it wasn't just a business meeting though? What if Project Phoenix was really what Christopher said it was . . . whatever that had been? I had a moral duty to go in there and find out. My whole relationship depended on it.

Turning that doorknob and seeing what was going on in there was what I'd gone to all this trouble for in the first place, right? I had to do it.

My heart was beating so hard in my chest. I was acting, I realized, like one of those heroines in Frida's books – the Too Stupid to Live kind. Going into that room would be a stupid thing to do. Any girl who'd do it was an idiot. If I was watching this unfold on a movie screen, I'd yell, 'Go home!' at the TV.

'Excuse me?'

I jumped nearly a mile and whirled around, then relaxed a little as I saw that the maid with the tray was behind me. Only she'd restocked her tray with glasses that were now full to the brim with sparkling champagne.

'I just have to get by you,' the maid said, sounding embarrassed.

'Oh, of course,' I said, and then, like it was the most natural thing in the world, I opened the door for her, since she had her hands full.

And after she went in, I followed her.

Nineteen

It was dark inside the room.

That's because it was some kind of media room, like the one Brandon had at his beach house, for showing movies. There was a huge screen at one end of the room, where images were flashing. All the Stark shareholders – even in the dark, I recognized the ladies I'd met downstairs from all the diamonds around their necks – were seated in wide, comfortable red velvet-covered chairs in front of the screen. They were watching the images flashing on the screen with rapt attention.

I shouldn't have worried about anyone noticing me come in. No one cared. They were too busy watching the presentation.

I found an empty chair and sat down to watch the show. The maid, noticing this, offered me a glass of champagne, which I accepted with a smile, just to be gracious. There was a little table next to my high-backed theatre chair on which I could set the glass, so I did so, knocking something over in the dark. This was embarrassing. Also dangerous. I didn't want to draw attention to myself, even though I was at the back, and there were only a few other people seated in my row.

I scrambled around on the carpeted floor for whatever I'd knocked over. I found it almost at once. It was some kind of gaming joystick, I realized as soon as my fingers closed over it. It had a cord attached to it that disappeared into the floor, but only a single button on the joystick. I was careful not to press the button, but I kept the joystick in my lap, since I noticed everyone else in my row was doing the same thing.

After that, I turned my attention to the presentation that was going on. The nice female voice I'd heard out in the hallway was much louder now. It belonged to an immaculately dressed, very beautiful Frenchwoman who was standing to one side of the screen. She was in charge of the presentation, I saw. She was holding a joystick too, but it was more of a clicker, like the kind you use during a PowerPoint presentation. In fact, that's what the presentation we were seeing was. PowerPoint.

I had to stifle an automatic yawn. Seriously? Power-Point? I almost wished someone *would* shoot me.

Then I saw what the PowerPoint was about and sat up a little straighter in my seat.

The slide the stunningly beautiful Frenchwoman was showing us was a photo of a muscular, slim-hipped young man who wore cargo trousers and no shirt, grinning into the camera with his arms around a collie. The collie had a bandanna round its neck.

'This is Matthew,' the Frenchwoman said in her cool, emotionless voice. 'Matthew is a twenty-year-old college student studying philosophy and is on his dormitory's fris-bee team. Matthew is six foot two and one hundred and seventy pounds and has a small tattoo of a fish on his left ankle. Matthew is a vegetarian and believes in abstaining from drugs and alcohol to keep his mind and body pure.'

With fingers that felt numb, I opened my bag and took out my cellphone. It wasn't easy to do without drawing attention to myself.

But I found the film application. And I pressed record.

I wasn't sure what was happening. But based on what Christopher had said on the phone, I was beginning to have a very creepy feeling.

And I just wanted to be on the safe side.

'Matthew has no history of heart disease or cancer in his family,' the Frenchwoman went on. 'And will become available when he leaves for a trip to Honduras to volunteer for Habitat for Humanity over spring break this April. Matthew is available for a starting bid at five hundred thousand dollars. Please begin your bidding now.'

Around me I heard the sound of clicking joysticks. I looked up from my cellphone, wondering if what I thought was happening could really be happening.

Because it just didn't seem possible to me that Christopher could have been right.

'Five hundred fifty,' the Frenchwoman said tonelessly. She was staring at a little computer monitor on her desk. 'Six hundred. Six fifty. Do I have seven hundred? Seven fifty. Eight hundred. Eight fifty. Matthew has a naturally fast metabolism and grew up in an area with fluoridated water, so no cavities or dental issues at all. He really is a prime specimen. You could not ask for a healthier young man. Nine hundred thousand. One million. I have a bid for one million dollars . . . Matthew, going once. Going twice. The bidding for Matthew is now closed at one million dollars. Thank you.'

The image of Matthew vanished from the screen, and the clicking of the joysticks around me stopped. Almost immediately – way before I'd even had time to process what I'd just witnessed – a new image appeared on the screen. It was of a young woman with long straight black hair. She was lying on a bed, laughing up at the camera, holding a grey and black tiger-striped cat. She was wearing a pair of cute shorts and a tank top. On her wall was a poster that said *Save Tibet*.

'This is Kim Su,' the Frenchwoman said in the same slightly bored but completely businesslike voice. 'She is nineteen years old and is five foot two and weighs one hundred pounds. She has no tattoos and is a lifelong vegetarian. She has no health problems, including no history of dental issues. She's a freshman at a prestigious university and works out regularly. Her family is extremely long-lived, including one set of great-grandparents who are still living and are now in their hundreds. Having yourself transplanted into Kim Su would make an outstanding investment, as she has not only incredible beauty, but longevity on her side. Because Kim Su is such an amazing find, the starting bid for her is eight hundred thousand. Kim Su will become available this summer when she leaves to be an au pair in the Hamptons.'

The clicking was even more enthusiastic for Kim Su

than it had been for Matthew. Bidding immediately went into the millions. I wasn't that surprised when the lady with the sparkles on the bottom of her dress got her for a cool three point five.

'Yes!' she cried, almost jumping out of her seat.

Several of the other ladies leaned over to congratulate her on her excellent buy.

I just sat there, feeling kind of sick. I think maybe I was in shock. I couldn't believe it was true. It was all true, everything Christopher had said on the phone. Project Phoenix was exactly that: people buying more attractive people's bodies to have their brains put into them.

Those kids we'd seen online – well, most of them had been kids. Teenagers, really – all the ones who'd bought Stark Quarks. The reason Stark had saved their information . . . the reason they'd combed through it so carefully, saving some and not others? It was because Stark considered them donors.

Like me.

I was Project Phoenix. The prototype.

Of course. The doctors at the Stark Institute for Neurology and Neurosurgery had said there was a waiting list of wealthy candidates wanting the surgery: candidates with perfectly healthy brain function but whose bodies maybe weren't all that they used to be – a little flab here, a little wrinkle there. Maybe some male pattern baldness. And that the only thing stopping the Institute from doing more surgeries was a shortage of donor bodies. And that the donor bodies they had weren't always the most desirable . . . the body Nikki got was of a drunk driver killed in a DUI.

And Nikki nearly died during her surgery because the body she got was so unhealthy. So why wouldn't Stark do this? What was stopping them?

Nothing. Nothing at all.

I felt cold all over. And it wasn't because of my way-too-short dress.

I don't know how long I sat there, watching image after image flicker across the screen and get bid on, before my view was obscured by a large male figure.

Not one of the males on the screen that I'd just seen sold off either.

This was a male dressed in Stark-security garb.

'Miss Howard?' he said softly. 'Will you come with me, please?'

I was busted. I shouldn't have sat there so long.

But how could I move? What Robert Stark was doing . . .

. . . it was the most disgusting thing I'd ever seen in my life.

All the Stark shareholders turned to look as I was escorted from the room, even though the Frenchwoman said in her calm voice, 'Please pay no attention to the slight disturbance at the back. It is only a minor interruption. Shall we turn to the next candidate?'

I heard the murmurs and whispers. And then I heard Robert Stark himself assure his shareholders, in his booming voice, 'Don't worry, everyone. It's only Nikki Howard.

You've all met her! She's one of you . . . or what all of you will be shortly. She just wanted to stop by to make sure you're choosing wisely!

This caused a ripple of laughter through the room.

I didn't hear any more. That's because by then the guard had pulled me out. I stood there in the hallway, staring at the floor, not really caring what was going to happen to me next. So what if Robert Stark had me killed, like he'd tried to do to Nikki?

I wasn't sure I wanted to live in a world where people did this kind of thing, anyway.

'Well, that wasn't smart now, was it?'

I glanced up from my feet to see Robert Stark himself standing in front of me, adjusting his tuxedo's bow tie, looking like a cat someone had stroked the wrong way.

'What did you hope to accomplish in there, anyway?' he asked. He leaned over and snatched my bag away. Then he opened it and dumped the contents on the floor. My iPhone fell out with everything else. He leaned down and picked it up.

'I suppose you were recording all that,' he said. 'And thought you'd be slick and send it to someone. CNN? Well, nothing's going to come of that.'

With surprising force, he turned and hurled the phone as hard as he could towards the far end of the hallway. It smashed into a thousand pieces when it hit the wall.

I flinched. The phone exploding reminded me of the way my body must have looked to Christopher, exploding under the weight of that plasma TV.

226

No wonder he was so messed up now.

Except . . .

Except that everything he'd been insisting was true about Stark Enterprises?

It had actually been true all along. *He* wasn't the crazy one.

The rest of us were, for not believing him.

'And not just because you don't have the recording any more,' Robert Stark said, turning back to me. He was speaking absolutely without rancour. That was the scary part. He wasn't even mad at me. He didn't care. He was completely cool and collected. Except for the part about destroying my phone.

'Those kids you saw in there?' he went on. 'The ones my friends just purchased? They're going to meet with accidents during their travels soon. The same kind of accident your sister is going to have this evening on her way back from her trip to cheerleading camp if a word about any of this gets out. Do you understand? Because believe it or not, I have people who would happily bid on her, as well.'

I stared at him, my heart suddenly feeling frozen. How had he known about Frida and her cheerleading camp?

But of course.

Frida had a Stark Quark. Robert Stark himself had given her one.

I nodded slowly. I understood. I understood perfectly well.

'One word,' he said. 'One word tonight when the Stark Angel show goes live – even though you might want to get

227

cute and try something? – and your sister never makes it back tonight to that little apartment she and your parents share down at NYU. Understand?'

'I understand,' I unglued my tongue from the roof of my mouth to say. 'You don't want me to tell anyone that Robert Stark is providing his shareholders with healthy donor bodies so that they can have their brains transplanted into them and be young again. If I do that, my sister dies.'

Robert Stark just looked down at me. His expression wasn't as cool and collected as it had been before. Now one of his dark, slightly greying eyebrows was raised a little.

'You just don't get it, do you?' he asked. 'We gave you an incredible gift – the gift of beauty – something most women would kill for. Do you know how many women would die to be in your shoes right now? You have the world on a string. And all you can seem to think about is bringing me down.'

'What about Matthew?' I asked him. 'And Kim Su? Do you think they're going to appreciate your *killing* them so that those rich old folks in there can live their lives for them?'

'Oh, they're not going to be living their lives for them,' Robert Stark assured me. 'They'll be living their own lives, just with new bodies. Sure, they're going to have to explain to their friends about how they had more than a "little work done". But that will only bring more clients in to me. And it will be worth it, not to have to wake up every morning with creaking joints, to have to take nine different kinds of heart medication – believe me, it will be worth every penny to them.'

'But what about Matthew's family?' I asked. 'What if they see him one day, walking around with some other guy's brain in his head, and he doesn't recognize them?'

'These people live in very different social strata,' Robert Stark said with a sneer, 'from the donors' families. They'll never see one another. You can be quite sure of that.'

I shook my head at his snobbery.

'You're going to get caught,' I said. 'It's murder. You can't keep it a secret forever.'

'Why not?' he asked. And now both eyebrows were lifted. 'I've managed to so far. How long do you think we've been doing this, anyway?' That's when he laughed. 'Nikki – and to me, darlin', you'll always be Nikki – we've been doing this for years. *Years*. With this latest technology, we've been able to offer our clients a more diversified and unique selection of products over a broader range, while still increasing our profit margin.'

Then he looked at the security officer and said, 'Clean that up –' he meant the mess emptying my bag had made on the carpet – 'and escort her back downstairs and to the car that's waiting to take her and her friends to the studio. She's late enough for the Stark Angel show as it is.'

To me, he said, 'The least you could do is say thank you, you know.'

Now it was my turn to raise my eyebrows. 'For *what*?'

'I've given you the greatest gift anyone could ever give

another human being,' he said. 'A second chance at life. Only this time,' he added, 'you get to do it beautiful.'

I just stared at him. Honestly, what could you even say to that?

I thought about spitting in his face.

But it didn't seem like the right thing to do.

Especially since he'd just said he knew my little sister's travel plans.

Did I really want to see Frida up there on that screen, being bid on like some kind of Ming vase at Sotheby's . . .

. . . only to have her skull sawed open and her brain lifted out to have it replaced by that blue-veined lady's?

I took back the bag that the security guard handed to me – minus my iPhone. Meanwhile, Robert Stark was already walking away, back into his macabre auction room. He never once looked over his shoulder at me.

Not that I'd expected him to, I guess.

It was just as well that he didn't. He'd have seen the murderous look in my eye.

And he wouldn't have liked it. He wouldn't have liked it one bit.

The security guard took me by the arm and began guiding me down the stairs. Not the back stairs Brandon had shown me, but the wide main staircase I hadn't been able to get up before, because I'd lacked a phoenix bracelet.

The other security guard was still standing at the bottom of it. He looked confused to see me being escorted down by one of his colleagues, but lifted the velvet rope and let me pass.

'Here you go,' the security guard who had my arm said, when we reached the coat check, where Gabriel and Nikki were standing waiting for me, with Lulu, who had my coat. They were all three flanked by other security guards.

'Oh my God,' Lulu whispered, holding my faux-fur coat out for me. 'Are you all right? You look pale as a ghost. Are you going to throw up?'

'Let's just get out of here,' I whispered back. 'Where's Brandon?'

'I don't know,' Lulu said. 'He disappeared a while ago with your agent.'

'Great,' I said sarcastically. The security guards were hustling us down the red-carpeted steps and out to the limo that was idling outside. Paparazzi snapped dozens of photos as we ducked inside the car, all calling out, 'Nikki! Where's your boyfriend?' and, 'Nikki! Did you have a nice time at the party?'

Once we were inside the car and the doors had been closed, Nikki said, 'It's so weird how they do that.'

'Do what?' Gabriel asked.

'Yell *my* name. But they're talking to *her*.' She pointed at me.

'It must be weird,' Gabriel said, but his voice was softer than when he'd ever spoken to Nikki before, as if he was sympathizing with her for once. 'You must miss it.'

'That?' Nikki's eyes widened. 'Being screamed at by the paps? *You* probably like it. But I'm sort of starting to appreciate this anonymity thing for a change.' She looked over at me and demanded, 'So? Did you find out anything?'

'Oh,' I said, leaning back against the leather seat and taking a long, cleansing breath, 'I learned a lot.'

'Oh?' Gabriel asked. 'Care to enlighten us?'

I reached into my bra and pulled out my Stark-brand cellphone. 'You have no idea,' I said. 'Can I borrow your phone? This one is bugged. I need to call Christopher.'

Gabriel fumbled around in his pockets, while Nikki just rolled her eyes.

'No one will let me have a phone,' she said. 'I'm not to be trusted, evidently.'

'Oh, for Pete's sake,' Lulu said, opening her gold Prada clutch and tossing me her phone. 'But you better tell us what you heard up there . . .'

I was already dialling.

'Oh,' I said. 'You're going to find out, all right. Hello, Christopher?' He'd picked up on the first ring.

'Em?' he said, confused, because his caller ID had said Lulu's name.

'Yeah,' I said, 'it's me. Listen, you were right. About all of it. Project Phoenix is exactly what you said it was. And I've got proof. On film. The problem is, I got caught. By Robert Stark himself.'

'Jesus Christ, Em.' Christopher sounded like someone had punched him in the stomach. 'Are you all right?'

'I'm fine,' I said. 'So far. They think they destroyed the only proof. That's why I can't email it to you or anything . . . because if I do, it will totally send up a red flag. Because it's on a Stark-brand phone they've got bugged, so that means it's also on their mainframe, I'm pretty sure.

Which means Felix could probably pull it up . . . but then they might notice. So just in case, I'm going to get Lulu and Nikki to hand-deliver it to him right now.' I looked at the two of them questioningly. They both glanced at each other, then nodded eagerly. 'So can you be there in, like, twenty minutes, Christopher, and be ready for it?'

'I'm already at Felix's,' Christopher said. 'He's ready for whatever you've got. What are *you* going to be doing in the meantime?'

'The Stark Angel lingerie show,' I said, unable to keep the sarcasm from my voice. 'Live.'

'We're already tuned in to Channel Seven,' I heard Felix yell in the background. 'All ten monitors! High def!'

I heard a crunching sound, then a cry of pain. I assumed Christopher had hit his cousin.

'Never mind him,' Christopher said. 'If you don't want us to be watching, Em, we won't watch. Besides, it sounds like we're going to be pretty busy.'

'No,' I said. I had to be mature about this, I realized. It was just a body. My body.

And with any luck, Christopher was going to be seeing it naked some day anyway.

'You can watch, if you want. Just do this other thing first. Only . . . whatever you're going to do with it,' I said, trying to control the shaking in my voice, 'can you wait until Frida's plane lands, and she gets home safe? Because Robert Stark said –' Suddenly I was holding back a sob.

'What, Em?' Christopher asked. He sounded as worried as I felt. 'What did Robert Stark say?'

The tender concern in his voice only made it harder to speak. I couldn't believe this was the same Christopher I'd been arguing with only an hour or so ago.

'He said if anything about Project Phoenix gets out,' I said, trying to keep from crying, 'he'll . . . he'll . . .'

'Don't say another word,' Christopher said. 'I know what to do.'

'But –' How could he know? I hadn't told him what Robert Stark had said he'd do. Something so awful, I couldn't even think about it.

'Em,' Christopher said. His voice was warm. Warm with love for me. For *me*. 'I know. Don't worry. Consider it done. Frida will be fine. We've got it handled here, OK? We're professionals.'

'But –' I said again. Now I couldn't help smiling a little. The idea of Christopher and his cousin as professionals was ludicrous – 'one of you is wearing an ankle bracelet.'

And one of you is an arch-villain, with fingerless gloves and a dark streak a mile wide.

'She's going to be all right,' Christopher reassured me. 'You did your part. Tell Nikki and Lulu to get here with that cellphone. And I'll do what I have to do. And, Em?'

'Yes?' I asked in a shaking voice.

'I'm really proud of you,' he said. 'Mad as hell at you, for putting yourself in danger. But really, really proud.'

'Yeah,' I said. Now the tears were coming.

But they were tears of happiness.

'Me too,' I said.

Twenty

It was chaos at the Stark Angel lingerie show. For one thing, Ryan Seacrest was there to emcee it. He hadn't been there for the two dress rehearsals earlier in the month because . . . well, he was Ryan Seacrest. He was a busy man.

For another thing, Gabriel and I were more than two hours late for our call time. That hadn't caused too much anxiety on the part of Alessandro, the stage director. He basically wanted to kill us.

'Dressing rooms for make-up and costumes,' he yelled when he saw me and Gabriel slinking in through the stage door. 'Now.'

I figured if Alessandro had his way, we'd never be asked to participate in another Stark production ever again.

Then again, after tonight, if things went the way I hoped they would, there wouldn't be any more Stark productions. Not ever again.

Jerri, the make-up artist, came darting in as I was wiggling out of my party dress, and the costume ladies were fretting about what to do about the indentations the seams of my tights had left on my belly. Seriously. These are the things we underwear models have to worry about.

'No worries,' Jerri said. 'I'll airbrush it. No one will see a thing.'

Jerri had a little machine that sprayed out liquid foundation the way self-tanning machines airbrushed bronzer on people. It was basically the same principle, only Jerri planned on spraying the foundation over my entire body, instead of just my face . . .

. . . which was what she did for most of her clients, a lot of whom were male sportscasters.

'They have to look good too,' she explained. 'Now that everyone has high-def TVs. You can't have any blemishes or anything. I do their hands too, for when they're holding the microphones, interviewing people. If you don't spray, you don't play.'

It was amazing. Here I'd been thinking Jessica Biel and all those movie stars had perfect bodies, when it wasn't even true. *Everything* on TV was fake.

Make that everything on TV, in magazines and in the movies too. No wonder those Stark shareholders felt like they needed to murder young people and steal their bodies.

'Oh, sure,' Jerri said as I stood there in my bra and panties, feeling the cold spray go all over my body. 'All the actresses do it for their nude scenes. They're all sprayed. It covers your cellulite too. Not that you have cellulite. Oh, wait. Yes, sorry. Even Nikki Howard! Ha, wait till I tell my sister. She thinks you're perfect. Not that you aren't –' Jerri popped her head around to look up at me. 'You know, you almost are.'

I smiled down at her queasily. 'It's OK. Can I borrow your cellphone?' I asked. 'I need to make a call. It's local.'

'Oh, go ahead, darling,' Jerri said. 'Make as many as you want. I'm getting holiday pay for this, it being New Year's Eve and all.'

She gave me her phone, and I quickly dialled my parents' number. My mom picked up after the second ring.

'Hello?' she asked curiously, not recognizing the number on the caller ID.

'Hi, Mom,' I said. 'It's me.' I didn't say it's me, Em, because Jerri was there. 'I was wondering . . . do you know if Frida made it to her plane all right?'

'Well, of course she did,' Mom said. 'She called me from the runway three hours ago. She should be landing at LaGuardia any minute. The girls are all sharing cabs back into the city. Why do you ask?'

'I just haven't heard from her in a while,' I said, trying to sound casual. 'That's all. Do you think you could have her call me the minute she walks in the door?'

'Of course,' Mom said. 'But aren't you a bit busy? I thought you were doing that, er, lingerie show tonight, on Channel Seven.'

Damn. I was kind of hoping that Mom had forgotten about that.

'I am,' I said stiffly. 'But that doesn't mean I don't worry about my little sister.'

'Well,' Mom said, 'I'll be sure to have her call you.'

Belatedly, I remembered I didn't have a cellphone. One was smashed to bits on the carpet in Robert Stark's upstairs hallway. And the other was on its way to Felix's basement in a cab with Lulu and Nikki. Hopefully it was there by now.

'Actually,' I said, thinking fast, 'could you have her call Lulu? My cell is messed up.' I gave her the number. 'It'll be better, anyway, in case I'm onstage.'

'All right,' Mom said. In typical Mom style, however, she didn't sound like she thought it was all right. 'Listen, honey, while I have you on the phone . . . about yesterday.'

'Yeah,' I said. I was conscious that Jerri was working her way up towards my head with the spray gun. 'I'm really sorry—'

'No,' Mom said. '*I'm* sorry. I realize now that when you asked me if you were pretty – well, that's such a loaded question, honey. I mean, for me. I don't want you girls to judge one another by your looks—'

'Mom,' I said. I couldn't believe we were even having this conversation. My boss had just threatened to kill my little sister if I exposed the fact that he was basically a murdering sociopath.

And if things went the way I hoped they did, I was just about to do exactly that.

And my mom wanted to have bonding time over the phone.

'I really don't have time for this. I just wanted to check on Frida.'

'But this is important,' Mom went on. 'I realize that maybe, at your school, that's what all girls do. Judge one another by their looks.'

238

'Not just at school, Mom,' I said. 'Try all of contemporary Western society.'

Hello, Mom? This is America. Welcome. This is called a McDonald's. Can you say that word? Mc-Don-ald's. They serve cheeseburgers here. And fries. Can you say the word *fries*?

'I know,' Mom went on. She sounded like she was practically crying. 'And it's just so wrong. I don't *want* you girls to judge yourselves that way. There's so much more to you than that. You're both just so amazing, you and Frida, so smart and strong and creative. I wanted to emphasize *that* part of you. But every time you turn on the television, what do you see? Well, skinny girls with big boobs, in tight trousers with shirts cut down to their belly buttons. And every time I'd take the two of you to the store, you'd both want exactly what those girls – like Nikki Howard – was wearing. *You* eventually grew out of it, but Frida – it's like a mother can't win. And my mother said I was exactly the same way, and that's why she stopped telling me I was pretty – that I let it go straight to my head when I was growing up . . .'

This was news to me. Grandma? Grandma always told Frida and me that we were pretty. So much so that it really didn't mean anything. Of course we were pretty. We were her granddaughters. It doesn't mean anything when your grandmother tells you that you're pretty.

But Mom? Mom never said we were pretty, or looked good. It was always, 'Your mind is all that matters!'

And of course that's true.

But it would have been nice to have heard our hair looked good, once in a while.

And now that I knew Mom had liked girly clothes? Mom, who always dressed so sensibly in grey suits and low-heeled shoes? Grandma had had to stop telling Mom she was pretty because she got so conceited about it?

This was fantastic stuff. I couldn't wait to tell Frida.

If I ever saw her again.

'And I guess,' Mom went on – she was practically babbling – 'I just thought if I followed her lead, you two would turn out like me . . . more interested in things academic than . . . well . . .'

What? What had Mom been like as a girl? I was dying to find out.

But by then Jerri had gotten to my head with the spray blower.

'Look, Mom,' I said. 'I have to go get ready for the show. I understand everything you're saying. I know it's all fake. No one knows that more than me. But it's still nice to hear your mom say you're pretty once in a while, you know? Anyway, don't worry about me, OK? Everything's going to be fine.' This was a boldfaced lie. I had absolutely no way of knowing this. But what else was I going to say? Look, Mom, because of my jackassery, my boss may be about to kill your youngest daughter? 'Just call Lulu as soon as Frida gets in.'

'I will,' Mom said. She hesitated, then said, 'I love you, Em. In case that wasn't clear. No matter what you look like. Or what you wear.'

240

This brought tears to my eyes. Because I so didn't deserve it.

'Thanks, Mom,' I said. 'Me too.'

I hung up and handed the phone back to Jerri.

'Moms,' I said to her, rolling my eyes in an effort not to burst into tears.

'Tell me about it,' Jerri said, tucking her phone back into her pocket. 'Mine smokes a pack of Camel Lights a day. Can I get her to stop? No way. Close your eyes now, hon, I'm gonna do your face.'

Forty-five minutes later – which Jerri claimed was a speed record for her – I was out of hair and make-up and tucked into the diamond bra and panties, my wings attached and floating behind me. I looked, when I saw myself in the mirror, like a cross between an angel and . . . well, a girl wearing a diamond bikini.

Oh, well. Hopefully Mom wouldn't be watching.

I strode in my platform heels towards the sound stage as Jerri trotted alongside me, blotting on the last dab of lipgloss.

'There you are.' Rebecca appeared as if from nowhere, still in her black evening gown. 'I heard you were late. What did I warn you about? Did I tell you not to be late? Did you eat anything? I can see your hip bones. I know you didn't eat anything. If you faint on me, Nikki, I swear to God . . .'

'I'm not going to faint,' I assured her. 'Is Brandon here with you? Because I really need to talk to him.'

'As a matter of fact, he is,' Rebecca said, looking

demure. Or as demure as it was possible for Rebecca to look, which wasn't very. 'You might as well know, we're an item now. And I know there's a bit of an age difference, but honestly, I think he could use a mature woman in his life. No offence, Nikki, but you haven't exactly been the most steadying influence on him. And he needs stability.'

'I really don't care about that,' I said. 'You can have him. That isn't what I want to talk to him about. It's about his dad, actually.'

'His dad?' Rebecca shrugged. 'Not exactly his favourite topic. But it's your funeral.' She pulled her BlackBerry from her Chanel bag and began banging on the keyboard. 'You sure you want to get into this now, right before the show? Can't it wait? You're onstage in five. And don't talk to Ryan, all right, darling? All the girls are talking to Ryan, and it's getting on his nerves.'

I looked up and down the hall. There were models in Stark-brand underwear and wings everywhere. I saw Kelley, my friend from the dress rehearsal, wave her cellphone at me and set off her ringtone. It played the *Journeyquest* Dragon Battle Cry. Kelley laughed and pointed at me, then gave me the thumbs up. I smiled at her like, *Ha! That's funny.*

But mainly I was thinking how much I wanted to throw up.

'I won't,' I said.

Rebecca shrugged and kept banging on the keyboard.

What was Robert Stark doing right now? I wondered. Was he trying to kill my sister?

And what about Christopher? Had Lulu and Nikki gotten him my cellphone? I felt so vulnerable not knowing what was going on.

I wasn't the only one. Gabriel stepped out of his dressing room in full make-up and his tux. He was with his band – all of whom were good-looking enough to cause a ripple of excitement to pass through the other models, Ryan Seacrest suddenly forgotten.

But Gabriel ignored it. When he saw me, in fact, he said to the rest of his guys, 'Hey. I'll be right there,' and fell back to whisper to me, 'So? Have you heard anything?'

I shook my head. 'Nothing. You?'

He shook his head. 'I'm sure it will be fine.'

'Or,' I said, 'we'll walk out on to the stage and a boom will fall on us, killing us both instantly, courtesy of Robert Stark.'

'It's always good,' Gabriel said, tugging on his lapels, 'to think positive.'

'Brandon will meet you after the show,' Rebecca announced, reading from the screen of her BlackBerry.

'But I really need to talk to him now,' I said, unable to keep the dismay from my voice.

'Well,' Rebecca shrugged, 'what do you want me to do? The man says he's busy. He'll meet you upstairs in the Stark Sky Bar, he says. There'll be champagne for all of us to toast in the New Year. It's where we're all going to watch the Times Square ball drop. There's a perfect view from there—'

'Places!' Alessandro came scurrying down the hallway,

clapping his hands. 'All of you. Backstage, now! What are you dilly-dallying for? Are you trying to give me a heart attack? The show's started! We're live! No more talking once you get through the soundproof door. Go! GO!'

I reached instinctively for Gabriel's hand. My own was ice-cold. But his felt warm . . . just like his gaze when it met mine.

'It's going to be all right,' he assured me with a smile. 'You did the right thing.'

'Did I?' I asked. I wished I could believe him. In theory, I did.

But Frida! My own sister! How could I have been so stupid?

'Oh, God,' Rebecca said, noticing our clenched hands. 'What is going on here? Are you two an item? This is perfect. Can I announce it to the press? Do you have any idea what this is going to do for your sales numbers, Gabriel? You're already in the stratosphere, but this, honey, we're talking Mars—'

By this time, I was going through the studio doors, and all the cameramen and sound engineers were shushing Rebecca to be quiet.

Still, she stood behind the doors, even as they were closing, whisper-yelling, 'You can't hide things from me, Nikki! You can't run away! I know all your secrets!'

If only she knew.

Inside the backstage space of the studio, where we were all gathered to wait our turn onstage, it was so quiet I could almost hear my own heartbeat. It was the front of the studio, where the stage was, where it was another matter entirely. There, it was thunderously loud. The live audience was screaming with appreciation for Ryan and the models who were already strutting out on to the stage, doing their catwalk up and down the runway, showing off their different bra-and-panty sets.

Gabriel and his band had ducked back behind the revolving set, to reappear on-stage just as soon as it was their cue to begin playing Gabriel's number-one hit song 'Nikki'.

This wasn't going to happen until the second-to-last commercial break. As I stood there waiting for my musical cue, I noticed Veronica, the model who'd hated me so much — because she thought I'd been emailing her boyfriend Justin, when actually, that had been the real Nikki — standing in front of me. She was pointedly ignoring me.

Because I needed something to take my mind off the fact that my sister, at that very moment, might be dying, I tapped her on the shoulder.

'Hi,' I said. 'I was just wondering. Did the emails stop?'

Veronica looked round. Her eyes grew huge when she saw me.

'We — we're not supposed to be talking,' she stammered.

'I know,' I said. 'But did they?'

'Yes,' she said, and turned back towards the show, nibbling on a press-on nail.

Ha. Because Nikki had better things to do these days.

Like torture Gabriel Luna.

A few minutes later, Veronica got her cue to walk – and she sashayed out on to the stage. And then I heard it.

'Nikki, oh, Nikki . . . the thing of it is, girl . . . in spite of it all . . . I really do think . . . I love you.'

My cue.

For a second, my heart hammering, I hesitated. I thought I was going to throw up. What was I doing? Who *was* I? Was I, Em Watts, the girl who wouldn't even shower in front of other girls during PE, really going to walk out on to that runway, in front of millions – maybe even a billion – of television viewers, not to mention however many people were in the live audience, wearing nothing but a pair of panties, a bra, a set of wings and a lot of body spray?

'It's not the way that you walk, girl . . . the way that you smile or the way that you look . . .'

On the other hand . . .

. . . if things went the way they were supposed to, and Christopher did what he said he was going to, because of me, Robert Stark, the fourth-richest man in the world, was going down tonight. What had happened to me was never going to happen to another person again.

And there might never even be another Stark Angel lingerie show ever again.

That would certainly make my mom happy.

'It's just the way you move me . . . the way that you move me . . . that makes me say, Nikki, oh, Nikki . . . the thing of it is, girl . . . in spite of it all . . . I really do think . . . I love you.'

'Nikki,' Alessandro whispered from somewhere in the darkness behind me, 'GO!'

I walked out into the blinding lights of the stage, moving my hips in time to the music, trying to follow the markings on the runway and step exactly where they'd told me to step and not run into Ryan Seacrest.

The reflections from the diamonds on my bra were making me crazy. I could hardly see where I was going. If something were to come loose from the ceiling overhead and tumble down, smacking me in the head, I would never know it. I was completely blind.

Who would wear one of these stupid things in real life? And *why*?

'Nikki, oh, Nikki . . . The thing of it is, girl . . . in spite of it all . . . I really do think . . . I love you.'

At least I had Gabriel's voice to guide me. The weird thing was, he actually sounded sincere.

But isn't that what musicians do? Like models and actresses, they make you believe what they're telling you.

Unless . . . he really did love Nikki. Not me. But the real Nikki.

Wouldn't that be funny? That as much as the two of them fought, they actually loved each other? They certainly seemed to be at each other's throat enough.

But wasn't that true of me and Christopher? We were always fighting. Always!

But then, when it came down to it, we really loved each other. At least, I really loved Christopher.

I hoped he really loved me. I thought I'd heard his

love for me on the phone when we'd spoken just now. I'd know for sure the next time I saw him . . . whether or not he really loved me. I'd be able to see it in his eyes. I was sure of it. We may not have had the easiest of romances, but it was one, I felt sure, that was going to last forever.

If Nikki and Gabriel fell in love, it would kill my sister, Frida.

Oh, God. *Frida. Why did I have to think about Frida?*

'It's not the way that you walk, girl . . . the way that you smile or the way that you look . . .'

'Ah, look at her, ladies and gentlemen,' Ryan Seacrest was saying. 'The number-one supermodel in the world, Stark's own Nikki Howard. She's wearing over a million dollars' worth of diamonds, ladies and gentlemen. I don't know when I've ever seen anything quite so beautiful. Except possibly for the low, low interest I'm receiving on my Stark credit card. Apply now for exclusive card-member-only sales and special financing offers throughout the year . . .'

Getting to the end of the runway, I looked out into the screaming, cheering audience and saw him. Robert Stark. Just sitting there, looking up at me.

Grinning. Grinning the way only someone who knows he's won can smile.

Why was he grinning like that? What had he done?

Gotten away with murder, that's what.

Except he hadn't.

Not yet. Not if I could help it.

Frida, my heart was crying, the entire time I was out there. *Please let Frida be OK.*

I made it off the runway without tripping or anything falling down on to my head. Only my heart hammering in my throat.

And no one, I was certain, had even been able to tell that much.

Because I was a professional now.

I was Nikki Howard.

It wasn't until I got to the Stark Sky Bar half an hour later – the diamond bra and panties handed back over to the security guards who'd been assigned to guard them, the angel wings put away and my street clothes put back on – that all hell broke loose.

Twenty-one

The Sky Bar, which was a huge circular restaurant at the top of the Stark Building, the walls made of floor-to-ceiling windows all the way around so that you had an unimpeded view of the sparkling lights – or in this case the crowds at Times Square and the New Year's ball drop – was crowded. Ryan Seacrest was there, along with his agent and his manager, enjoying some Dom Pérignon. I spied Rebecca there as well, hanging on to Brandon like they were attached at the hip – gross – and Gabriel and his band.

Everywhere else I looked were celebrities from the party at Robert Stark's house, as well as the shareholders I'd met.

The same ones who'd been bidding on 'donors' for their brain transplants. Of course, they didn't know that I'd filmed their little auction and smuggled that film out and that two computer geniuses were (hopefully) at this very moment doing whatever it is those kind of people do with that kind of thing.

What *were* they going to do with it? I wondered.

'Hey,' Gabriel said, coming up to me with a glass of sparkling water a few minutes after I'd walked in. He was a welcome sight. I'd been surrounded by Stark shareholders, wanting to chat with me some more.

I knew what they really wanted, of course. To talk to the Project Phoenix prototype, a living, breathing, actual brain-transplant recipient. They didn't say as much, but it was totally obvious. They were dying to know what it was like to die . . . and then be resurrected as someone totally hot.

If they'd come right out and just asked, I could have told them: it was hell. And heaven. At the same time.

Would I do it again?

Not a chance.

'Glad we're not down there,' Gabriel said, indicating one of the many flat-screen TVs that hung from the ceiling, showing close-ups of Anderson Cooper reporting live on the impending ball drop from Times Square. It was so cold, you could see Anderson's breath.

'Me too,' I said.

'Have you heard anything?' Gabriel wanted to know. He wasn't talking about the ball drop.

'I don't have a phone,' I reminded him.

'Right,' he said, wincing. 'Sorry, I forgot. I haven't heard anything either.' His gaze drifted towards Robert Stark, who was laughing at something Rush Limbaugh had said, and slapping him on the back.

'Nikki!' Robert Stark cried, having spotted me over Rush's shoulder.

I winced. Brandon's dad was holding an arm out, beckoning for me to come over, a big smile on his face. Surrounded by adorers, he was holding court. Everyone was smiling and holding champagne, clearly enjoying themselves.

And, of course, there was a bunch of photographers there, itching to take some publicity pictures for tomorrow's papers.

'Oh no,' I said under my breath. Gabriel looked sympathetic.

'Here she is, the star of the evening,' Robert Stark called, waving to me again to come over. 'Nikki Howard, ladies and gentlemen. Wasn't she lovely this evening? Didn't she look beautiful in all those diamonds?'

I had no choice but to go over to him. What else could I do? I tried to plaster the nicest smile I could on to my face. I knew what was going on.

And I knew the role I had to play . . . at least until I found out whether or not Frida was safe: Robert Stark was showing me off. I was his finest product.

I was the original phoenix.

When I got to his side, Brandon's dad slipped his arm around me. It was like being embraced by a python.

'Such a great girl,' Robert Stark said, hugging me to him. 'So glad to have her in the Stark family.'

I kept the smile plastered on my face. Flashes went off. The photographers said encouraging things like, 'Great! That's just great, Nikki, Mr Stark. Over here, now. Sir, could you put your chin up? Chin down now. Nikki, look over here. Great. Fabulous. You two look great together. Thanks so much.'

But the whole time, all I could think about was how much I wanted to throw up.

When the purple splotches from the flashes faded, out

of the corner of my eye I thought I saw some people coming into the restaurant. I had to do a double take, not sure I believed my eyes, before I registered who they really were . . .

Lulu, in her outlandish black cocktail dress with its bright red crinoline, sassily striding up to the bar and demanding a cocktail, pulling Steven Howard – *Steven Howard* – in her wake . . .

Steven's sister, Nikki, with her jet-black hair and matching black corset, sashaying up to the bar behind her brother like she owned the place . . .

And Christopher – *my* Christopher – escorting a very young-looking girl with curly hair, who was peering all around the place with her mouth slightly ajar in the manner of someone who seemed *way* too excited to be there . . .

Frida. *My sister, Frida.*

I'm pretty sure some sick *did* come up into my mouth when I saw that. Frida? They'd brought *Frida* here? Were they crazy? Hadn't they registered the part where I'd told them Robert Stark had threatened to *kill* Frida?

'Um,' I said, ducking out from beneath Robert Stark's arm, 'will you excuse me?'

'Of course,' he said, looking a bit confused as I darted away.

I raced towards Frida until I was able to grab her by both arms and spin her round – she'd been pressed up against one of the vast windows, looking down over Times Square at the crowd below.

'Frida,' I cried frantically. 'You're all right?'

'I'm great,' she said, pushing away some of the hair I'd caused to fall into her eyes by the violence of my gesture. 'What do you think? Those guys came and got me. Em, what's going on? No one will tell me. Is everything OK? And what happened to Nikki? She's all hot now. Also, have you seen the way Gabriel looks at her? It's not fair, I saw him first –'

I hugged her to me.

'Never mind about Gabriel,' I said into her hair. 'He's too old for you anyway.'

'What?' Frida said. She was hugging me back, but obviously had other concerns. 'He's only, like, eight years older. That's nothing. Edward Cullen was, like, a hundred years older than Bella—'

'Seriously.' I pulled her away from me and looked down into her eyes. My own were filled with tears. 'There will be lots of boys your own age who are going to be crazy for you. So just shut up.'

Christopher had come over, holding two glasses of soda. 'Problems, ladies?' he asked lightly.

'None at all,' I said, turning my tear-filled gaze towards him. 'Is everything—'

'Oh,' he said, handing one of the glasses to Frida. 'It's all good. Look up.'

'Up?' I looked up, not knowing what he was talking about. But all I saw were the flat-screen TVs hanging overhead.

'That's right,' Christopher said. 'Keep watching. Hey, has anyone talked to Brandon?'

'Brandon?' I took the sparkling soda he offered me. I'd lost the one Gabriel had given me a while ago. 'Why?'

'Because he just might want to prepare himself for—'

That was when all the television screens in the room started showing that the Times Square ball was beginning to drop. And everyone began hurrying towards the windows to see it for themselves.

'Ten,' everyone began to chant. 'Nine . . .'

Everyone, that is, except for Nikki – the *real* Nikki. She walked right up to Robert Stark with a great big smile plastered across her bright-red-lipsticked mouth.

'Hello again,' she said, grinning at Robert Stark.

He seemed a bit startled to be interrupted while counting down to New Year. But not unpleasantly so, because Nikki was one hot little number.

'Well, hello there,' he said, grinning back at her. 'Miss, er . . . Prince, is it?'

'That's right,' Nikki said. 'Good memory. But that's not actually my real name.'

And she lifted the remote she'd snagged from the bar and turned up the sound on all the TVs.

'Five,' everyone was screaming. 'Four . . .'

'It's not?' Robert Stark asked, seemingly only interested for politeness's sake. 'What is it then?'

'Nikki Howard,' she said. 'You should have just paid up, Robert.' Then she cocked her head to look at him a little bit harder. 'On second thoughts . . . I should have just turned you in in the first place.'

'Happy New Year!' everyone screamed.

Over by the bar, I saw Lulu throw her arms around Steven and kiss him. Rebecca and Brandon had already wrapped themselves into such a tight clench I had to look away a little shocked. Even Nikki scampered off from a confused-looking Robert Stark to go up to Gabriel Luna, who was hugging his band mates, pull him away by his shirt front and plant a huge kiss right on his lips . . . much to the dismay of Frida, who let out a faint whimper at the sight.

Christopher, meanwhile, was grinning down at me. He looked more devilish than boyfriend-like. I was so alarmed by everything that had just happened in the past five minutes, I took a step away from him. I really wasn't sure how much more I could take.

'Oh,' I said, holding up both hands to ward him off, my heart having begun to stutter. 'No . . .'

But it was too late. He'd already caught me around the waist and hauled me back towards him, crushing my body to his and then dropping his mouth over mine.

I think I let out a whimper that was not unlike Frida's – only for different reasons, of course – before I found myself melting, as always, at the touch of his lips. Why couldn't I resist him? It was so infuriating! Was this how it was always going to be between us? We were always going to be making each other mad, then kiss and everything would be fine . . . *more* than fine, actually?

Christopher had his arms around me, seeming to be in no hurry to finish our New Year's kiss. Not that I minded.

Who knows how long we would have stood there

kissing (and in front of poor Frida! I did feel badly about that) if right then every single television in the room hadn't flashed the same orange message: *Breaking News*, and a news anchor hadn't come on to say urgently, 'We're interrupting our New Year's Eve coverage to inform you of a breaking story out of New York City concerning Robert Stark, the entrepreneur who founded Stark Enterprises, known worldwide for its chain of large discount department stores.'

A ripple of excited chatter went through the Stark Sky Bar when this announcement was made. Rebecca and Brandon actually disattached themselves long enough to pay attention to what was going on. The Stark shareholders all stood looking up at the television screens in confusion, some of them weaving on their feet a little, because they'd had so much to drink.

Robert Stark stood absolutely still, staring in shock at what he was seeing.

I reached for Christopher's fingers with one hand and Frida's with the other. Frida glanced at me and asked in a whisper, 'Em. What is this?

'Just watch,' I whispered back. I'd be lying if I said my heart wasn't hammering a little though.

'This evening,' the news anchor went on solemnly, 'CNN has exclusively obtained video – video CNN can verify is authentic – which proves that Stark Enterprise shareholders, including Robert Stark himself, have been knowingly participating in a highly experimental surgery known as a full-body transplant –'

Somewhere in the room, a woman screamed and dropped a glass, which smashed to the floor.

'– in a secret laboratory in Manhattan called the Stark Institute for Neurology and Neurosurgery. Here's CNN chief medical correspondent, Doctor Sanjay Gupta, to explain this controversial – not to mention illegal – procedure.'

'Thank you, Wolf,' a new voice said. 'In a full-body transplant, a patient's brain is completely removed from his or her body and placed into a new body, usually from a donor who has been declared brain-dead. In the case of something the corporation was calling Project Phoenix, however, living donors were being handpicked from—'

'What is this?' Robert Stark thundered, whirling round to glare at the rest of us. 'What is this? Turn it off. Did you hear me? I said turn it off!'

No one moved to turn the televisions off, even though I was pretty sure the bartenders had the remote controls. In fact, I saw Nikki lift one of the remotes and deliberately turn the volume up.

'– in this exclusive video, representatives from the corporation can be seen auctioning off the profiles of young people who, it is alleged, will be placed into a vegetative state at a later date so their bodies can be harvested for the highest bidder, to have their brains transplanted into them when –'

The footage I'd shot at the auction began to play. I have to say, that Stark-brand cellphone had done a pretty good job of capturing what I'd wanted it to. The images of Kim

Su, the Frenchwoman presenting her and the shareholders bidding on her were clear as day. You couldn't really see their faces, but you got the gist of what was going on really well.

And the sound, after I'd had to slide the cellphone into my bra to hide it?

Still crystal clear.

'*You*,' Robert Stark raged, whirling round to face me as the recording of him – recognizably the deep voice of Robert Stark – was saying, '*They'll be living their own lives, just with new bodies . . . And it will be worth it, not to have to wake up every morning with creaking joints, to have to take nine different kinds of heart medication – believe me, it will be worth every penny to them . . .*'

I stumbled back a step. He looked angry enough to lift me up and throw me bodily out one of the plate-glass windows that were all around us, like in one of the *Die Hard* movies. I totally wouldn't have put it past him.

I wasn't the only one who noticed either. Christopher moved in front of me, placing himself as a human shield between me and the billionaire who wanted to kill me.

If that wasn't love, I don't know what is.

'*You*,' Robert Stark growled again, completely ignoring Christopher. '*You* did this! I destroyed that phone! How is this even possible?'

On the television screen, our voices went on – his and mine, with a written transcript provided for the viewer, in case anyone couldn't understand what we were saying on the tape.

'*You're going to get caught. It's murder. You can't keep it a secret forever.*'

Did I really sound like that?

No. Of course I didn't.

But Nikki did.

'*I've managed to so far. How long do you think we've been doing this, anyway? We've been doing this for years.* Years. *With this latest technology, we've been able to offer our clients a more diversified and unique selection of products over a broader range, while still increasing our profit margin.*'

Profit margin. That's all it had ever been about for Robert Stark.

And that's what was about to destroy him.

'You destroyed my iPhone,' I said to Robert Stark in the steadiest voice I could summon, speaking from around Christopher's broad shoulders. 'But you didn't find my Stark-brand phone.'

'The one you've been bugging all this time,' Christopher added. 'All that film and audio was up on your own mainframe. We just transferred it over to CNN. Wolf Blitzer has it all now. And after this, the world.'

Robert Stark stared at us like we'd just told him Mariah Carey was really a man.

'Stark!' one of red-faced shareholders shouted. 'You told us this would never get out! You swore!'

'– two teen hackers in the New York City area who discovered that the new Stark Quarks actually contain spyware that enables the corporate giant to upload all the users' data to their mainframe,' Wolf Blitzer went on, 'and sent us this recording of Robert Stark and super-model Nikki Howard at a Project Phoenix auction this evening . . .'

The Stark shareholders, I noticed, were suddenly beginning to head for the doors of the Sky Bar, their expressions panic-stricken.

But it was going to be difficult for them to leave.

Because just then the doors were thrown open, and dozens of New York's finest, in their dark blue uniforms, began to stream in, their gold badges gleaming under the disco lights.

'Everybody stay where you are,' one of them said, using a megaphone to be heard over the sudden cacophony of shocked partygoers. 'Nobody's going anywhere.'

'I need my blood-pressure medicine,' the husband of the lady with the sparkles at the bottom of her dress screamed.

'We'll make sure we get it for you,' a cop assured him, 'over at Rikers.'

'Is this really happening?' Nikki came over to ask me.

'I think it is,' I said, feeling as dazed as she felt.

Over by the bar, Brandon, finally realizing this was his big moment, hurried to face the photographers who'd been taking the publicity photos of me and his dad earlier.

'In light of the recent discoveries about my father,' he said, suddenly sounding as if he hadn't had a single thing to drink all night, 'with whom my relationship has always been troubled, I'd just like to say that I'll be taking over the day-to-day operations of Stark Enterprises for the foreseeable future, and that I'll be doing my best to make Stark a greener, more earth-friendly corporation. I'll definitely be thinking of the employees, who for so long have laboured without a union or proper health care. I'll be working to correct that, as well as the impression Stark may have given that it doesn't care about the small-business owner –'

But none of the reporters was listening. They were only interested in what was happening in the centre of the room.

'Robert Stark?' asked a police captain, striding up to Brandon's dad and showing him his badge. 'We'd like to ask you a few questions downtown, if you don't mind.'

'Not without my lawyer.' Robert Stark bristled.

'I wouldn't dream of it,' the police captain said politely.

That's when he handcuffed Robert Stark and led him away.

Twenty-two

It was months before it all settled down.

And even then, I couldn't go anywhere without some-one wanting to shove a microphone into my face to ask me about it.

I wasn't allowed to discuss it though, because of the tes-timony I was scheduled to give against Robert Stark – and all the Stark shareholders who'd been at the auction the night of the Project Phoenix auction, and Dr Holcombe and, yes, Dr Higgins too – at the grand jury.

I wasn't the only one testifying of course. Because of what we'd done, Dr Fong was able to come out of hiding and tell what he knew about the goings-on at the Stark Institute for Neurology and Neurosurgery too, in exchange for immunity from prosecution.

Some of the surgeries, he maintained, had been medically necessary to save the life of the patient, and completely above board.

But a lot of them . . .

Well, let's just say, not so much.

The families of some of those 'donor bodies' had come forward to testify as well. According to the legal experts I saw occasionally on the news, this wasn't something Robert Stark was going to be able to wiggle his way out of. This was multiple counts of murder, attempted murder and, in Nikki's case, assault with a deadly weapon (a scalpel). Robert Stark, formerly one of the world's most powerful men, was going to go away for a long time.

A long, long time.

Dr Fong wasn't the only one who was safe now. Nikki, Steven and Mrs Howard were safe too, because of what we'd done, and able to go back to their normal lives.

Except, of course, that for some of them this wasn't so simple.

Mrs Howard was excited and eager to go back to Gasper and her dog-grooming business.

I was sorry to see her go. I'd really grown to think of her as a second mother.

But Gasper was the place she knew and loved, and where all her best friends were. And Harry and Winston didn't like being cooped up in tiny New York apartments. They missed having a yard to play in.

I went with her to the airport and hugged her goodbye. It was sad, but it was better for everyone all round, especially Mrs Howard. Too much togetherness with her daughter had been giving her chronic migraines, and was perhaps too much for anyone to put with, long-term . . .

. . . including Steven, since he went back to his naval unit. He sort of had to. I guess it had something to do with the fact that he'd signed up to be on this submarine and couldn't exactly just leave, especially now that he'd found his sister, which was the only reason they'd let him off in the first place.

Lulu was devastated. I had to order her a banana split every day for almost a week before she started to look on the bright side.

'At least,' she pointed out, 'he can't cheat on me. There aren't any girls on his sub.'

In the meantime, she says she's really and truly going to finish her album. She's already finished a song based on their (daily) emails to each other called 'Hot Love Down Under (the Sea)'.

I don't know. I think it's got real potential. I'm not the only one. She was the first artist to be signed on the Stark label under Brandon's new management as CEO.

He hasn't actually done a bad job of being in charge now that his dad's in jail (without bail). Of course, Brandon has a lot of talented people to help him (not the least of which is Rebecca, from whom he's seemed to become inseparable. In fact, she's quit the agenting business. But that's all right. Really it is. I like waking up to find only people I've invited over in my bedroom).

One of the first things Brandon did upon taking over Stark Enterprises was hire Felix and Christopher to come up with a free software patch for all the people who purchased the Stark Quarks to download, so they could fix the pesky little spyware problem. This was a far better strategic move than recalling all the PCs (which was what a lot of people advised him to do), and went a long way towards improving consumer confidence in Stark after everything his father had done to ruin the company. Because of the free patch and all the publicity the case is getting, the Stark Quarks are actually the highest-selling PCs of all time.

Which just goes to show: there's no such thing as bad publicity.

Felix and Christopher did such a good job coming up with the patch solution so quickly (not to mention bringing down his dad as CEO) that Brandon hired them as heads of Stark's IT department, since whoever was running it before sucked so badly that a couple of teenagers could break into the mainframe and basically run rampant through their entire network.

Now Stark's firewalls are impenetrable, their encryption codes unbreakable, and their IT department takes a two-hour lunch every day so they can have *Journeyquest* marathons.

And Felix, who got his ankle bracelet removed a few weeks ago, has started using Accutane and wearing a suit to work. He actually looks almost presentable . . .

And because of Stark's newly implemented sexual-harassment training seminars (mandatory for all staff administrators – Christopher's suggestion), Felix can actually speak to women without making lewd and offensive innuendoes.

Which still doesn't make it OK that he asked my sister Frida to his alternative high school's prom.

'It's not like a real prom,' Frida said when I made a big deal about this while we were shopping at Betsey Johnson the other day. She was actually planning on getting something there to wear to Felix's prom with high-tops (thus the 'not like a real prom' part. If it had been a 'real prom', she said, she'd have worn heels). 'We're not *going out* or anything.'

'But it's still a prom,' I said. 'He's still *Felix*. He's going to try to kiss you. Probably worse.'

'And that is a bad thing . . . how?' Frida replied.

'You'd let Felix kiss you.' I could not believe this was happening. 'Christopher's *cousin*?'

'You let Christopher kiss you,' Frida pointed out, flicking through a rack of off-the-shoulder numbers with big puffy skirts. Total prom wear. 'All the time, I might add. I hardly ever see you two when you *aren't* kissing. Including in school. Which is disgusting.'

'That's different,' I said huffily.

And it was. Christopher and I had known each other our whole lives, practically. We were made for each other. We finished each other's sentences.

Sure, we still fought sometimes.

But what two headstrong people deeply in love don't fight from time to time? Especially two people who'd been friends for so long before falling in love. We knew each other so well, we could tell what the other person was thinking, half the time.

Like just the other day, in Public Speaking, when Whitney Robertson poked me in the back before class even started and leaned over to ask, 'Hey. Is it true, the rumour I heard . . . that you had one of those brain transplants they're talking about on the news all the time, and you're really . . . um, *Em Watts*?'

She said my name like it was a dirty word.

Also, I could tell there was no way she believed it was true. How could I, Nikki Howard, lithe, swanlike creature, ever be associated with someone as odious as that hideous, hobbit-like Emerson Watts?

It had been Christopher who had leaned forward in his seat and said to Whitney, with obvious pleasure, 'You know what, Whitney? It *is* true. And because you were always so mean to her when she was Em, you can pretty much kiss away any chance you might ever have had at getting to meet Heidi Klum and Seal at any of the fall fashion shows. Right, Em?'

Whitney and her little crony, Lindsey, had both turned their horror- and guilt-stricken gazes towards me. You didn't have to be a mind-reader to see what they were thinking: *Please let what he said not be true. Please!*

I thought about putting them out of their misery. As the other thing that had come out of all of this (besides an end to Robert Stark's newest commercial sales campaign, to sell hot young bodies to his old friends, for them to be hot and young again), was an end to all the lies.

So, 'He's right,' I'd said with a shrug. 'I'm really Em Watts. I just use Nikki Howard as my modelling name now. And I'm not really interested in being BFFs with you guys. Unless, of course, you stop spiking volleyballs at other girls' heads on purpose. And torturing them about the size of their butts in the hallway. You do remember when you used to do that to me, don't you, Whitney?'

Now Whitney's eyes were the size of quarters.

'B-but,' she'd stammered, 'I – I was only kidding around.'

'Huh,' I said. 'Did you notice how I wasn't laughing back then? It doesn't hurt, you know, Whitney, to be kind to people, no matter what they look like. Especially because, these days, you never know who they're going to turn out to be later.'

'I . . .' Whitney blinked. 'I'm so *sorry.*'

'Yeah,' I said. I believed she *was* sorry. Now. 'I bet you are.'

The best thing about everyone knowing who I was – who I *really* was – was that my old grades were combined into my new ones and brought my grade point average up quite a bit. Suddenly I went from being a mediocre student to an above-average one. Not straight As, by any means, like I used to be.

But considering what I'd been through, and how many classes I'd missed, it was still a relief. With hard work, I'd managed to keep my head above water, grade-wise . . . hard work, and Nikki's career-management skills.

Because Nikki, another witness in Robert Stark's grand-jury trial, had decided not to go back to Gasper but to stick around in New York . . . as my new agent and manager.

Well, why not? She knows everything about the modelling business – especially as it concerns Nikki Howard – and obviously has a shrewd business sense (except when it comes to blackmailing people, which she swears on the Clairol Midnight Black she uses to keep her hair so dark that she's not going to do any more).

She turned out to be serious about business school. She took her mom's advice and enrolled in classes and is already making her professors miserable.

Hey. No one can say Nikki Howard's not bossy and doesn't know how to get what she wants . . . especially for her clients (of which, so far, I'm the only one. But she's working on that).

It made sense that I give Nikki a cut of what I earned, anyway, since my career was the one she'd launched. We worked out that she got a percentage of all my future earnings, plus everything that had been in the accounts I'd found when I'd been declared 'legally' Nikki Howard.

And since, immediately following the makeover Lulu gave her, Nikki regained her va-va-voom factor with men, she lost all interest in swapping brains (not that we'd have been allowed to do this, even if we'd wanted to: there's been a total ban on the surgeries, except in the case of life-threatening injury). I don't know how much of this had to do with the fact that Nikki seemed to get really into being goth 'Diana Prince', the name and persona she took for her new body, and how much of it had to do with Gabriel Luna being . . . well, into *her*.

But I do know she has no interest whatsoever in selling the loft. She's perfectly happy staying where she is, living in Gabriel's apartment, driving Gabriel nuts by taking up all his closet space and insulting his band mates . . .

. . . and he, in turn, is the most creative he's ever been, having written three new *albums* of songs – all about the same whacky girl he lives with – in four months.

Instead, I'm paying Nikki rent, same as Lulu.

My living situation had been the source of heated discussion with my parents, who'd assumed I'd move back home once my true identity was revealed.

But to me, in a weird way, the loft *is* home now. How could I leave Lulu, who had no family, other than me and Steven (who was still away at sea)?

'Maybe when he comes back,' I'd explained to Mom and Dad over pizza at their place one night – pizza I could now enjoy without worrying anyone was spying on me, 'and he and Lulu do get married some day . . .'

Frida snorted. 'Right.'

'What's that supposed to mean?' I demanded.

'You're not coming back, even if Lulu does get married. You like living in a bachelorette pad,' Frida said accusingly. 'Face it, Mom and Dad. She only wants to stay there so she can have Christo—'

'That's not true!' I interrupted, although it was, of course, partly true. 'And it's not that I love you guys any less. It's just that I still have a very busy schedule, what with work and school and—'

'Oh, please,' Frida snorted.

'She's gotten used to being in her own space,' Mom said very diplomatically, 'and wants to keep it that way. We understand.'

Dad didn't look like he understood exactly, but he didn't say anything. He clearly felt that he was outnumbered by females in this instance, as often happened in our household.

'I don't care,' Frida said, shrugging. 'So long as I get invited over for your parties once in a while . . .'

'Done,' I said. Like I said, Frida had really gotten very mature lately.

'. . . and I can bring Felix.'

'Oh my God, no! Are you serious?'

'Felix saved my life,' Frida said truculently. 'And yours. How can you be so mean about him?'

'He didn't save your life,' I said. '*I* did. Felix and Christopher helped. A little.'

'That's not true. They were equally as important as you. He told me all about it—'

'Girls,' Mom said. 'Please. Both of you are smart, vibrant, beautiful girls with wonderful, talented, handsome boyfriends. Please stop fighting and clear the dishes so your father and I can have some alone time.'

Alone time is important if you want to build a strong romantic relationship. Christopher and I try to grab as much as we can. Especially at Balthazar, which is one of our favourite restaurants to go to together for dinner . . .

. . . with an appetizer *and* dessert, despite Lulu's assertions that high-school boys couldn't afford to take their girlfriends there (they can, if they also work part-time in the IT department of a major corporation. And their girlfriend insists she pays once in a while, because I work too, and it's only fair for the girl to pay sometimes. I don't know where this archaic idea that the boy always has to pay comes from).

It was at Balthazar the other night that I was sitting

across from Christopher, happily stabbing a piece of lettuce and goat's cheese, when a little girl came up to our table, holding a pen and a piece of paper.

'Excuse me,' she said to me shyly, 'but are you Nikki Howard?'

I looked at her, surprised. She couldn't have been more than seven or eight years old. I saw her parents sitting at a neighbouring table, smiling at her encouragingly.

The truth was, I didn't know what to say. I was Nikki Howard . . . sort of.

Except I also wasn't, any more.

But the little girl's expression was one of such hopefulness . . . she was in New York City for the night, all dressed up (she was probably going to a Broadway musical later).

And here she was in a fancy restaurant, and she'd spotted a celebrity. What was I going to do? Say, *No, little girl. Actually, I'm Em Watts.*

'Yes,' I said, 'I am.'

Her face burst into a delighted smile. She was missing her two front teeth.

'Can I please have your autograph?' she asked, shoving the pen and paper at me.

'Of course,' I said, darting a look at Christopher, who just grinned and kept on eating his salad. 'What's your name?

'Emily,' the little girl said.

I refrained from saying, 'Em is my name too,' and wrote *Best wishes, Emily, love, Nikki Howard* on her piece of paper, and handed it and the pen back to her.

'Here you go,' I said. 'Have a nice night.'

'Oh, thank you,' she said, and scurried back to her table and her parents, looking overjoyed.

'That was nice of you,' Christopher said as soon as she was gone.

'What was I going to do?' I asked. 'Kick her in the face?'

'To tell her you were Nikki Howard, I mean,' he said.

'I *am* Nikki Howard,' I said. 'As long as I'm stuck with this face, I'll always be Nikki Howard.'

'Yeah,' Christopher said. 'But it's not such a drag, is it? I mean, being Nikki Howard has its perks.'

'It does,' I said, smiling. 'But it has its drawbacks too. As you might have gathered, since even the real Nikki Howard doesn't want to be Nikki Howard any more.'

'Well,' Christopher said, 'maybe this will make you feel better about it.'

And he reached into the pocket of his jacket and pulled out a long rectangular velvet box, which he slid across the table towards me.

'What's this?' I asked, surprised, since we weren't exactly the kind of couple who showered each other with gifts. We sort of had everything we'd ever wanted . . . which was each other.

'Open it and see,' he said, a mischievous twinkle in his blue eyes.

I widened my eyes at him in mock astonishment, then opened the box . . .

274

. . . and my astonishment turned to the real thing.

Because lying there inside, on a whisper-thin necklace chain, was a heart-shaped platinum tag, surrounded by tiny diamonds, on which the words *Em Watts* had been inscribed in elegant cursive.

'I thought if you wore that, no matter what face you saw every morning in the mirror,' he said in his deep voice, 'you'll never forget who you really are.'

My eyes filling with tears, I held my hand out across the table top. He grasped my fingers, his grip strong and reassuring.

'As if I ever could,' I said, my voice clogged with emotion, 'with you around to remind me.'

meg cabot

air head

She's a brainiac trapped inside the body of an airhead . . .

Teenagers Emerson Watts and Nikki Howard have nothing in common. Em's a tomboy-brainiac who couldn't care less about her looks. Nikki's a stunning supermodel, the world's most famous airhead. But a freak accident causes the girls' lives to collide in the most extraordinary way – and suddenly Em knows more about Nikki's life than the paparazzi ever have!

The first book in a spectacular romantic trilogy with a spine-tingling twist!

air head

Being Nikki

meg cabot

Em Watts is gone. Nikki Howard is here to stay.

Teen-supermodel Nikki Howard has a secret. She's not the gorgeous golden airhead she seems – on the inside she's someone else. Literally. Em Watts is stuck in the body of glamazon celebutante Nikki. And it's not easy. Especially when Nikki's past is about to catch up with her, her boss is spying on her, and Em's heart wants one thing but her lips keep kissing someone else . . .

The funny, crazy, super-glamorous sequel to *Airhead*.

JINX

Meg Cabot

Does Jinx have bad luck – or special powers?

Misfortunc has followed Jean Honeychurch all her life – which is why everyone calls her Jinx. And now her parents have shipped her off to New York to stay with relatives – including her sophisticated cousin, Tory – until the trouble she's caused back home dies down.

Could she even be . . . a WITCH?

Tory is far too cool to bother with Jinx – until Jinx's chronic bad luck wreaks havoc in Tory's perfect life. Only then does Jinx discover that beneath Tory's big-city glamour lies a world of hatred and revenge. Now it seems that the jinx that's driven Jean crazy may just be the only thing that can save her life . . .

A selected list of titles available from Macmillan Children's Books

The prices shown below are correct at the time of going to press. However, Macmillan Publishers reserves the right to show new retail prices on covers, which may differ from those previously advertised.

Meg Cabot

Airhead	978-0-330-45382-0	£6.99
Airhead: Being Nikki	978-0-330-45383-7	£6.99
All American Girl	978-0-330-41555-2	£5.99
All American Girl: Ready or Not	978-0-330-43834-6	£5.99
Avalon High	978-0-330-44687-7	£5.99
Teen Idol	978-0-330-43300-6	£5.99
How to Be Popular	978-0-330-44406-4	£5.99
Tommy Sullivan Is a Freak	978-0-330-44407-1	£5.99
Jinx	978-0-330-44201-5	£5.99

All Pan Macmillan titles can be ordered from our website, www.panmacmillan.com, or from your local bookshop and are also available by post from:

Bookpost, PO Box 29, Douglas, Isle of Man IM99 1BQ

Credit cards accepted. For details:
Telephone: 01624 677237
Fax: 01624 670923
Email: bookshop@enterprise.net
www.bookpost.co.uk

Free postage and packing in the United Kingdom